Classified Documents:

World Wars

www.amazon.co.uk
Kindle Direct Publishing

A CIP catalogue record for this title is
available from the British Library.

ISBN-13: 979-8652004187

T
his is a work of fiction
Names, characters, places and incidents originate from the writers imagination.
Any resemblance to actual persons, living or dead, is purely Coincidental

Published in 2020

Other publish titles in order by release dates

Blood Warrior and the Three Weapons of Darkness Book 1 2016

B.M.Ts L.O.A.Ds aka Lords of All Dimension Prequel Story 2020

B.M.Ts Classified Documents: World War prelude Story 2020

Blood Warrior and the Wrath of Darkness Book 2 2020

B.M.Ts Dawn of a New Warrior alternated Story 2021

Blood Warrior and the Era of Darkness Book 3 2021

Brilliant Masterful Transcripts Ltd

Prologue

Two men wearing protective uniform enter into what it seems like an office, with them armed man standing outside of the office, and in the room sitting in a chair a man. One of the men wearing the protective clothing places a folder on the table in front of the man sitting down, and the man picks it up reading the front of the folder.

"Classified Documents, World Wars."

Speaking in Russian one of the men wearing the protective clothing spoke out, "All of the files are there, with every single detail even the assassination hits."

"Is he in here?" the man in the chair asked.

"All of them Sir."

As the man moved his hand the two men in protective clothing leaves the office, as they started walking away the hallway two gun shots echo's back into the office, and one of the armed men came in. The man sitting in the chair speaking in English said, "Clean that mess up out there."

"Yes boss."

The armed man exits the office and the man in the chair opens the folder, immediately looking at a name.

14th of June 1907 the First Super-human experiment was successful on U.S.A soil by American and Russian scientists

Name: Kwame Xavi Iwu, now known as X-Hamstring

Gender: Erased

Height: Erased

Build: Erased

Features: Erased

Nationality: Erased

D.O.B Erased

17th of April 1912 President of Austria assassinated

Cause of death: Sniper Bullet to her chest

Assassin X-Hamstring instructed by the C.I.A. however it was intended for X-Hamstring to assassinate President Ferdinand not his wife, so the C.I.A cover their trace by manipulating the blame onto Serbian.

20th of November 1912 X-Hamstring retires from C.I.A heading back to his home country Libya

28TH OF June 1913 President Ferdinand was assassinated

Cause of death: dagger to his back two bullet holes one in his forehead and one in his chest

Assassinated by French special force ops this triggered Austria-Hungry alley Germany in which Serbian had surrendered to them and putting German on the path to invade France.

The scene changes to the man in the office this time he was standing up with the papers from the folder spread across his desk.

"July 2nd 1914 German's invasion of France," out spoke the man.

The Man was putting in order the paper on the desk, while he was a knock on the door happened, the man looked up at the door, as he opens with one of the armed man drops down onto his floor. The man draws for his pistol and in walks a guy moving to the shadow of the room, holding his own pistol in his hand aiming it at the man, the man could barely see the who the guy was.

"Put it down," said the guy.

The man drops his pistol to his desk, "You're meant to be dead?" asked the man sweating from his forehead from the heat in the room.

"I am very much alive, as you can see."

"How did you find me?"

"It's over, hand over the files now."

"You will have to kill me?"

The guy shots the man in his forehead the man drops straight to the floor, and the guy comes out of the shadows, walking over to the desk looking at the paper spread all over the man's desk.

"Impossible."

The guy drops to one of his knees throwing his hand around to his back pulling out a knife, blood pours out at an incredible speed, and then the guy drops to the floor. The man then sits back down into his seat, as the files were now in order, he starts to read them.

Chapter One

Inside Man

2nd of July 1914 England, London

The time was roughly 14:00pm; the Prime Minster of England was sitting down in his office, discussing what actions he could use to help the French troops defeat the German troops.

"Prime Minster you must give the order, Paris will be taken by the German troops."

Prime Minster Asquith replied, "Blunt I understand, but have you looked at our numbers; we have only a few hundred troops based outside of Paris, Germany has at least over a thousand."

Blunt replies, "You have to do something, France is our allies."

Prime Minster Asquith replied, "I will not give the order."

Blunt replies, "You leave me without any other choice."

Blunt moved backwards aiming his pistol downwards towards the Prime Mister, Asquith moved upwards and back, as he did more armed men came in pointing their weapons at Asquith.

July the 2nd 1914 the time was 19:00pm France, Paris.

"President Raymond, we must retreat now."

President Raymond replied, "No the British will help us."

"Their troops haven't started too move, Asquith will not give them the order.""

President Raymond replied, "I will not retreat, Asquith will give the order."

"President."

President Raymond replies, "What is it?"

"What are those?"

President Raymond replies, "The impossible is possible."

Moments later these aircrafts came flying pass in incredible speed, the aircrafts started to blast away the German troops.

"Who is that?

The Aircrafts landed down onto the ground, out-came Asquith and some British troops in special design amour, with advance weapons.

"Impossible."

President Raymond and his advisor moved over to Asquith, the French Troops kneel down to Asquith, in pure fear of him.

Advisor said, "How is this possible, these kind of equipment, cannot be, not for at least hundred years from now."

Blunt replied, "Open your eyes, it is, and has been."

President Raymond said, "Are you here to defeat us?"

Asquith said, "Step aside Blunt, let me answer this."

Asquith then started to float up into the air floating over to the German Troops which were fighting the French ones; Asquith then attacked the German Troops eliminating them, without Asquith knowing someone in the shadow was recording him doing the few acts he had performed.

A few weeks later

White House, Green room, a meeting was taking place.

"President we like to introduce you to someone."

"Hello Mr President, I am Leeroy Blair."

"Not to be rude young man, but why are you here?"

"I have some important footage to show you."

"Footage?"

"Yes President Wilson, He's a professional at his art."

"Yeah if I take it out, yes and put this in here, that's it. Yeah like this, I hmmm, yeah turn it this way. That should do, plug this in right here, ok that's good, and switch this on."

President Wilson said, "What the hell is he doing?"

Leeroy begun to say, "I created both devices, this device records images, and this device shows the images. It'll only come up in black and white, but you will get the feel on what is taking place."

As the images came up onto the wall President Wilson and Joseph which was the President's secretary, with the congress men, leaned forward looking at the images before them.

Leeroy looked backwards at one of the President's personal bodyguards, as he was reaching for his pistol ready to shoot the President, Leeroy grabbed one of the other PB's pistol shooting the personal bodyguard before he could kill the President.

President Wilson said, "What in god's name is happening?"

"Sir, Leeroy has just saved you're life."

The Personal Bodyguard said, "Never touch my weapon again, you nigger."

President Wilson replies, "George, god damn it, mined you're tone around me."

Leeroy replies, "It's ok President, I don't expect any less."

President Wilson replied, "Please, call me Mr Wilson."

Joseph said, "Mr Wilson, I think this calls for the special weapon."

President Wilson replied, "I believe so."

One of the Congress men said, "With that kind of power, Britain will turn against us."

Joseph said to Leeroy, "You're a professional ain't you?"

Leeroy replies, "You could say something like that."

Joseph replied, "You're good at tracking people down right?"

Leeroy replies, "Well only recently since my parents were murdered."

President Wilson said, "I'm sorry to hear that, how did they die?"

Leeroy replied, "I don't want to talk out of my league, but from some damn racist white folks."

Joseph replies, "How about you take on a job, which pays highly, very highly."

Personal Bodyguard said, "Are you people ok, because you're asking a kid, no older than thirteen to work with the secret service."

President Wilson replied, "Exclude yourself from this room."

Leeroy said, "I'll take the job, how much, and what I gotta do."

Josepha replied, "Hundred Thousand now, and hundred Thousand afterwards, Leeroy Jacobs Blair. You're going to Egypt, Africa. There you will locate this man," Josepha passes Leeroy a photo of the man and carried on to say "Bring him back here, I think it's time the world gained a hero."

Leeroy replies, "Who is this man?"

President Wilson replied, "This kid is smart."

Josepah said, "He's well kinder a friend, he'll help us against this threat."

Leeroy wasn't too sure as when he was recording the events which took place in Paris, France. He noticed that Prime Minster Asquith, wasn't doing nothing to alarming, but hey ho, Leeroy was just thinking about the money.

Leeroy said, "I do it."

President Wilson replied, "You're be followed by four Secret service, just in case you get yourself into a bit of trouble."

Later day that Leeroy was in a Bar drinking some milkshake, and then he came out of the bar, two things Leeroy noticed was someone following him and he knew who. Leeroy moved through the crowd trying to blend in, until the person which was following pushed the people out the way, Leeroy turned around to see the President's Personal Bodyguard which called him a nigger earlier, reach out his pistol firing it off, the bullet went into Leeroy's chest Leeroy flew backwards down to the ground as people were screaming everything went blank.

"It looks like he pulled through, Mr President."

"Doctor, we thank you're service so much."

"President, what should we do now?"

"It's been two months, they say, he should be fully recovered."

The President and his Secretary Josepha walked into Leeroy's hospital room, escorted by a few Secret Services.

President Wilson said, "Leeroy, Leeroy, do you remember me?"

Leeroy replied, "Mr Wilson, I don't think I'm suffering from any brain damage."

Josepha replies, "We caught the person responsible for this."

Leeroy replied, "Good."

President Wilson replies, "He's serving life in prison."

Leeroy replied, "Maybe there is justice in this country after all."

Josepha said, "We were wondering if you were still interested, that's if you can remember our last conversation."

Leeroy replied, "Yes, but I want my own secret Service, watching over me, plus their blend in much better in Africa, than yours would."

Chapter Two

German's Wrath Part 1

Late 1914 location Africa

"Barbertunda, Barber, the Germans are a few miles away."

"Alert X-Hamstring, it's time."

As one of the soldiers of Nyeri a small town in Kenya came into the hut, where X-Ham was sitting down with his legs crossed onto each other, the solider quickly said.

"Germans have taken over, "Sirte, Sabha, and Awbrai."

As the soldiers said that X-Ham had flashes of each city's names, X-Ham stood up tall.

"X-Ham, they are making their way here, we believe they want Libya, so they can take over Egypt."

X-Hamstring said, "Prepare the defence line."

While that was happening there was a conversation taking place, somewhere in England.

"Prime Minster, we believe the Germans, intend to take over Egypt. Take all their gold, diamonds and enslave the people, to grow their empire."

Prime Minster Asquith replies, "Where are the British troops?"

Personal Advisor replied, "Sudan, with the King's army."

Prime Minster replies, "They won't make it in time."

Personal Advisor replied, "I greatly advise you to take action now."

Prime Minster said, "Ready the Hover-Jets."

"Prime Minster."

"Not now."

Back in Libya X-Ham was at the defence line.

X-Ham said, "Barbertunda my oldest friend, I will not think any difference of you, if you choice to go to Egypt with your family."

Barbartunda replied, "X-Ham, you are more than a friend, we stand here as brothers."

X-Hamstring pulled out two Machetes, one which was covered in diamonds and the other which had a bright Golden shine surrounding it, X-Ham started running towards the German troops, and then he had a flash back.

One year before September 1913

"Barber, Barber, you need to come see this."

Barbertunda followed one of the village people into a hut, where he saw his friend X-Ham, out cold. The village doctor waved these thin sticks over him which smoke started to come out from them.

Barber said, "What's the meaning of this?"

"We found him in the fields."

Barber replies, "X-Ham."

"Barbertunda, something is happening, you need to come."

Barber could see from a far flames burning down this building, Barber raced over to it, until he saw something from the sky smashed down into the ground.

Barber said to himself, "X-Ham."

X-Ham then blazed along the ground over to the battle rushing in, and grabbing people after people, and getting them to safety. As X-Ham looked back he saw a young boy, screaming out a window, somehow X-Ham power jumped off the ground and into the window, and the building blew to pieces as X-Ham jumped out of the building crashing into the ground.

As Barbertunda got to where X-Ham landed he saw burn marks all over X-Ham, and X-Ham release the young boy and the boy run into his mother's arms, just like that X-Ham started to heal all the burn marks disappeared.

Barber said, "X-Hamstring, how, what has happened to you?"

X-Ham replied, "The Americans and Russians, they know everything about me, I am the prince of Inspiron where I truly come from, they did experiments on me; they help advance my abilities, I am now like a superhuman, I age very slow as well."

Barber replies, "X-Ham, you know you will always be my friend, no matter what."

Late 1914 Germans invasion on Africa completes

X-Ham with many Libyan soldiers dived into the German troops, Barber watched X-Ham as he got lost within the thousands of thousands of German troops marching towards him.

X-Ham sliced and diced down the German troops all around him, X-Ham stabbed and rammed his two machetes into bodies after bodies, the German troops were getting forced back by the forces of the two Machetes, X-Ham flew through the air slicing of the heads of more German troops, and legs, X-Ham rolled through killing more German Troops.

Until he got forced backwards by unknown force, one which he couldn't understand, as the Machetes flew out of his hands and then shot up into the sky until he couldn't see them no more.

The Machetes went into outer-space hitting each other making sparks fly off them, until they merged into another universe and in that universe they came landing down onto a planet which one half was Dark and the other half Light.

Righteous walked forward reaching out his hands, and the Golden Machete flew into his hands, and the one covered in Diamond turned into liquid and then vanished into the planet.

Back on Earth, Libya Africa

German Troops mounted X-Ham pinned him down to the ground.

"You're not so great, without you're weapons."

X-Ham replied, "I understand you."

"Impossible."

X-Ham forced them off him racing into them, grabbing a pistol and started shooting the German Troops, until the Libya Soldiers came behind him and started killing the German Troops.

X-Ham looked over at Barber getting taken down by a few German Troops, and some more entering into Libya. X-Ham power jumped of the ground, and came crashing down behind the German Troop which were about to kill Barber, X-Ham quickly took them out and helped Barber up.

Barber said, "You're my guardian angel or something."

"Look, they've entered Libya, come on."

X-Hamstring and Barbertunda looked back at the Libyan soldiers getting killed and the other Soldiers in Libya struggling to hold back the German Troops.

Reports came back to England

"Sir, the Germans have taken over Libya."

"George, are the Hover-Jet ready?"

"Yes Prime Minster."

"It's time."

October 7th 1914 Death of Barbertunda X-Hamstring's non-blood brother, cause of death German soldier stab wound to the left leg and bullet to the head.

X-Hamstring was about to attack a group of German Troops, but Barber held him back.

"No, there's more over there, we're out-numbered."

X-Ham stood up looking at all the rest of the Libyan Soldiers hiding; he knew what he had to do. X-Ham said, "There's less than an thousand, and yes only a handful of us, but if we don't fight them they will cause more damage. I know what I will do, but will you follow me into war."

X-Hamstring raced out and started to attack the last group of the German Troops, X-Ham came flying in the air taking down Troops after Troops, as they looked back watching the last of the Libyan Soldiers getting killed. X-Hamstring carried on killing German Troops after German Troops, until they were only a few left.

X-Ham got up as he did he got knock by two German Troops, they shot him in the chest four times, and then went to stab him but he held their weapons back, and pulled them forward killing them .

X-Ham looked backwards at Barbertunda as he did; the German Troops Barber was fighting against, stabbed him in his leg and shot him in the head. X-Ham dropped to his knees as he did, the last of the German Troops came over to X-Hamstring, aiming their pistols and weapons at him.

One of the German Troops said, "Emperor Wilhelm said no survives."

Another German Troops said, "He can't understand us, kill him."

X-Ham replied, "I can understand you."

As the German Troops went to finish X-Hamstring off, some more Libyan soldiers killed the last of the German Troops, which were about to kill X-Hamstring.

Barbertunda's burial location by a childhood tree in X-Hamstring's home country

X-Hamstring buried Barbertunda near a tree, this tree which he buried Barbertunda by, meant a lot to him and barber, when they were much younger. That would be the place they first met each other, so he knew this would be a perfect spot for Barbertunda.

X-Hamstring said, "This enemy will pay for what they have done here."

As the Libyan soldiers walked off, X-Ham took a moment for himself, and then just like that a faded out Barbertunda stood to the side of X-Ham.

X-Hamstring said, "Is this a dream?"

Barbertunda replied, "No friend."

X-Hamstring replies, "How is this possible?"

Barbertunda replied, "It's you're powers X-Ham, you're powers allow you to see me, even after death."

X-Hamstring replies, "How does it feel?"

Barbertunda replied, "They allowed me to have peace, I now understand what peace is."

X-Hamstring replies, "There must be a reason why you are here?"

Barbertunda replied, "Yes, you must travel to Egypt, there help will seek you. You're path has just begun you must leave now, a very and I mean very large group of German Troops are still heading this way."

X-Hamstring replies, "You want me to leave my home?"

Barbertunda replied, "Only so you can truly save it."

X-Hamstring replies, "What kind of help is in Egypt for me?"

Barbertunda replied, "A young boy will seek out for you, he will need your help, you must follow and protect him."

X-Hamstring looked behind him as he did his eyes zoomed in, he could see the very large group of German Troops, and then he looked back at Barbertunda, but Barbertunda was not there no longer.

A low but yet peaceful voice said, "In your dark hours, I will be you're rock to lean on."

X-Hamstring quickly got back to his hut, he started to dig up the ground, until he got to this large rug, he uncovered it and his old weapons were there. He took out a dragon designed sword, a Machete, a few daggers and knives. X-Hamstring head out moving through Libya as the German Troops destroyed and took over Libya.

George said, "Prime Minster, "We'll be in Egypt by the morning, and one more thing Prime Minster."

Asquith replied, "Speak."

George replies, 'the Americans have some kind of footage of you, what you did in Paris, and they believe you to be a threat."

Asquith replied, "Americans always believe everyone's a threat, we'll have to clear that up after Egypt."

Chapter Three

Enemies alike

November the 17th 1914 Somewhere in Tokyo

Outskirt of central Tokyo something impossible but yet possible had just happened, as the Rebel of Japanese imperial soldiers, gathered around what it seemed like smoke spreading out after an impact. The Rebel Soldiers armed themselves quickly as the smoked cleared away, and what it seemed like a naked Caucasian woman curl up, into a ball, the Rebel Soldiers moved in slowly.

The Second in command said, "Cover her up, and bring her to General Okuma."

Moments later the female gets thrown to the ground in front of General Okuma, and his second in command.

General Okuma said, "Who is she?"

Second in command replied, "She came out from the sky, crashing down into the ground, that's all we know."

General Okuma replies, "She looks American, she is American, she's an enemy."

"I am not American, never ever call me American."

Second in Command said, "She speaks Japanese?"

General Okuma replied, "Who are you?"

"Call me Eight, I guess I'm you're good luck charm."

General Okuma replied, "You sound American?"

Second in Command said, "Good luck Charm?"

Eight replied, "I believe the year is nineteen fourteen?"

Second in Command replies, "Yes, that's correct."

Eight replied, "World War one."

General Okuma said, "World War one."

Eight replied, "You against the Americans, British and Russians against the Germans, and the rest of the world against each other."

Second in command replies, "Correct again, but you seem, not off this world?"

Eight spoke in English, 'time to fuck things up."

General Okuma said, "What did she say, what did she say?"

As the Rebel Soldiers went to attack Eight, Eight killed them immediately, and took their weapons as more Rebels soldiers came at her, she took care of them like no one's business. The General got up laughing his head off, and his Second in Command watched General Okuma laughing in joy.

General Okuma said, "I like her."

Eight then dashed a blade towards the Second in command slicing his neck open, and then the General went silent, and Eight kneel down to him.

General Okuma said, "Get up on to your feet, you are now my second in Command."

Eight replied, "I know how this war will end, and it will not end well for you, but with my assistances it will."

While Eight settled in on her new life, somewhere else across the seas, Leeroy came off a ship on the docks of Egypt, Leeroy dropped to the floor and said.

"Mother-land, I am home."

As Leeroy walked around and looked around he saw someone holding a sign up with his name on it, Leeroy headed over to the person, and the person looked up and down.

"I can tell you are not from here, but change in to these."

Leeroy replied, "What the flip?"

"Yeah, that's matter better."

Leeroy replied, "Who are you?"

"Just call me the Driver."

Leeroy replied, "I need to find this person."

The Driver replies, "No point showing a picture of a random person, I'm only the Driver, I get you here and there that's all."

Leeroy replied, "No shit."

The Driver replies, "How old are you?"

Leeroy replied, "Just turned fifteen, why?"

The Driver replies, "I hope for your sake, you don't get kidnapped here."

Leeroy looked behind him at these four random black guys, which he believes have been following him, he knew they had to be the secret services.

Leeroy said, "I won't."

The Driver replied, "Where too young man or young boy?"

Leeroy replies, 'the Pyramids."

The Driver replied, "Very interesting."

Leeroy replies, "What did you say?"

The Driver replied, "Nothing this way "Sir."

Leeroy said, "Wow, is this your motor-vehicle?"

The Driver replied, "Yes."

So just as Leeroy thought the four black guys got into their own motor-Vehicle, and followed him, but not too closely.

Leeroy said, "Who are these people?"

The Driver replied, "Don't mind them; they cloud the road, all the time."

Leeroy looked backwards but he couldn't see the four guys no more, as the people blocked his views, just like that the four guys came to a stop and suddenly they were under attack.

The people cleared the road and Leeroy could see the four guys again, Leeroy leaned before as he did, the Driver stopped racing out of the car and he started running.

Leeroy looked behind him at the other car which was following him with the four guys, which he thought was the secret services, nut they started shooting at the motor-Vehicle which Leeroy was in.

Leeroy said, "What the flip?"

Just like that the four guys dropped one by one, and then out of the shadow came a random person, he grabbed Leeroy and they headed into a building.

Leeroy said, "Wait, who are you?"

X-Hamstring replied, "I believe you are looking for me?"

Leeroy replies, "X-Hamstring."

 X-Hamstring said, "ssshh, the Germans have paid a handful of people of, to catcher both of us."

Leeroy replied, "I guess we must move fast."

X-Hamstring replies, "Before me we do, I must ask you, what you know?"

Leeroy replied, "Yes."

X-Hamstring replies, "Why have the Americans, sent you to find me?"

Leeroy replied, "I think they believe the Prime Minster of Asquith, intention will turn against them, and he has some kind of powers."

X-Hamstring replies, "Ok, this way."

Leeroy replied, "No, the Germans are here."

As Leeroy saw a group of Germans Troops moving through the city, the Hover-Jets came flying around, blowing up where ever the Germans were.

Leeroy said, 'the ship is about to leave, we must go now."

X-Hamstring and Leeroy raced through the city getting back to the docks, as they did, a group of German Troops cut them off from their path.

X-Hamstring flew at them but they blasted him backwards, and down to the ground, and four German Troops pinned him down.

From a far Leeroy could see the American troops fighting off the Germans Troops, allowing the ship to move away.

Leeroy then looked upwards at the Hover-Jet, the door opened up and standing there was Asquith, Leeroy quickly jumped into cover not thinking that Asquith was there to help the America Troops.

Asquith got the few Hover-Jets to firing upon the Germans Troops, and also the Troops which had X-Ham pinned to the ground, X-Hamstring quickly got over to leeroy grabbing him, and they both run towards the ship.

The Ship blew to pieces and X-Hamstring covered Leeroy as a piece of the ship came flying towards X-Hamstring slicing into his side, X-Hamstring pulled out it slowly.

Leeroy dropped to the ground and then looked up at X-Hamstring pulling it out, and then healing slowly back, X-Hamstring and Leeroy then found themselves surrounded by Germans Troops again.

X-Hamstring said, 'stay back."

X-Hamstring raced forward towards the German Troops, but the Germans Troops got blasted down, X-Hamstring looked upwards at a Hover-Jet, and it landed down near to him.

Asquith said, "Over here."

X-Hamstring tightens his grip on his Dragon Sword, and was about to race off towards Asquith, but Leeroy grabbed his hand X-Hamstring looked down and back at Leeroy.

Leeroy said, "Not here, not now."

Asquith held out his hand calling for them, X-Hamstring and Leeroy came to the Hover-Jet.

George said, "Get in."

X-Hamstring held Leeroy back, and said, "Why."

Asquith said, "I believe you want to go to America."

Leeroy replied, "Yes."

Asquith replies, 'so do I."

George said, "Get in then."

Elsewhere another conversation was taking place.

""Sir Wilhelm, the Prime Minster, is no longer in England."

Wilhelm replied, "Prepare the Troops, we take England tonight."

So X-Hamstring and Leeroy were in a Hover-Jet with the Prime Minster Asquith, and his advisor also a few British troops in special design amour.

Leeroy said, 'so what do you call this?"

Asquith replied, "Hover-Jet."

X-Hamstring replies, "How is this possible, where did you get the power and equipment to build this?"

Asquith replied, "I'm from a place, my Being calls the True world, but better known as Ruthon."

Leeroy said, "I knew there were aliens."

Asquith replied, "Aliens, I'm not an alien, I'm a Supreme Being if anything you're the aliens to me."

X-Hamstring replies, "I should kill you where you sit."

George said, "Stand down Troops."

Prime Minster Asquith said, "Why would you want to do such a thing?"

Leeroy replied, "It's my fault, I recorded you on something like this, and showed it to the President. He believes you are now a threat to him, and that's why I was in Egypt, they told me to find him."

George said, "Who is he?"

X-Hamstring replied, "I'm the....."

Prime Minster Asquith replies, "Super-Human, the Americans and Russians made, back in nineteen ten."

X-Hamstring replied, "Yes that's right."

Prime Minster Asquith said, 'the first success of creating a super-human, but that factory was designed by the Chinese."

X-Hamstring replied, "Wrong that was a cover up story, so that the Americans could go into China, I destroyed that factory and any source of the Super-Human formula."

Prime Minster replies, "Good man, nothing good would have come off that."

As Asquith said that it looked like X-Hamstring took wrongly to Asquith remark.

X-Hamstring said, "When we get to American, you will meet you're end."

Leeroy turned to X-Hamstring and replied, "Can't you see the Prime Minster is not the bad guy here, and he just saved our asses back there."

 X-Hamstring replies, "Young boy, you will learn in this line of business, no one does favours for free."

Prime Minster Asquith said, "Like I said Before Smart man."

While they were still travelling to America in a Hover-Jet, Eight had other plans for General Okuma and his Rebel soldiers.

General Okuma replies, "What do you mean?"

Eight replied, "War will come to you, but not only wipe you out, but also half of Japan."

General Okuma replies, "How do you know this?"

Eight Replied, "Put it this way, I'm from the future, and I've read my history."

General Okuma replies, "What should I do?"

Eight replied, "I need you're soldiers, if I can make it to Russia, I can rewritten history."

General Okuma replies "Yes take my soldiers, take them all."

Eight said in English, "Grandmaster my ass-hole, what a Fool more like."

Eight walked out of heading straight to the army before her, she looked ahead of herself, and she knew what her true plans were, but she was surprise how foolish the General was, by giving him a bit of herself she had him wrap around her little finger.

Eight stand in front of more than a million soldiers ready to take mother Russia.

While Eight's new army was preparing to leave for Russia, the President of USA, was not ready for what was about to hit him. All the President, his Secretary, Secret Services and people of America saw were a few dozen flying craft heading straight to the white house.

President Wilson said, "What in God's name are those?"

Secretary Josepha replied, "Looks to me like flying machines."

President Wilson replies, "Ready the army around the White House."

Prime Minster Asquith said, "I guess you don't see this every day."

Leeroy replied, "No doubt "Sir."

George said, "Are you sure we will be safe?"

Prime Minster Asquith replied, "Man up you pussy, even this fourteen year old."

Leeroy said, "Fifteen, "Sir."

Prime Minster Asquith replied, "Yeah, even this fifteen year old, has more guts than you."

X-Hamstring said, "That's true."

Prime Minster said, "Stand down Troops, no violence here."

Josepha said, "Who do you think it is?"

President replied, "It doesn't matter, those machines, look like they could rip this white house in with a new arse-hole."

Josepha said, "Indeed Mr President."

Chapter Four

Allies alike

Early 1915's

General Hudson said, "Emperor, the Troops are ready."

Emperor Wilhelm replied, "Begin invading England."

General Hudson replies, "The Bank of England?"

Emperor Wilhelm replied, "Destroy the house of common, and also the palace, today we will catcher a Queen, and then the Bank of England."

While that was happening the Prime Minster of England was in the White House, with a few Secret Services, plus the President's Personal Bodyguards, standing closely to him.

X-Hamstring said, "Sir, I'm just waiting for the call."

President Wilson replied, "Well you can wait a bit longer."

Prime Minster Asquith said, "So, can we stop the Germans?"

President Wilson replies, "Their Empire is five times bigger than, yours, mines and the Russians, they've paid off many more people. Anyone could be a threat no one is safe, too many snakes in the wood works."

Leeroy said, "Finally someone is talking some sense."

President Wilson turned to the wall turning the machine which Leeroy placed the images in, and switched it on.

The President's Secretary Josepha said, "Are you a threat or a friend?"

Prime Minster Asquith replied, "I'm a friend can you not see."

President Wilson replies, "If you are, you will share those machines out there with us, we believe you have created more."

Prime Minster replied, "I am a friend, and I do intend to share, those crafts out there with you."

Josepha said, "Where are you keeping the rest, we may need to move them, to somewhere untouchable."

Prime Minster Asquith replied, "Under the Bank of England."

The Prime Minster Advisor came running in shouting, 'the Germans have started to invade England."

President Wilson said, "Ready as many Troops as you can, many people can fit on one those?"

Prime Minster replied, 'two hundred and sixth."

Secretary replies, "We must leave some troops here, in case of an attack."

President Wilson replied, "Yes of Course."

"Prime Minster....

Asquith replied, "No President, I'm going to defend my country."

Secretary Josepha said, "Leeroy the President's Secret Services will take you and him somewhere safe."

Asquith said, "George, I'll fully understand if you want to stay here…

George replied, "Yes."

X-Hamstring said, "Coward."

Asquith said, "X-Hamstring I take that as you are with me on this one?"

X-Hamstring replied, "Yes "Sir, someone has to keep you in check."

President Wilson replies, "Good luck Asquith."

X-Hamstring said, "Asquith, does the German know, anything of the weapons?"

Prime Minster Asquith replied, "If they do we are in real danger, there's newer equipment like guns, amour, missals, tanks, rockets and more aircrafts."

X-Hamstring replies, "Why did you built them?"

Asquith replied, "To protect us from a threat like this."

X-Hamstring replies, "You might have just handed over all of lives to them."

Prime Minster Asquith and X-Hamstring climbed into Hover-Jets with some Americans heading into others, they then flew off.

The Germans Troops storm the House of Commons, placing bombs all over the place, and leaving the House of Commons, blowing it to pieces.

Elsewhere some other Germans Troops stormed the Palace, killing all the King's knights and guards, moving towards where the King and Queen was seated with a handful of knights shielding them.

General Hudson walked in behind his troops holding up their weapons at the Queen, and the Knights.

King George said, "Stand down my Knights; I will deal with this matter, myself."

The Knights looked back at the King, and the King moved forward, as the King moved forward General Hudson shot him in his chest, the King dropped down to the floor. The Knights rushed forward but the German Troops took them all out, General Hudson looked straight into the Queen's eyes.

General Hudson said quietly to himself, "I will breed her."

"Sir."

General Hudson replies "Pretend you didn't hear that."

"No "Sir, I prefer you as a leader, than Wilhelm."

General Hudson moves quickly and smoothly over to the troop stabbing him in his ribs, and twisting it upwards and inside.

General Hudson said, "I still respect Wilhelm, He's playing his part, but for me no one needs to fear yet."

The Troop dropped to the floor and Hudson walked out of the room.

Asquith said, "How long until we are in England?"

The Pilot replied, 'two or maybe three more hours."

Asquith replies, "Go full power."

"Yes "Sir."

Back in England Blunt and a very large handful of British troops blocked off the German troops, from taking central London.

Blunt said, "Stand your ground."

A grenade came down near to Blunt blasting him off his feet, and over a motor-vehicle, German Troops stormed passed him.

Blunt slowly got up as he did one German Troops threw his fist towards Blunt's face connecting Blunt's face forcing him downwards, and then the German Troop went to knee Blunt in his face. Blunt blocked it moved forward onto the Troop, grabbing his knife, and slicing the Troops neck, other German Troops shot Blunt backwards, Blunt falling down some stairs into the underground.

As Blunt heard Troops marching down the stairs, he quickly made his way to the train, jumping on it and ordering the few British Troops to get the train moving. The German Troops started firing the train to pieces, as it was slowly moving away.

Blunt looked at the map searching for something one of the British troops came to him.

"Where do you think they'll attack next?"

Blunt replied, "It wasn't attack, it was distraction."

"What do you mean?"

Blunt replied, "This train can cut into the secret path way, to the Bank of England."

'there's no path way."

Blunt replied, "Yes there is, it leads under the Bank of England."

"How do you know this?"

Blunt replied, "I'm not a hopeless Agent."

"What's under the Bank?"

Blunt replied, "Our Prime Minister's secret weapons, if the Germans know anything about this, they will be unstoppable."

The German Troops along with Emperor Wilhelm stormed the Bank of England, killing most of the employees, and also catching some.

Emperor Wilhelm said, "One of you will tell me, where the weapons are."

"Through there, "Don't hurt me, don't kill me, please."

Emperor Wilhelm said, "That was easy, you and you go."

As those two German Troops headed over to the doors, they both stepped on the ground, and they felt they got slightly lowered, just like that a force impacted them moving them backwards.

Emperor Wilhelm moved through a few Troops as the flames covered them, and Emperor moved forward at the person who pointed their hands towards that door.

Emperor Wilhelm held a gun to that person's forehead.

"I'll proudly die protecting my country."

Emperor Wilhelm said, "More the fool you are, this country wouldn't give a damn about you."

Chapter Five

German's Wrath Part 2

February 19TH 1915 German's Invasion of England

Blunt and a few handfuls of British Troops entered through the secret pathway to the Bank of England, but were they too late.

Wilhelm informed his Troops to blew the floor to pieces, in which they did after and after, until the floor came apart, and beneath them where no longer than the weapons.

Emperor Wilhelm said, "Silly British."

Wilhelm and his forces gathered the weapons together as they were, Blunt and a few handfuls of British Troops, came through another secret door, to find that the hidden room was being cleared out.

Blunt said, "Stop them."

Emperor Wilhelm replied, "We have what we want, hold them back."

As Emperor Wilhelm got into a more advance Hover-Jet, Asquith and the rest came flying in and started blasting, but THE Craft Wilhelm was in was much more powerful.

X-Hamstring said, "He's escaping, wait watch out."

A tank fire a cannon towards the Hover-Jet X-Hamstring was in; X-Hamstring flew out of the craft as it blew to pieces, and fall into the Bank of England which was half destroyed.

Asquith said, "Fall back, they have tanks, we are too late. Wait what are they doing?"

"Sir, they are America, that's what they do."

A few other Hover-Jet heading after Emperor Wilhelm, but the tanks were shooting them out of the sky.

Asquith said, "Fall back; we need all of the Hover-Jets we have, fall back."

The Hover-Jet Emperor Wilhelm was in turned around while flying backwards, aiming at the Hover-Jet Asquith was on, and firing towards it. This missal came flying towards the Asquith, and then the Hover-Jet blew to pieces, Asquith was on the ground with a force field over the few British and America Troops.

Asquith said, "This is very bad."

X-Hamstring rolled onto the ground, watching in front of him, someone running towards him blasting this Machine Rifle, X-Hamstring quickly flick the bullet of his sword blade, moving him kicking down the unknown person.

X-Hamstring then found himself being under attacking by other British Troops, X-Hamstring dive for covered, but also throwing out a few daggers which spin in the air. They cut and sliced into the Troops body, the unknown person to X-Hamstring but known person to us which was Blunt got taking out an Axe.

Blunt said, "Bring it."

X-Hamstring came out of cover facing Blunt, Blunt started running towards X-Hamstring, just as Blunt was going to place his Axe in the way of X-Hamstring Asquith appeared in the middle of them both forcing them back.

Asquith said, "What are you both doing?"

X-hamstring replied, "You know him." Blunt replied, "You know him."

Asquith said, "You're both on the same sides."

X-Hamstring said, "Why couldn't you stop them?"

Blunt replied. "Unlike you I'm not a super-human, and I only had six British Troops with me, against a few thousand of them."

X-Hamstring replies, "How did you know I was a Super-Human?"

Blunt replied, "Guessing by your raw strength, and reflexes."

X-Hamstring replies, "Yet you still decided to fraught me."

Blunt replied, "Because I fucking love my country."

Asquith said, "I'm just wondering what German's, next plan is."

General Hudson was sitting across from the Queen, back in Germany.

General Hudson said, "Eat, please, do not insult me like this."

The Queen of England replied, "Why are you doing this, you seem like a decent lad?"

General Hudson replies, "Wilhelm is forcing me to, but don't worry, as long as you're with me I'll look after you."

The Queen replied, "Why is Wilhelm doing this?"

General Hudson replies, "I am not sure, maybe out of power."

The Queen replied, "Please free me, please."

General Hudson replies, "I cannot he'll kill my son and mother, if I had a say all this wouldn't be happening."

The Queen replied, "Why are you so nice to me, when you are not around, his troops."

General Hudson replies, "I'm sorry my Queen, but when I'm around them, I have to put up an act pretend that I am heartless."

The Queen replied, "When the British come, I'll make sure no harm, comes to you."

General Hudson replies, "Please eat, you need you're strength."

Emperor Wilhelm came back with a handful of new and very advance equipment and weapons, this would make his army the strongest in the world, people haven't experience so far, but now they will.

This would enable Wilhelm forces too travel the world more quickly, and taking over cities and countries, more quickly, Emperor Wilhelm empire was about to triple the size and within only a short period.

More than half a year went by Asquith and Wilson had to do something, German had already taken over twenty new countries, the Emperor's forces were growing.

Elsewhere a very large group of Russia rebels decided to stand their ground against the Chinese forces, this was perfect for both Eight and Emperor Wilhelm.

Emperor Wilhelm said, 'today my soldiers, you will attack Russia, and take it from them there I will build the greatest empire."

Eight said, "We are very close to the broader of Russia, there I will build my weapon, which will wipe out all of my enemies."

The Chinese came into the other side of Russia; the Russians were holding them back, unaware of another two attacks which were going to take place.

Finn which was the Russia Rebel leader said, "Kill them all."

Finn jumped off where he was standing racing into the crowd of Chinese soldiers, killing them one by one, the Russia seem very powerful on this side of their country, but on the other side trouble had just begun.

"Alert President Nicolas, the Germans are attacking, they've taken over five cities already."

The news travelled far in fact it travelled all the way over to Finn.

Finn said, "I did warn the government of the German intentions, not my problem."

Eight could just about see land until one of her ships got blasts, Eight turned to the side of her, and saw the Japanese Imperial Army.

Eight said, "Why are they attacking us?"

"We are Rebels."

Eight replies, "A figure of speech."

"I do not understand."

Eight said in English, "Course you wouldn't understand."

Eight ordered her troops to push forward, and had the other ships turn, to attack the Japanese Imperial Army.

"It's General Okuma."

Eight replies, "Why is he working with the Imperial Army?"

"He never wanted a war with Russia; he believes Russia could destroy Japan."

Eight replies, "Keep pushing, we are very close."

Deep in Russia President Nicolas had ordered a massive group of Russia soldiers to march towards the Germans, once word somehow got back to Eight she was pleased this was what she wanted. Eight ship crashed onto one of the beaches of Russia, Eight gathered her small group of Rebel Troops together, and marched into Russia undetected. Eight aimed was to get to one of the greatest labs known to earth, which was located somewhere in Russia, so that she could help the Russian's scientists finish build an ultimate machine. The German forces came across the Russia soldiers, but this time around the Russian soldiers weren't so powerful, as the German forces wiped them out like nothing. After Finn had defeated the few Chinese's soldiers, plus scaring them back to China, he decided to help the President of Russia.

Finn said, "We will help our brothers, defeat this German fiend, they will not be so powerful against our wrath."

Eight had got to the mountain in which the secret lab was hidden; Eight stormed into the mountain, just like that the Russian Scientists surrendered.

Eight said, 'that machine will not work without my blood, your machine will be become my machine."

Chapter Six

Russia's downfall

Mid 1916's Germans took over of Russia

Finn watched as the German Troops stormed into the President's palace, Finn held back his last rebel soldiers, and looked at all of them.

Finn said, "We are no longer any help, we must leave."

"There's no where we can go."

"Yes, one place, America. There will seek help."

Emperor Wilhelm walked into the throne room, where the President was sitting along with many troops, Wilhelm laughed out loud.

President Nicolas said, "You cannot do this."

Emperor Wilhelm replied, "You will be the last emperor of Russia, this country will be called, Republic of German."

Emperor Nicolas replies, "Republic of German, don't make me laugh, this man is ill kill him."

As Nicolas troops march forward towards Emperor Wilhelm, Wilhelm's soldiers jumped forward, in the advance armoury. Nicolas's troops found out that they were no match for, Emperor Wilhelm's advance soldiers.

Emperor Wilhelm said, "Join me or die like you're ex-leader."

Nicolas's troops looked back at him at that moment of time, Nicolas got up racing towards Emperor Wilhelm, holding his pistol in his hands. Nicolas troops moved in front of him, knocking out his pistol, and then pinning him down to the floor.

Emperor Wilhelm said, "Wise choice to make."

Wilhelm moved forward towards Nicolas getting onto his knees, and going up close to his ear, speaking in Russian.

"You're Downfall will shake the Earth."

Emperor Wilhelm then sliced open Nicolas throat killing him immediately, while that was happening, Eight's few hundred rebel soldiers were trying their best to hold back the Imperial Japanese army, but they were struggling.

"We should surrender."

"Never!"

Somewhere else in Russia deep in the mountains, Eight and a few dozen of her rebel soldiers, were fighting off some Russian troops.

Eight moved forward taking out her two pistols shooting down some Russian troops, and then flying forward kicking some more Russian troops down.

More Russian troops came out from the back surrounding Eight and her few Rebel soldiers, Eight headed into them dodging their attack, and killing the rest of the Russian troops. As Eight moved forward to the scientists, the scientists quickly kneed down to her, like she was an goddess.

Eight said, "What kind of metal is this?"

"It came out from space, its very advance, but we are having trouble."

Eight replies, "What kind of troubles?"

"We need a source of pure energy, so when we finish building the machine, the machine will be online."

Eight sliced her arm and drain some of her blood into a tube, and passed it onto one of the scientists.

Eight said, 'test this."

While that was happening Emperor Wilhelm had taken over Russia, in fact a spy came back to him, saying that he saw a group of Russia rebel heading to a ship.

Emperor Wilhelm said, "Kill them, wait, no instead bring me their leader alive."

While Finn with a handful of Russia Rebels, they scanned ahead over at the docks, looking for any German troops, but he saw none Finn had a weird feeling about this.

Finn said, "We will not take a ship, in fact we will take, one of those flying machines."

"You really want to kill us."

"Calm down."

"I won't calm down; I'll join the Germans, that's the smarter move."

Finn replies, "You're become their slave, what's wrong with you?"

"Better than them killing me."

"You mean us."

"See Finn, I'm not alone on this one."

Finn said, "I can't let you go."

"Try and stop us."

Finn moved forward passing his loyal troops, and forcing down the troop wishing to leave, and holding his blade up against the troop's throat.

"What are you waiting for, kill me already, I rather you kill me than them."

Finn replied, "It doesn't have to be like that."

"Watch out behind you."

An impacted happened near them knocking more than half of Finn's rebel troops down to the ground and out, the troop which wanted to go, got up and started running towards the German soldiers, holding their arms up basically surrendering.

"What should I do?"

"Kill them all."

The German soldiers was holding a Rifle with a scope on it, as the Russia rebel troop was running towards him, he shot the troop down. Finn and a few other Russian Rebel troops saw this, and Finn got up as he did, he got shot by the same person. Finn went flying backwards onto the floor next to one of his troops, the troop moved down next to Finn, and then Finn started breathing again.

"What the hell?"

Finn rolled around into cover and the other troops, saw Finn wound heal back to normal, Finn looked down at the side of his body noticing it as well.

Finn said, "I remember."

Finn grabbed a Rifle from one of his dead troop's, moving forward to the German soldiers, as the German Soldiers were firing at him, Finn was twisting and moving pass the bullets.

"Who is that guy?"

Finn came in on the German Soldiers, taking the blade out of the Rifle; he stabbed two German Soldiers, rolling forward throwing the blade into another German soldier's neck. Finn picked up a machine gun while moving forward at the other German soldiers, and he started blasting the hell out of the rest of the German soldiers, as that was happening a tank from Finn's side fire at him, as the impact came down on him, Finn somehow placed a force field around himself. This event which just took back travelled fast back to Emperor Wilhelm; Wilhelm rushed out of his chair, grabbing a knife of the table moving unbelievable quickly to his soldier ramming the knife into the soldier's side.

Emperor Wilhelm said, "What are the rest of you looking at, get into the Hover-Jets, and get after him."

After Finn destroyed the tank Finn turned around to only a few of his Troops, they came up close to him.

"What are you?"

"I am Finn Between, I am not from this Earth, but a place we call the True world. Better known as Ruthon, I came through a black hole after my brother Asquith Between, we are only here to gain knowledge, but being here we have changed events badly."

"Finn Between, we are with you until the end, to make things right again."

Finn Between replied, 'to America we shall go."

Finn and the last remaining of his rebel Troops boarded an Hover-Jet, Finn moved to the front of the Hover-Jet, and one of the troop looked at him funny.

"Do you know how to fly this thing?"

Finn replied, "It's has an similar systems as a Magic-Craft, I can fly this."

"A Magic-Craft?"

So as Emperor Wilhelm and a great force of his soldiers came to that side of the country, they saw Finn fly away.

"Emperor, what now?"

"Let them go, we have important matters to attend to."

One of the Rebel Troops said, "I wouldn't believe this to be the downfall of Russia."

Finn between replied, "Believe me it is, but we will fix this, and make sure Emperor Wilhelm pays for killing our brothers and sisters."

While Finn and few of his troops were travelling off towards America, back in Germany General Hudson was in bed with the Queen, just like that a few German soldiers bushed through the doors. Hudson got up placing on his gams, and was about to go for his handgun, but it was too late as the German soldiers knocked him down to the floor.

"When word of mouth, of this situation gets to Emperor Wilhelm, he will not be grateful off you're intentions."

The Queen of England replies "Leave him alone."

"Take him away."

While Hudson got dragged out of the room else where a few German Soldiers were being taken out, and moved forward was two masked man, as they stealthy moved through the kingdom, taking out soldier after soldier, until they heard screams.

The German soldier smashed the Queen of England of the bed over onto the floor, moving around to her.

"I show you what a real man is."

While unbuckling his bait the two masked men came into the room, the German Soldier move around aiming his handgun at them firing it off, the two masked men move out of the way of the bullets, and knocked the handgun out of the German soldiers hand, and grabbing him up against the wall.

"If you don't mine my Queen, please turn away for a moment two three."

The mask man who had the German Soldier up against the wall, started to cut into the soldier's throat, and then threw the soldier down to the ground.

The Queen of England said, "Who are you two?"

Both the masked men refill their faces to the Queen; they were no other than X-Hamstring and Blunt.

"My name's Blunt, I'm one of British MI6 agents, and this here is X-Hamstring He's the President of American secret service."

AS Blunt and X-Hamstring escorted the Queen through the kingdom, Blunt and X-Hamstring were killing soldiers after soldiers, until they got to a room, where they saw General Hudson getting beating to death.

"Pain first, and then tell the Emperor, of your actions."

As one of the German soldiers said that Blunt came behind him, snapping his neck in half, and then the other started firing his handgun at Blunt. Blunt sliced of the Soldier's arm. just before Blunt went to ram his blade into General Hudson, the Queen screamed out.

X-Hamstring said, "What's wrong with you?"

Queen replied, "He's a good guy, He's been looking after me, He's treated me brilliantly."

Her scream did alert some more German soldiers over to them, but as General Hudson got untied, he step in front of his German soldiers.

General Hudson said, "Stand down men."

"Emperor Wilhelm will not…

"What he will or will not like, I show no care for, stand down or you join you're other comrades."

Many more German soldiers came from behind them, and to the side of them, General Hudson wasn't sure on what was about to happen. The next few actions which took place, was going to be important for the survival of Germany's Empire, the German soldiers kneed down in front of Hudson.

"We respect you move as a leader, then the Emperor, what is your orders General?"

General Hudson replied, 'thank you my soldiers, I order you to let these few go, and also to company me to Russia. It's time Emperor Wilhelm dies, but I can't do this alone, will you join me."

"Yes."

The Queen of England said, 'thank you Hudson, I hope we meet again soon."

General Hudson replied, "We will meet again, I'll make sure of that."

So as Blunt, X-Hamstring and the Queen of England got into a Hover-Jet which was an upgraded from the Hover-Jet, they flew back into England. While General Hudson's own plans were setting in nicely, as he was in a Hover-Jet headed towards Russia, but what was his true intentions, was what he said to the Queen of England a lie or some part the truth. General Hudson said, "After the Emperor is dead, so that you few know, I do not wish to be you're leader."

"If we do not have a leader, then who will manage this war, you must become our leader. You are strong, smart, better in every way."

General Hudson replies, "I only wish to free you from his will."

"You are the next Emperor, which will make German's Empire, a much feared and ruthless one."

Chapter Seven

Japan Imperial Army

January the 15th 1917 Japan allied with the new German forces

So the Japanese Imperial Army destroyed the last of the Rebel soldiers, storming onto one of Russian's beaches, as they marched off their ships and onto the land.

The new German force awaited there for them, with less than half a million soldiers to face, General Okuma and Emperor Taisho, came off the ship to meet with the new German force.

"Emperor Wilhelm wishes not to war with you, as he believes he could whip you clear of the surface of the Earth."

Emperor Taisho replied, "We too do not wish to war with him, we are after a person leading a small group of Japanese rebel soldiers, we believe she came through here."

General Okuma said, 'she goes by the name Eight, she does believe she is from the future, and she can help win the war against the U.S.A and Great Britain."

"I think you both have been fooled, let me guess she requested something of yours?"

General Okuma replies, "Yes to lead my Rebel soldiers."

"What for and why Russia?"

President Taisho replies, 'she's after something that the Russia Scientists has been trying to create."

"If that is so, the rumours are true, they are building the machine I must report this back to Emperor Wilhelm."

General Okuma replied, "I believe I cannot allow you to do that."

Okuma moved forward with his Samurai slicing into the German Soldiers chest, forcing it out, and slicing of another German Soldiers head.

President Taisho said, "Move forward and attack."

So as the Imperial Army was attacking the New German soldiers, word got back to Emperor Wilhelm that the Japanese Imperial Army had started warring against him?

While that was happening it was perfect for China to invade Japan, in which they did.

Emperor Wilhelm was trying to figure out why the Japanese Imperial Army was warring against him, even though he had nothing to worry about, as the Japanese Imperial Army was losing against him.

One of the new German soldiers bottled it, and run away back into the city, while most of the Japanese Imperial Army retreated back to their ships.

A Hover-Jet landed down outside of the Emperor's new palace, and out came German soldiers into the palace carrying the Emperor of Japan, and getting him to inform to the Emperor that his Japanese Imperial Army was retreating.

Emperor Wilhelm said, "You must be foolish."

Taisho replied, "I never knew you took over Russia."

Emperor Wilhelm replies, "Why did you come here?"

Taisho replied, "With honour I'll never tell you."

Taisho trapped both of the German soldier to the ground, grabbing one of their blades, as he was about to stab himself, General Hudson shot the blade out of Taisho hand Taisho went mad and started heading his head against the ground.

Emperor Wilhelm said, "General Hudson, why are you here, where is the Queen?"

In walked General Hudson with a few rebel soldiers.

General Hudson replied, "Let's stop this guy from killing himself first."

The German soldiers came down to Taisho as they lift his head up, they knock him out with the back of their Rifle handle, and then took him away.

Emperor Wilhelm said, 'start talking Hudson."

General Hudson replied, 'the Kingdom was invaded, I don't know how they did it."

Emperor Wilhelm replies, "Impossible, invaded by whom?"

General Hudson replied, 'the Americans and British."

Emperor Wilhelm replies, "What about the Queen?"

General Hudson replied, 'the last of us were outnumbered, we had to leave, get here to inform you."

Emperor Wilhelm replies, "How could my Kingdom get invaded, when I have more than a hundred thousand soldiers, defending the Kingdom."

General Hudson replied, "I believe it to be an inside job."

Emperor Wilhelm replies, "Are you saying, that I have double agents, working within my house?"

General Hudson replied, "Yes, but do not worry, they didn't take any of the equipment's back, only the Queen."

Emperor Wilhelm started walking slowly around his long table, looking at his other German soldiers, and then looked at General Hudson.

Emperor Wilhelm said, "How long have I known you?"

General Hudson replied, "I'm not sure, about eighteen years."

Emperor Wilhelm replies, "You're like family aren't you, and family don't betray their own blood do they?"

General Hudson replied, "What are you getting at?"

Emperor Wilhelm replies, "All my soldiers are not my blood, but I consider you as, my blood."

Emperor Wilhelm looked pass General Hudson, and said, "Kill them."

General Hudson German Rebel troops marched through, shooting all of the German soldiers sitting around the table, more German soldiers came into the room, and the Rebel troops killed them as well.

Emperor Wilhelm said, "I'm so lost, I'm so helpless, lead me General Hudson show me what to do next?"

General Hudson looked at the Emperor and laughed out loud, taking his handgun out, and shooting the Emperor's leg the Emperor dropped to the floor.

Emperor Wilhelm screaming out more and more German soldiers came rushing into the room, but the German rebel troops took care of each and every single one of them.

General Hudson shot the Emperor in the upper part of his chest, by the force of the bullet the Emperor moved backwards, to the bottom of his chair.

General Hudson walked in close to the Emperor kneeling down to him, as he did the Emperor went to stab Hudson into his neck, but Hudson knocked the blade out of his hand, and shot Wilhelm in his other leg.

Emperor Wilhelm said, "You're the inside man?"

General Hudson replied, "I've been waiting so long to do this, it disgusts me to even be called a German, even though I am only one half German. Oh didn't you get the memo, my mother is Russian, so yes my mother was one of them. One of them which you threw out, but you see both my parents were smart giving me none of their last names, yes I'm lucky enough to have my last name German hiding my true identity."

In Wilhelm weak voice he replies, "Why are you doing this?"

Hudson in a proud and powerful tone replied, "It was my father's last wish, before you sent troops to murder, any man whom lay down with Russian woman."

Wilhelm replies in a lower quiet struggling voice, "We could have made this Empire great."

Hudson in an angry tone replied, "No, I will destroy this Empire, and build a greater one."

Hudson then took out his Axe placed it against Wilhelm throat, and moved it back, and raced it in cutting of Wilhelm head.

Hudson then hangs up Wilhelm head and as more German soldiers came into the room, they saw Wilhelm head, and Hudson sitting down. The German soldiers dropped their weapons and surrendered to Hudson, Hudson got up moving towards them and stops and he looked down at one of the German troops, and noticed something about him.

Hudson talking in a strong Russia tone said, "You are Russian?"

Asking back in a worrying tone, "Yes."

Hudson replies, "Stand up, be proud."

Hudson walked out onto the ledge of the palace; he then talked into this mic-phone.

"I am you're new Emperor, today our Empire will become greater, as the person stands before you, shares both German and Russian bloodlines, and this country will be reclaim as Mother Russia."

As Emperor Hudson walked back into the Palace royal room, he heard both sides cheer his name.

April the 27ᵗʰ 1916

The Queen of England was sitting down in front of the last members of the House of Commons, the Prime Minster, and the MI6.

One person from the MI6 said, "Our spies have returned, it's seems like good and bad news my queen."

The Queen looked down at her new born daughter, with a hopeless smile, and replied, "You may shed the bad news first."

"Hudson, has become the new Emperor, and he has renamed the Republic of German, he is calling it Mother Russia."

The Queen replies, "The good news?"

"Well that Wilhelm is dead and that there will be no further attacks on Great Britain."

The Queen replies, "We need a work force, so that Britain can be rebuilt, and carries its name proudly."

"My Queen the work force had already arrived; Britain is slowly becoming Great Britain again."

"Good job."

Prime Minster Asquith said, "We should be thinking ahead, I am not sure of Hudson intentions."

Blunt replies, 'thinking ahead it's the year nineteen fifteen, we act now before Hudson does."

Prime Minster Asquith replied, "India is off the subject."

Blunt replies, 'they are a few miles from, a rise to power, Emperor Hudson will notice this and act on it. Why don't we beat him to it, they could be great, as our allies."

The Queen of England replied, "We are in dark times, we should be thinking of building back an army."

Prime Minster replies, "All of our resources went into building, those machines, equipment's, arsenals, and don't forget getting the labour to build Great Britain back."

Member of the House of Common's replied, "He's right, we can't afford travelling to India, what if we cause worst things to happen?"

The Queen of England replies, "It's a risk we must make."

Blunt replied, "I agree with the Queen."

Head chief of the MI6 said, 'the only honest thing we can do is, borrow from the US."

The Queen of England replied, "Do it."

Blunt replied, "Being in debt with the US for more than a hundred years doesn't sound good."

The Queen of England replies, "I agree, but what choice do we have, Emperor Hudson could be looking to invade again, especially if he founds out the truth."

Prime Minster Asquith replied, "What truth, am I missing something?"

"Can I speak with you my Queen?"

"Yes Blunt speak out loud, we do not hide any secret from each other."

'this one should be privately."

As the Queen and Blunt went into the next room the Head Chief was MI6 was quick to say, 'that guy he thinks he so special."

"He's one of your best agents isn't he?"

"Prime Minster with all respect He's an asshole, look at him."

"I think you're being a bit harsh, he saved the Queen."

"Look at this, a super-human; of course you would be thinking like that, if that's the case he should be the Director of the MI6."

"He's better than the MI6," said X-Ham.

"What did you just say?"

"Guys leave it."

As Blunt and the Queen walk out of the other room, the Queen's personal bodyguard escorted her away, Blunt came back into the room.

"Well, I have to go back to America," said X-Ham.

"The land of the great aye," said Prime Minster Asquith.

"Tell that kid, Leeroy his Visa was accepted, he should receive it in the post any day soon," said Blunt.

"One of his biggest dreams come true, to set up a business in this country."

"He's got that chance to do that now," said Prime Minster Asquith.

Head Chief of MI6 turned to Blunt, "You will stay in the palace for now; we need someone on the inside, just in case anything crazy would to happen."

"Yes "Sir, no problem "Sir."

"X-Ham, before you leave, I will need your help with something."

"Yes Prime Minster, anything."

Chapter Eight

Mother Russia's Wrath part 1

Late 1917's

As Emperor Hudson was about to take his seat, three of his soldiers came into his royal room, throwing down this unknown person.

Emperor Hudson said, "Who is this person, well who is he?"

One of the soldiers replied, "A spy working for Great Britain."

Emperor Hudson moved forward throwing out his hand, smacking the guy upwards, and then kicking him backwards to the floor, making him land onto his bum also holding his handgun at his forehead.

Emperor Hudson said, "What is your name?"

"I am Agent A1389574602."

Emperor Hudson said, "Who do you work for?"

"I am Agent A1389574602."

Emperor Hudson looked at his soldiers, and said, "Do I really have to play this pathetic game?"

Emperor took out an army knife stabbing it into the Agent's leg, and digging it in some more, slowly slicing through his leg.

Emperor Hudson said, "Now let's do this again, "Who do you work for?"

In a painful weak tone the Agent replied, "MI6."

Emperor Hudson replies, "What is the MI6?" squeezing the knife into the Agent's leg some more."

The Agent screamed out, "Mother's Intelligences sector six."

Emperor Hudson replies, "Where is this MI6 located?"

"Agent A1389…… Emperor pulled out the knife and stabbed it into, the Agent's shoulder, forcing him down to the ground.

Emperor Hudson said, "Where is this……

"England, London, next to the Bank of England."

Emperor Hudson replies, 'that wasn't hard was it, you're free to go."

"I'm free to go?"

Emperor Hudson replies, "They will clean you up."

As the Agent was about to walk out with the three soldiers escorting him, Emperor turned back around to the Agent.

In English the Emperor Hudson said, "Agent A1389574602?"

As the Agent turned around Emperor Hudson threw the knife into the chest of the Agent, the Agent immediately dropped backwards hitting the ground and his eyes rolled in.

Emperor Hudson replies, "Someone clean that mess up."

As Emperor Hudson walked back to his table one of his loyal soldiers turned advisor came to the side of him, talking in Russian.

"We must attack England, destroy the MI6, they could become a problem and we don't like problems."

Emperor Hudson replied, "Problems, no I don't like problems at all, you are right. Ready the army but this time we only take a quarter of them, I have other plans for the rest of the army."

As the Queen entered her bedroom to find her husband King George sitting there holding their baby in his arm, with a pistol in his hand, the Queen went to move forward but King George didn't allow her any closer.

King George fired the pistol of near her, and said, "Don't move."

The Queen replied, "Why are you doing this?"

King George replies, "You haven't been faithful to me, have you?"

The Queen replied, "I don't understand, I don't know what I have done wrong?"

King George replies, "The baby, she isn't mines is she, who's baby is that?"

The Queen replied, "Course the baby is yours, this is not the right time, to be thinking like this."

King George replies, "When is the right time to think like anything?"

The Queen replied, "Give me my baby, and we can talk."

King George replies, "We"re talking right now."

The Queen noticed that the King has been drinking as well, the look of things; He's been drinking a lot.

The Queen said, "Just hand over the baby please."

King George moved forward nearly dropping to the floor, and the Queen Rushes forward, grabbing hold of the baby, King George fired off the pistol.

As the King looked at his wife he saw blood rushing down out of her, the Queen dropped to her knees still holding her child, and the guards and Knights came rushing into the room.

As that happened something crashed into the side of the Palace, Blunt came into the room, and saw what had happened.

Blunt said, "Oh no, the Russian are invading again, come on my King you must leave."

King George holding onto his wife the Queen saying, "No, no, nooooooooooooooooooooooooooo."

Blunt took the Princess moving forward the Palace as he saw behind him Russian soldiers killing Knights and Guards, Blunt got to the back of the Palace, X-Hamstring and Asquith was in a Hover-Jet, Blunt raced over to them jumping into the Hover-Jet.

"Get the hell out of here."

Asquith replied, "This is the only Hover-Jet left, what about the Queen and King,"

Blunt looked up at Asquith and he knew by Blunt's body languages that something bad had happened to both the King and Queen.

X-Hamstring said, "Where are we going?"

"America?" Asked Blunt.

Asquith replied, "No, India."

"Sir this Hover-Jet hasn't got enough fuel to get us to India, maybe north of France, but not India."

Blunt replies, "Just get us from here."

As they looked back at the Palace they saw it blow to pieces, and then three Hover-Jets popped up, and started firing on them.

X-Hamstring said, "Asquith what are you doing?"

Asquith replied, "Giving you guys a way out."

Blunt replies, "That's suicide man."

Asquith said, "Fly right towards them, I'll meet you guys in France or India."

As the Hover-Jet flew over one of the three Hover-Jets, Asquith jumped out of it, crashing through the top part of the Hover-Jet breaking his way inside of the Hover-Jet. As hr did Russian soldiers came at him, he punch one back forcing the rest to drop down, Asquith then sent a force to the rest killing them like nothing. Asquith came up near to the pilot slicing the back of his neck, and flying the Hover-Jet near the other Hover-Jets.

Asquith opened the door as the Hover-Jet crashed into the other Hover-Jet jumping into that Hover-Jet, some more Russian soldiers came at him, one stabbed him in the shoulder and the other stabbed him in his side, holding him up in mid-air, another soldier punched Asquith forcing him from the blades.

Asquith dropped to the floor blooding while a soldier kick Asquith to the face, making him roll near to the edge of the Hover-Jet's door, another Russian soldiers aimed his machine gun down at Asquith, at this time Asquith quickly rolled out of the Hover-Jet, back climbing around the bottom of it, to the other side of the Hover-Jet, climbing inside as he saw the Russian soldiers looking over the edge.

One Russian soldier said, "Where is he?"

Asquith replied, "Behind you."

Asquith throws a grenade moved backwards as it exploded killing the soldiers, but also destroying the Hover-Jet, Asquith forced jump forward into the last of the three Hover-Jets. As he entered into the Hover-Jet Emperor Hudson, was standing their holding a handgun, and he started shooting the hell out of Asquith, Asquith dropped to the floor, and started healing back but very slowly.

Emperor Hudson said, "I know what you are, so I made sure these bullets, were made out of gold."

One of his soldiers came forward stabbing him with a gold blade, and another stabbed him, and another stabbed, until he was left with six blades in him, pinning him up against the inside of this Hover-Jet. Emperor Hudson shot Asquith three more times, blood was just dropping from Asquith, Emperor Hudson moved forward grabbing hold off Asquith's throat.

"What about the others?"

Emperor Hudson replied, "Don't worry about them; we're get it out of him." Emperor then stabbed Asquith into his stomach with his army knife made out of gold.

Asquith's eyes closed and everything went blank.

Chapter Ten

Russia's secret Prison

November the 22nd 1917 Emperor Hudson catcher Prime Minster Asquith

Emperor Hudson said, "I just like the feel the look of gold, it doesn't wonders for me."

His army came through the doors of the MI6, as the Agents went for their handguns; Hudson's army destroyed them like nothing.

Emperor Hudson said, "Don't kill him."

As Asquith came through the doors carried by six soldiers, with the blades in his back this time, Asquith looked up at Hudson and Hudson punched him knocking him out again.

Emperor Hudson said, "Lock him up there, this would make a fine prison, one no one would think of looking here."

"You won't get along with this, someone will kill you."

Emperor Hudson replied, "I'm guessing you're the leader right?"

"Yes, but that doesn't matter."

Emperor Hudson replied, "Who knows of this place?"

"No-one does, it's a secret."

Emperor Hudson replied, "Perfect place to build a prison, what do you think?"

"You are truly crazy."

Emperor Hudson replied, "Crazy a simple word to use, I'm far from crazy, I'm just doing what best suits me."

"What's that?"

Emperor Hudson moved forward punching pass the Head Chief face, but through a wall, in which a hidden safe was.

Emperor Hudson said, "What's this?"

"Nothing important, just some information, plans on the underground."

Emperor Hudson replied, "I can't read English, something I should learn, but the way things are going I doubt I would need to."

Emperor Hudson moved backwards to an MI6 Agent blooding out badly, and threw down the file, and said read it."

Agent said, "Agent A1235678932."

Emperor Hudson replied, "Really?"

Emperor Hudson while looking at the Agent blooding out, aimed his handgun at the Head of Chief, firing his handgun, as she looked at the Head of Chief, one of Hudson's soldier's dropped to the floor.

Emperor Hudson said, "Oopppss."

Emperor Hudson then shot the Head of Chief, he flipped to the ground, and the Agent started reading.

Emperor Hudson said, "What does it say?"

"It's a DNA result."

Emperor Hudson replies, "DNA result, for whom."

"The Princess of England."

Emperor Hudson replies, "Stating what?"

"That King George is not her biological father."

Emperor Hudson thought to himself, if that is correct almost two years have passed by, when he laid in bed with the Queen, it came to his knowledge that he may be the father to the Queen's daughter.

"This means nothing."

Emperor Hudson replied, "No, it means everything."

The Agent looked back at the Head Chief as she got shot in her head, Emperor Hudson moved around to Asquith.

Emperor Hudson said, "This will be you're new prison, imagine that, you being imprisoned in your own country."

Asquith lift up his head something he was trying to say, Emperor Hudson jumped back, and then bend down grabbing Asquith's head.

Emperor Hudson said, "He's about to say something, wait for it, wait for it."

Emperor Hudson placed his ear closer to Asquith mouth.

Asquith in a very quiet voice, said, "Go to hell."

So X-Hamstring and Blunt landed down somewhere north of France, they knew they had to move out of open, into cover as some Prussia soldiers were in France already. They named themselves Prussia instead of Russia, because they were mix with both German and Russia troops.

So somewhere near the middle of France, President Raymond, and his army had got caught.

Raymond said, "My army will rise up against you."

A Prussia soldier replied, "Most of your army has joined us already, it's over."

Raymond replies, "Where are you taking us?"

The Prussia soldier replied, "Who said we're taking them anywhere, you're the person Emperor Hudson wants."

As Raymond looked over his shoulder at his troops, the Prussia soldiers killed all of Raymond's last loyal troops, and then knocked Raymond out.

Elsewhere deep in France Blunt and X-Hamstring found themselves running through the back streets carrying the Princess of England

Blunt said, "Where are you going, it's this way."

X-Hamstring replied, "If we go that way, we will run into, the soldiers."

Blunt replies, "Come on."

X-Hamstring replied, "It's getting dark, and you're carrying a baby, we need to find somewhere to stay."

Blunt looked passed X-Hamstring at the Prussian soldiers, marching towards them, Blunt moved through the back roads of France, with X-Hamstring.

A stranger said, "Over here in here."

Blunt replied, "Who are you?"

The Stranger replies, "Friend."

X-Hamstring replied, "It's better than being out in the open."

So Blunt and X-Hamstring climbed down inside of this house.

"Put the baby over there, It'll be fine, go on."

Blunt placed the baby down onto the soft clothes, and quickly went to the gap, and looked up out of it as the Prussian soldiers marched pass.

X-Hamstring said, "Who are you?"

The Stranger replied, "A friend like I said."

Blunt replies, "What kind of friend?"

The Stranger replied, "I work for the French special forces."

X-Hamstring replies, "You sound a little Prussia, to me."

The Stranger replied, 'that's because I joined the German forces at a young age as a spy to blend in, I'm one of hundred Special Forces that are looking to destroy the Prussia forces from the inside."

Blunt replied, "Ok kid, what's your name?"

The Stranger replies, "Does that matter?"

X-Hamstring replied, "Not really."

Blunt replies, "No, it matters to me."

The Strange replied, "Fine, my name is Eric."

Blunt replies, "How old are you?"

Eric replied, 'twenty, what does that matter?"

X-Hamstring replies, "He's only two years older than you."

Blunt replied, 'this is why it matters."

Blunt raced forward towards Eric drawing out his sword, but X-Hamstring knocked Blunt off his feet and backwards. The baby started to cry Eric moved over to the baby, holding a small dagger at the baby's throat, while X-Hamstring and Blunt was fighting.

Suddenly Prussia soldiers bashed through the door, and Blunt and X-Hamstring looked towards the baby in which Eric, had a small dagger at the baby's throat.

Eric said, "Do not move."

X-Hamstring throws five daggers stabbing into five Prussia's soldiers, while Eric went to slice the baby's throat, Blunt shot Eric downwards, Blunt quickly moved over to the baby grabbing it. As more Prussia Soldier's came into the house, X-Hamstring killed them swiftly, coming out of the house to see more soldiers coming towards them.

X-Hamstring said, "Back inside."

Blunt replied, "What now?"

X-Hamstring replies, "Out that where."

Mid 1918's

The Prison was built in fact Hudson connected it to the Bank of England, with Asquith and Raymond both imprisoned in it.

Asquith's Brother

Early 1919's

Finn walked into the President safe house, as he did the President's secret services surrounded him quickly, Finn hold his hand around his Blade handle ready to pull it out.

Leeroy said, "Stop, stop, he's a good guy."

President Wilson replied, "Who is he?"

Leeroy replies, "He was the next person on my list."

Josepha said, "What list?"

Leeroy replied, "A person who will be known to you, but right now isn't important to mention."

President Wilson said, "Why are you here?"

Finn replied, "I need your help, to take back Mother Russia, from Emperor Hudson."

Josepha replies, "What kind of help do you think, we can give you, don't you see we're all in the same position."

"It took me almost two year just to get here standing in front of you, if it was for no reason, then I wouldn't have a reason to want Mother Russia back on the right path."

President Wilson, "Over these years we lost many; I doubt I want to lose anymore, let's hear him out."

Leeroy said, "Sir, tell them to place down, their weapons."

President Wilson said, "Stand down men."

Josepha said, "Come this way so we can talk."

As Finn walked into a room and the few Russian Rebel troops stood around, watching the secret service watch them, Leeroy came into the room as well.

Josepha said, "Does the boy have to be here?"

Finn replied, "Yes, I like him, he stays."

President Wilson replies, "You're English is good, for a Russian."

Finn Between replied, "It should be, I've studied it well enough, where is my brother?"

Josepha replies, "Who is your brother?"

Finn replied, "Asquith Between."

Leeroy replies, "Asquith, yeah it makes sense."

President Wilson said, "I believe He's been caught, by the Prussia soldiers."

Finn Between replied, "Trouble hasn't even come yet."

Josepha replies, "What did he just say?"

Leeroy said, "So where are you from, how did you get here, as we don't know much about Asquith other than his abilities?"

Finn Between replies, "Ruthon, through many dimensions leading into black holes, we've been studying Earth for a long time, in fact my younger brothers. They have come to Earth before, way before, but this time something has happened."

President Wilson replies, "What has happened?"

Finn Between replied, "I and Asquith are way too involved."

Josepha replies, "How can you just say that?"

Finn Between replied, "It's true, to you we are aliens, to us you are less than aliens. In Ruthon it is known as the True World, you Beings are just science, experiments, for something greater to toy with."

Leeroy replies, "What kind of powers do you have?"

Finn Between replied, "Super-Strength, different forces, flying, speed, teleporting, healing and with the gifts of wisdom and knowledge, but all that has been reduced since we came here."

Josepha replies, "So being here you have less of those powers?"

Leeroy replied, "Its abilities."

Finn Between replied, "Yeah, the longer we are here, the weaker we are. Together I and my brother can open a portal, sending us back to Ruthon."

President Wilson said, "So you plan on leaving us?"

Finn between replies, "Yes, but after we have fixed our mess."

Leeroy replied, "It's funny, because Asquith hasn't mentioned a thing about this."

Finn Between replies, "That's because of the brain damage he is suffering with, being on this planet so long."

Josepha said, "So what is the plan?"

Finn Between replied, "Find my brother, together I and him, will win this war for you."

President Wilson said, "May you both step outside, I must talk with my Secretary alone."

As Finn and Leeroy came out of the room.

Josepha said, "If we help the British now, they will be indebted to us, for a very long time.

President Wilson replied, "We will send our troops in."

Josepha replies, "Smart move Mr President."

President Wilson replied, "This country will one day be built up by others owning debt to us."

So President Wilson gave the order for the America troops to prepare to take Britain back, and locate Asquith which was going to be hard.

Leeroy replies, "Do you think we will win this war?"

Finn Between replied, "With my help course we will."

Leeroy replies, "You're an honest man, or should I say Being."

Late 1919's Emperor Hudson forces were becoming to be feared across the planet

Emperor's advisor was informing him on something, which would lead the empire way into the future.

Emperor Hudson replied, "What do you mean?"

"The middle-east not the king but his son the Prince, he wants to surrender to you; he wants to give you a gift, so long as you do not enslave his people."

Emperor Hudson replied, "Get them to repair that Hover-Jet, we will leave Great Britain, once it's fixed."

February the 4ᵗʰ 1920 four days before Great Britain was reclaimed

Finn Between said, "How long until we reach Great Britain?"

"Less than four three days."

Emperor Hudson, "Our spies report, large number of ships, have left America heading here."

Emperor Hudson replied, "I still have some matters to intend to here."

"Emperor the few Hover-Jets will be ready on time, should we use them to destroy their ships?"

Emperor Hudson replies, "No, they can have back Great Britain, if they want, we go to Dubai."

Four days later

"Emperor Hudson we must leave now, they will be here by drawn."

Emperor replied, "Lock down the Prison, it's time we go to the Middle-East, visit the Prince."

Chapter Twelve

Britain's up rise

Early 1920's

Emperor Hudson and some of his Prussian soldiers, and the rest left Great Britain in many more Hover-Jets, as the ships crashed into the beaches east of the Country. Finn Between and the American troops stormed through England hunting down any Prussian forces, they found nothing; Emperor Hudson and his forces were gone.

"What now "Sir?"

Finn Between replied, "I have not a clue."

So Finn got to Buckingham Palace, which was rebuilt, reasons unknown for now.

"What's going on, was Hudson ever here?"

Finn Between replied, "This is what you call, they've done a number on us."

So Finn Between scanned the rest of the England trying to find out if Asquith his brother was hiding anywhere, but he had no luck, everyone was too scared to say anything only that the Prussians came and went.

"I guess back to America?"

Finn Between replied, "We rebuild an army for England first."

"I agree."

Finn Between said, "Get word back to President Wilson on the situation."

"What situation?"

Finn Between replies, "Just say something."

Finn Between looked at the areas of the country which needed protecting, and started rebuilding it with the help of the Irish, Finn travelled far out until he got to the edge of south England, from a far he could see an Island.

Finn Between returned to Central London into the House of Commons, he looked for anyone, but no one was around, Finn Between left and went to the Library of England.

Scanning through the books and geographic of England, finding out any knowledge of any Islands close to England, and something came up an Island called Mesink became famous due to the Last dragon in the world was slayed there.

Some troops dress in America uniform came in after Finn Between, Finn Between noticed them searching the library, Finn moved out of cover.

Finn said, 'soldiers what are you looking for?"

One soldiers replied, "You."

Finn replies, "What's the problem?"

Another soldiers replies, "You are the problem."

The fifteen soldiers race off towards Finn, Finn went in between them punching and kicking them back, as they fired off at him, Finn dodged the bullets rolled forward onto the ground.

Finn said, "What are you lot doing?"

A soldier replied, "It's just training day."

One soldier sliced Finn's armed and another kicked Finn over a table, and then the rest surrounded him.

Finn said, 'training day, I doubt you're meant to use, real blades?"

Some other American's troops came into the Library, and saw that these soldiers were attacking Finn, as Finn got blasted through some book shelves, and onto the floor.

The American soldiers started shooting the non-American soldiers, and then Finn came behind one, releasing his sword from his waist, and then sliced three soldiers, rolling forward kicking out other soldier's leg and then slicing into that soldier's neck.

"Sir, are you ok?"

Finn replied, "Yes, what the hell was that about."

"We believe there are still some more enemies inside our walls."

Finn replied, "I believe so as well, I guess it's cleaning up time."

One American troop came running at Finn as he came out of the Library of England.

Finn said, 'slow down, breathe, what's wrong?"

"It's the ships, it's the Prussians."

Finn jumped into a motor-vehicle racing over to the beach as he was in the vehicle, a Hover-Jet popped up and started firing down at Finn.

Finn grabs both the driver and troops teleporting them out from the Motor-Vehicle, which blew to pieces, Finn found himself on the beach side with the driver and the troops.

As Finn looked over at the ships he saw the Hover-Jets destroying them, Finn then teleported into one Hover-Jet, stabbing the pilot flying the Hover-Jet into another.

Finn turned around as a blade was about to cut his face, Finn moved around the blade, grabbing the soldier by his neck, and slamming his head into the inside of the Hover-Jet. While other soldier came to the side of Finn, Finn quickly side kicked the soldier downwards, as three moves forward Finn sent the soldier blade into his hand and jump forward at them killing them.

As Finn stood at the edge of the Hover-Jet he looked into the small valley, and saw the people of valley fighting back, in fact this started to happening all around England.

Finn dropped backwards out of the Hover-Jet teleporting himself, in the middle of a group of Prussian soldiers, as he did he attack them straight away. All of the Prussian soldiers dropped straight to the floor, and then he saw the people of Britain reclaim their land.

"Finn, Finn, over here."

Finn started running over to the American troops, as the British came rushing downwards to them, as the Americans made a defence line ready to fight the British.

Finn said, "Drop you're weapons."

"Never, they will kill us."

Finn replies, "No, they won't."

"What do you mean?"

Finn replies, 'this is Britain's upraise."

Chapter Thirteen

India's Rise to power Part 1

Mid 1920's

Blunt and X-Hamstring was in line with the Force Drill, ready to take New Delhi back from the Prussian soldiers.

22nd of December 1919

Blunt said, "Where are we?"

X-Hamstring replied, "We're in Pakistan."

Blunt replies, "How so?"

X-Hamstring replied, "I remember a hit I had to do."

11TH of June 1910 X-Hamstring was assigned a mission to assassinated General Khan of the Iran army in which he was staying with the Pakistan's castle cause of death machete wound slices all over the body and throat sliced open

As Blunt and X-Hamstring started moving through the back ways of Pakistan, carrying Princess Elizabeth with them, they saw a Hover-Jet flying all over.

X-Hamstring said, "What the hell is going on?"

Blunt replied, "If there's Hover-Jet flying, that means Mother Russia, has taken over Pakistan or something."

Early 1920's the meeting between Emperor Hudson and Prince Shah

Emperor Hudson landed down in Dubai, meeting with Prince Shah, as Iran and Majlis were about to go into chaos with each other. Emperor Hudson and his Prussian soldiers came of the Hover-Jet, being escorted into the palace.

Prince Shah said, "Emperor Hudson, what a greeting this is?"

Emperor Hudson replied, "I heard…

Just before Hudson was going to say what he was going to say, he saw Prime Minster Farman' Farmam being executed right in front of his own eyes; Emperor Hudson looked back at his soldier's excitement.

Prince Shah replies, "What were you going to say?"

"You know what you have done right, what the USA tried to do, you will cause both countries to clash Farman was keeping the peace."

"Are you upset with me Emperor Hudson?" asked Prince shah.

"Upset, no, I am pleased to see you take action."

"Good, good, please sit," said Prince Shah.

Emperor Hudson replies, "So I heard you're in some kind of trouble, and you want to make a deal with me."

Prince Shah Replies, "You're forces are feared across this side of the world, I've had to execute must of the other higher rank leaders across this part of the world," said Prince Shah.

"You murdered other ones not from this side of the world, by doing so you have upset so many people, creating a war in which you do not need to fight in, meaning you will profit from the outcome."

"Emperor Hudson, you are a wise man, my father always told me you were."

Emperor Hudson replies, "Prince, all I care about is what this deal is?"

Prince Shah replies, "Oil, all of the oil you will ever need, pumping through Mother Russia non-stop."

Emperor Hudson laughed out and replied, "You want me to help you destroy India for your oil, how about I take it up from under you."

As Hudson said that Shah's forces surrounded him and his Prussian soldiers, Hudson leaned forward nudging his head; Prince Shah looked at his forces.

Emperor Hudson said, "Well played new friend, but the Russia government and British government did ware you of your actions before, but as the British are no our allies and weak at the moment, you're only choice for survival is me."

Prince Shah replied, "Will you provide your forces, and kill my enemies, with my oil you're empire will advances ahead of your enemies."

Emperor Hudson replies, "I respect you're father more than I respect you, but young prince I respect you even more now. I will move a large part of my forces into India, after you look at this."

Prince Shah replied, "That's located in the red dessert, it's just a myth, if it was true……

Emperor Hudson replies, "I will have my resources here to help you find it."

Prince Shah replied, "Fine."

Emperor Hudson replies, "Nice doing business young prince, oh do say hello to your father for me."

Prince Shah replied, "Where are you going, what about my enemies?"

Emperor Hudson replies, "My forces will be in India a few months from now."

Prince Shah replied, "You're a smart man."

Emperor Hudson speaking in German said, "And you're a foolish man."

Hudson boarded his Hover-Jet as he saw his forces flying into Iran, Hudson was informed about a movement happening New Delhi.

27th of August 1920

Blunt said, "You sure these bicycles, will be any force, against the Prussians?"

X-Hamstring replied, "It's the only thing the Force Drill has."

As Blunt and X-Hamstring with a handful of British, plus American Troops, and new British army known as Force Drill which was made up of Indians marched into New Delhi.

4TH of August 1920 Prussian forces are within India

"General Townshend forces are nothing against the Prussians."

Karabeki replied, "Get a message to General Pasha, to set up the defence for New Delhi."

"What do you mean?"

Karabeki replies, "I will not be trapped here in Kut, we retreat, if General Townshend wants to die, let it be."

"If we do nothing, the Prussia forces, will take New Delhi."

Karabeki said, "Who are those two?"

"Commander Karabeki, this is Blunt and X-Ham, they travelled from Great Britain."

Karabeki said, "Will the British help us?"

Blunt replied, "Last time I was in Great Britain, the Prussia forces took it again."

Karabeki replies, "How long have you both been travelling for?"

X-Ham replied, "Almost three years."

Karabeki replies, "Rumours say the American troops has help Britain to reclaim the lands."

Blunt replied, "Is there anything I can use to get a message to Great Britain?"

Karabeki replies, "Yes in New Delhi."

Karabeki turned over to his soldiers and then looked back at Blunt.

Karabeki said, "Where are you going?"

Blunt replied, "If I can send a message back to Britain, maybe they would help."

Karabeki replies, "You cannot go anywhere with her."

Blunt replied, "Yes that's true."

Karabeki replies, "I will sent her over to Kolkata, my sister will look after her, until it is safe."

Blunt replied, "Thanks."

Karabeki replies, "I guess that Commonwealth agreement will be signed after this mess."

Blunt and X-Ham both travelled on motor-cycle travelling through India, making their way slowly to New Delhi.

Blunt said, "It says here on the map, that's it's just over this mountain."

X-Hamstring replied, "Look over there."

Blunt replies, "Impossible, the Prussian forces are already moving in on New Delhi."

X-Hamstring replied, "Let's waste no more time."

"Commander Karabeki we've last Kut."

Karabeki replied, 'the British will not be happy, when they find out this."

As Blunt and X-Ham raced into New Delhi suddenly being surrounded by General Townshend forces, Townshend came out of cover.

General Pasha said, "Karabeki, told me of you, it's this way."

Back in England Finn and a small group of American Troops, were in the old MI6 hidden building, as they scanned through it Finn could near a funny noise.

"What is that?"

"This way."

As the American Troops and Finn came into this room, to find a machine typing out codes onto a paper, Finn quickly grabbed it.

"What is it?"

Finn replied, "It's a message from Blunt."

"What does it say?"

Finn replied, "Help is needed in New Delhi, Kut has been lost to the Prussian forces."

"What are we to do?"

Finn replied, "He said there's a beach near Surat, and he'll meet us in Agra in over three weeks."

Back in New Delhi Blunt had just received a message back from Finn.

X-Hamstring said, "What does it say?"

General Pasha said, "What was that noise?"

"General Pasha, the Prussia has started to invade New Delhi."

General Pasha replied, "We retreat to Agra, help will arrive in three weeks" time."

Blunt said, "He's sending a message to American."

General Pasha said to his soldier, "Inform Commander Karabeki of this."

August the 27ᵗʰ 1920

Finn with a great number of American and also British Troops marched into Agra to meet Blunt and X-Hamstring, and the few last of the Force Drill.

Finn said, "What's the plan?"

General Pasha replied, "Commander Karabeki, start an attack once, we give him a sign. That will allow us to creep up behind the Prussia forces and take back New Delhi, what do you think?" Finn replies, "Depends on the number of Prussian there are?" General Pasha replied, "Karabeki reports, that they more than thirty thousand."

Finn replies, "What about their equipment?"

General Pasha replied, 'tanks, Rifles but no flying machines."

Blunt said, "What do you think?"

Finn replied, "All together it's sixty thousands of us."

X-Hamstring replies, "We can take them."

Finn replies, "You and X-Hamstring will take twenty thousand troops with you, attacking at the west side, and I will attack from the south, and Commander Karabeki will attack from the east.

Blunt replies, "When will this begin?"

Finn replied, "We have a well-rested night, and move out in the morning, and should reach they within two days."

X-Hamstring replies, 'sounds good."

Finn said to Pasha, "What will be the sign?"

General Pasha replied, "Red smoke."

Blunt replies, "How far can someone see the red smoke?"

General Pasha replied, 'that's the problem, half a mile from the centre of New Delhi."

Chapter Fourteen

Mother Russia's Wrath Part 2

Mid 1920'S

Emperor Hudson had his own plans; he had sent a great force of Prussia soldiers to invade South African, as he was informed of a mining company shipping gold to American. Emperor Hudson walked into a palace closed to the mining area, as he did African soldiers came at him, but his Prussian forces killed them.

Emperor Hudson said, "Where are you going?"

Prince of Africa replied, "I have done nothing wrong."

Emperor Hudson replies, "Liar, I've been informed on, what you're father has been doing."

Prince replied, "What do you mean?"

Emperor Hudson replies, "You don't even know."

Prince replied, "Whatever he has done, let me repay you, I have much gold and diamonds."

Emperor Hudson replies, "That's why I took, Namibia, Botswana, Zimbabwe, Zambia, Nyeri, Nairobi and Kenya."

Prince replied, "You will not have the whole of Africa."

Emperor Hudson replies, "This is where my new empire will start, in time Africa will be mines."

Prince replied, "Why Africa, why here?"

Emperor Hudson replies, "You've heard the rumours."

Prince replied, "You cannot be talking about the temple of Kano?"

Emperor Hudson replies, "Yes."

Prince replied, "The temple is a myth."

Emperor Hudson said, "Imagine having army of dead at your own will, imagine that, can you imagine that?"

The Prince replies, "You've lost it."

Emperor Hudson moved forward cutting open the Prince's throat, and then said hold back the Prince's neck, pulling him in close.

Hudson said, "No regrets."

"Emperor Hudson, what would you like us to do?"

Emperor Hudson replies, "General Harris, you manage Africa for me, tonight the rest of the Prussia soldiers will take the gold back to Mother Russia, and you will take you're forces, and take the rest of Africa."

General Harris replied, "Most of my men have come down with this fever."

Emperor Hudson replies, "Talk to me."

July the 17th 1920

Word had got back to the Secret service; the President had a meeting with a few of his closest advisors and government members.

One member of the Congress said, "We've been distracted."

Secretary Josepha replied, "Who's to know what Hudson true motive is?"

President Wilson replies, "I may not be out there, but I can sure tell you."

Head chief of the Secret service replied, "You think you know more than you're secret service does?"

Secretary Josepha said, "How about you Vice President?"

Leeroy replied, "He has nothing to say?"

Head Chief of the secret Service replies, "Who let this kid in on this meeting?"

President Wilson replies, "I did, and I consider him as my advisor."

Secretary of Defence Josepha said, "Well Leeroy what's you're angle on this situation?"

Leeroy replied, "Emperor Hudson…

Josepha replies, "Please just call him Hudson, he ain't no one's Emperor."

Leeroy replied, "Fine, Hudson I believe his plans is something more deadly."

President Wilson replies, "What do you mean deadly?"

Leeroy replied, "Before I went to Africa, Egypt, I done some research."

Head Chief of the Secret Service replies, "What kind of research?"

Leeroy replied, "Just the normal stuff, like the history of Egypt, and someone called Roman James the First had wrote a piece on what he found when he was in Africa."

President Wilson said, "What kind of information?"

Leeroy replied, "Black magic…

Secretary Josepha replies, "Black Magic the kid has some great imagination."

President Wilson replied, "Hear him out."

Leeroy replies, "So I've sent a letter to Roman James the First, and he has invited me, to his research lab located on an Island called Mesink near the south coast of England."

Head Chief of the Secret Service said, "What's you're aim?"

Leeroy replied, "The truth about this Army of Dead?"

Josepha said, "Now He's talking fairy tales."

President Wilson said, "It is a little far fetch."

Leeroy replies, "What if this Army of Dead is true."

President Wilson got up and came over to Leeroy, Leeroy got up out of his seat, and President Wilson walked with him to the door, as Wilson opened the door. President Wilson handed Leeroy a piece of paper, Leeroy looked up at the President Wilson.

Leeroy said, "What is this?"

President Wilson replied, "On this letter I and the next President have signed it, it will allow you to open up, any kind of business, or something like a journalist firm."

Leeroy replies, "Thanks, Mr Wilson."

President Wilson replied, "You may not know this, but you have done so much for us, you brought us a little closer into the future with your inventions."

Leeroy replies, "Mr Wilson, becarful I don't trust any of those men, just becarful."

Chapter Fifteen

India's Rise to Power part 2

July the 29th 1920

So Blunt and X-Hamstring marched onwards into New Delhi with a handful of the Force Drill, moving stealthy through the city. X-Hamstring saw a large group of Prussia forces patrolling the area near to the centre of the city, as Commander Karabeki was outside of the centre of the city waiting for the sign.

"Commander, Commander, look the red smoke."

Just like the Blunt and X-Hamstring and the handful of Force Drill were under attack by the Prussian Forces, as the Force Drill's bodies were dropping, and then a very large group of more Force Drill came marching in holding back the Prussia forces, Blunt and X-Hamstring got into cover, as they watch Commander Karabeki appeared out from the blue with his army.

Blunt said, "About time."

X-Hamstring replied, "Oh that great British humour, I've missed."

As X-Hamstring said that a Prussia soldier came behind him, and was about to stab him in his back, but Blunt shot the soldier down to the ground.

Blunt replies, "We need to keep moving."

Word got back to Emperor Hudson that the British had a new and much bigger powerful army, this was not warming to his ears, Hudson screamed and shouted.

Hudson said, "No matter what I do, they come back, and they come back better."

"I have a plan."

Hudson replies, "Yes."

"Send a Hover-Jet loaded with C4 into New Delhi, destroying the British forces."

Emperor Hudson replies, "Yes, and no."

"What's the plan?"

Emperor Hudson replies, 'send the Hover-Jet with the C4, but we must travel to Japan, it's time to make ourselves some new allies as well."

Blunt and X-Hamstring racing through the city killing Prusian soldiers one by one, cleaning the whole city out, until the Prussian forces surrendered.

As General Pasha was walking forward towards Blunt and X-Hamstring, Commander Karabeki flew out of nowhere, shooting General Pasha to the ground.

Blunt said, "What was that all about?"

Karabeki replied, "He's working for Hudson."

X-Hamstring replies, "With what proof?"

Karabeki replied, "My guts."

Blunt replied, "Watch out."

Pasha Rebel soldiers started to firing towards Blunt, X-Hamstring and Karabeki, but the new British forces which was mix with, English men, Americans and Indians destroy the rebel soldiers, with not a lot of effect.

As Blunt and X-Hamstring looked down at Karabeki, he was bleeding out, Blunt came down to his knees, placing his ear near to Karabeki's mouth.

"They know where the Princess is, she's not safe."

X-Hamstring shouted, "Blunt where are you going?"

Blunt shouted back, "Get back to England, I'm going to save the Princess."

While that happened Finn destroyed the last of the Prussia forces, and he saw Blunt running form a far distances, Finn looked over at X-Hamstring and saw a large group of hidden Prussian forces ready to attack. X-Hamstring turned around as he did the Prussian forces came out of cover and started blasting back the new British forces, but the new British forces held back their attack. X-Hamstring then found himself surrounded outnumbered cornered off from the rest, as he did he pulled out his dragon sword, and place his Machete away.

X-Hamstring said, "Well boys, what are you waiting for?"

As the Prussian forces started to blast the hell towards X-Hamstring, X-Hamstring was trying his best to flip the bullets of his blade, but some hit him forcing him back into a wall, and then man explosive happened near him making him break through the wall. X-Hamstring dropped to both his knees as he did one Prussian soldier came forward, pulling out his blade, tipping it to X-Ham's jaw lifting his head upwards. As the Prussian soldier was about to drive his blade into X-Ham's throat, Finn teleported behind the soldier, quickly grabbing his head in a lock with his arms and snapping it from his body taking his head facing it at the rest. As Bullets came flying into the Prussian soldiers, Finn kicked the soldier forward, and punched the ground sending a force along the ground over to the Prussian forces forcing them downwards. Finn turned around throwing out his hand to X-Ham, x-Ham looked up and grabbed Finn's hand, and Finn helped him to his feet.

Finn said, "Are you good?"

X-Hamstring replied, "Just need some rest."

Finn replies, "Where did Blunt go?"

X-Hamstring replied, "Something about the Princess, she's in danger."

September the 1st 1920

Blunt got to a hill over-looking a large camp he saw a massive group of Prussian forces, and Rebel soldiers searching the camp. Blunt climbed down the hill moving into the forest hiding from the Prussian forces, Blunt then moved quickly into the camp, moving through passing a few huts.

"Over here, over here, quickly."

Blunt looked to the side of him and then to the other side, as he saw one Rebel soldier looking at him, Blunt went to grab a knife form his waist but they were gone. The Rebel soldier run off and Blunt headed into a tent, as he came into the tent, Blunt got knocked down to the ground. Blunt could hear a child crying as he lift up his head the person went to swing the bottom of his rifle at Blunt again, Blunt moved passed it, as he did he watched as the woman got her throat cut opened. Blunt kneed the person and grabbed the Rifle shooting it off, and the rest of the Prussian forces and Rebel soldiers heard, Blunt had to move quickly as the Prussian soldier was about to do harm to the Princess, Blunt grabbed the back of the soldier's neck, and threw his head backwards and placed his knee upwards snapping the soldiers neck to pieces. As a few Prussian and Rebel soldiers came into the tent no one was there, Blunt had started moving through the camp, and then Blunt was forced backwards. As Blunt hit the ground his grip on the Princess was loosened, and the Princess rolled over in front of no other than Emperor Hudson.

Emperor Hudson said, "Hello Blunt."

Blunt tried to move upwards back he got shot again in his shoulder, forcing him backwards to the ground. Emperor Hudson said again, "I'm not going to kill you, but I'm going to leave you here hopeless, but I'll let those Rebel soldiers tear you apart."

Blunt again tried to move upwards with all his force, but Hudson gave the order, and his General shot Blunt three more times, Blunt was bleeding out to his death as Hudson took the Princess and got onto his Hover-Jet, Blunt's vision starts to go blurry everything slowed down the Hover-Jet flew up into the sky and starts flying away slowly. As Blunt looked forward he saw Rebel Soldiers moving towards him; but also dropping to the floor Blunt closed his eyes, only for a few seconds.

October 1920 location Great Britain

As Blunt opened his eyes again he was in a hospital, Blunt tried to move forward, but couldn't.

X-Hamstring said, "It's ok Blunt, Finn saved you're life."

Blunt replied, "Where am I?"

X-Hamstring replies, "King Cross hospital, it's been a few weeks."

Blunt replied, "What about the Princess?"

X-Hamstring replies, "Hudson has her."

Blunt replied, "I failed."

X-Hamstring replies, "No Blunt, you did you're best."

Blunt started having flash backs, as he open back his eyes, he was back in Kolkata on the ground bleeding out, as the Rebel soldiers moved in close. This bright light came from nowhere, and he barely saw what events took place, as Finn moved forward slicing the soldiers backwards, X-Hamstring came down near to him.

X-Hamstring said but to Blunt words were missing, "Everything,ok, hold in, we, get,here."

Blunt woke back up screaming out and the doctors and nurses raced in.

"Give him a shot; He's having an panic attack."

The doctor looked at the nurse, as he knew she was a junior nurse, "For god's sake woman, I'll do it, fucking rookies."

Chapter Sixteen

The assassination of Ex-President Wilson

3rd of February 1921

No one had heard a thing of Emperor Hudson, and what his next plan was until, the Ex-President Wilson started walking to greet the new President, in the crowd something else was taking place, as the Ex-President got onto the stage. Someone had given the order and just like that blood was flying out of Wilson's head, as his body dropped to the ground. The Secret Service moved through the crowd as they did, one by one they were getting taking out, and then the Prussian soldiers showed themselves, as they attack the White house, the American troops moved forward defending the White House, but half of the building blow to pieces, in that half Leeroy was, and he got forced through a wall into the next room. The Prussian forces popped out of nowhere shooting random people, killing hundreds of people, moving forward towards the White house, the Prussian forces placed something onto the ground, like a message. Vice President ordered in the Canada's troops to help hold back the Prussian forces, as he looked down from the White house, at the message it said.

"NOONE IS SAFE THIS IS JUST THE BEGINNING."

Names: Thomas Wood Wilson

President of U.S term Served: 1913 – 1921

Height: Five foot Ten

Build: Average below medium

Features: Short Black and grey hair no facial hair

D.O.B: 12/28/1886

D.O.D 03/02/1921

Cause of Death: Bullet to the head

Prussian forces carried on killing the American troops, this attack the Americans were not prepared for, as most of the American troops were in India helping rebuild the country. Even though Emperor Hudson had the very young Queen of England by his side, he was anger as the Indian government was more powerful, he couldn't afford to send any of his forces into Indian, this alley that the British and Americans made was a smart move one Emperor Hudson never expected. As news got back to him off Wilson death, and the new President's death as well, and that American was in chaos. Emperor Hudson could still search out for this hidden temple, in fact he got obsessed with it, he put all his power and resources into it, but he didn't plan for Americans comeback as the attack on them would lead to some backtrack.

As Leeroy got up a few Secret Services rushed into the room, to find Leeroy getting up, as he was getting up the Prussian forces stormed the White House killing the Canada's troops and the Secret Service.

"Get your head down, boy."

As a few Prussian forces came rushing into the room, Leeroy dropped backwards out of the window, along the edge onto the grass, as he saw bullets flying out of the window and the Secret Services flying out of the window too.

The Prussian shoulder planted C4 all over the White house, as Leeroy got into the city looking back at the White House, he saw a few Hover-Jets landing down onto the grass, and then the Prussian Forces boarding them. The Hover-Jets then flew by him as he looked back at the White House it blew to pieces. Leeroy shield his eyes from the bright blast of the White House, but also fall backwards to the ground, word got back to Great Britain.

"Prime Minster, Wilson has been assassinated and the new President."

Blunt replies, "How so, weren't they prepared?"

Prime Minster replies, "Active the defences, it's time we prepared for a third attack."

5th of April 1921

As half of the New British Forces came back from India, they only had a short break while being on those ships; they were back building a whole new defence for Britain.

X-Hamstring replied, "I should have been in America."

Finn replies, "Died along the rest of them."

7th of July 1921 Mother Russia

Emperor Hudson was sitting next to the now Queen of England teaching her how to speak German and Russian, also Hudson was anger from the defeat in India, but his plan worked in America.

"Your daughter my blood, you must ensure you have learn your mother tongue."

"Yes father."

General of the South unit walked in on the Emperor, "Emperor, the New British Army, has retuned back to England."

Emperor Hudson replied, 'send a dozen Hover-Jets to India, and destroy the whole of India, or better much make them beg to join the Empire."

"Yes, Emperor."

Mid 1921's

The new Prime Minster had been thinking, and thinking, he arranged a meeting with the new members of the House of Commons, Director of the MI6 and leaders of the New British Army. The new Prime Minster said, "We need to go back to India?"

"Why "Sir, what's the problem?" asked Director Zack of the MI6.

Prime Minster replies, "I believe Hudson plans to attack, and attack hard."

"If this is so we've lost India already, It'll take us three weeks, by ships. We have not a lot of resources left, gold, diamonds to build Hover-Jets," said the Lord of House of Commons.

"Why do you think he'll attack India?" asked Director Zack.

Prime Minster replied, "They may not have much natural resources, but labour they do."

X-Hamstring said, "I will go just me, there's a few Hover-Jets left."

Prime Minster replied, "When was I going to be aware of that?"

X-Ham answers, "We had to keep it lowkey."

Director Zack said, "Where?"

X-Ham replied, "Mesink."

In walked Finn, "You're not going friend, I will"

X-Hamstring replies, "Max space in a Hover-Jets is forty people, there's three crafts left, so that's hundred and twenty people."

"In that case I will give you a few of my best skilled agents."

Prime Minster said, "Of course you will have some soldiers at your command."

Finn replied, "I haven't tried this before, but what if I teleport a very large group?"

Prime Minster replies, "Can you do that, if so will they be any backdrop from it?"

"Backdrop?"

X-Hamstring, "It's an English term, he means side-affects?"

"I haven't personal done it before, my abilities are weaker here, but we may have to try," as Finn said that in walked Leeroy.

X-Hamstring said, "You're alive."

Leeroy replied, "It was chaos, they came from nowhere, and it was horrible, so many died."

"Here take this Leeroy, sit, sit here, just take it easy."

Blunt said, "We believe Hudson plans is indeed to attack India."

Leeroy replied, "He wouldn't have attacked America for no reason, I think it was to set us back."

Blunt said, "I'm coming on the journey as well."

Finn replied, "It's too dangerous, for a science being, you're better off staying here."

Leeroy replies, "How about you company me to meet Roman James the First."

Blunt replied, "You got a meeting with him, no one ever gets a meeting with him."

Leeroy replies, "Will you come with me?"

Blunt replied, "It would be an honour, to meet this mysterious person, of course I will."

So as X-Hamstring gathering everyone together Finn instructed them to all hold hands he placed both his hands onto one of the New British soldier, "Do not break the link, if you do you will be lost in limbo." Just like that all hundred and twenty people were teleported outside of Roman James the First Mansion.

"Thanks for the transport Finn."

"No problem Leeroy, good luck with your meeting."

Finn dropped to the floor, "What's wrong Finn?" asked X-Hamstring

"Just as I thought I am becoming less."

"The Hover-Jets are this way, let's go."

As X-Hamstring escorted everyone else into the forest where the Hover-Jets were, they all start to board the Jets, as X-Hamstring was about to step on the Jet this mysterious portal opened up behind him.

E-Man Phillip Armstrong's son, first time being seen in this part of history to this day no one knew where he took X-Hamstring.

August the 6ᵗʰ 1921

"Welcome to Mr First's home, please follow us this where."

"He owns all of this land, it's so massive."

"He inherited, from its true owner, when they passed away, they treating him as their own son."

Chapter Seventeen

India's downfall

August the 9th 1921 Finn Between catcher by the Prussian forces

Finn found himself separated from the rest as the New British Army was placed all over India, they quickly started to get their forces together. As Finn looked upwards seeing a dozen Hover-Jet entering India blasting the building to pieces, Finn quickly teleported into one Hover-Jet, but he dropped straight to the floor.

"He must be another one of them, the gold is affecting him."

"He'll make a fine collection to Hudson trophies."

"I agree."

Finn moved upwards as he did the soldier sliced Finn in his chest, with the gold bladed sword, Finn moved backwards as he got kicked, Finn went sliding over to the edge of the Hover-Jet as he watched India being destroyed, and the New British Army dying. Finn moved onto his back as two Prussian soldier came down pinning him to the ground, one other sliced his chest some more.

"I'm going to cut into you."

"No, the Emperor would want this one alive."

Four soldiers behind the one which sliced Finn moved forward ramming gold blades in through Finn chest, pinning him up against the inside of the Hover-Jet.

Blood was dropping from Finn as his eyes kept closing and opening, punch after punch was landed against Finn, while the other Hover-Jet destroyed some parts of India. Until India surrendered to Hudson force news of this travelled back to Great Britain, as the Prime Minster heard.

So as Finn was travelling in the Hover-Jet it entered Mother Russia, he was still weak, the Prussia soldiers carried on punching the life out of Finn.

"No, let me have a go."

"Fine, take over."

The Hover-Jet landed down outside of the Palace, as Finn was being escorted with the blades still inside him, Emperor Hudson stood up as his soldiers carried in the infamous Finn.

Emperor Hudson said, "All this trouble you've made, look how pathetic you look."

Finn in a struggling tone blurred out, "Free, see, pathetic, I'll, you."

Emperor Hudson came up close to Finn everyone was moving slow and in complete silent, his soldiers placed the spares down onto the floor, placing in place. Forcing Finn to stand upright Hudson moved backwards and then rushed into Finn kicking him, the force made Finn fly out from the blades, and along the ground.

Hudson said, "Get up, and show me!"

As Finn got up he slowly started to heal back, Finn moved forward disappearing for a second, Hudson moved back in shock, and then reappearing closer. Hudson prepared himself as Finn disappeared again, and reappeared again in front of him, Hudson trapped Finn making him twist upside down in mid- air, and quickly grabbing his body slamming him to the ground.

Emperor Hudson said, 'see, you are pathetic."

As Hudson started walking away he said, "Just kill him."

As his soldiers moved in on Finn, Finn hold Hudson blade, and he killed the soldiers, as Emperor Hudson turned around Finn was up close and personal, holding the blade against Hudson throat.

Finn said, "Where's my brother?"

Hudson replied, "I'll never tell you."

Finn started to slice the blade into Hudson's throat, blood started to appear.

Hudson said, "London."

Finn replied, "Where in London?"

Hudson replies, "Under the Bank of England."

Finn released the Emperor kicking him backwards over to his chair; the Emperor reached for a cloth, and wipes the blood from his throat. Finn then turned around and said, "By the way." As Finn was about to throw the blade into Hudson, Hudson had already shot Finn, four times with golden bullets. Finn dropped the blade and dropped to his knees, as he did the Prussian soldiers rushed in, stabbing Finn with their golden spares.

Emperor Hudson said, 'too you I look like the bad guy right, well to me I am not the bad guy, power needs to remain here in mother Russia."

Introducing Roman James the First

August the 12th 1921 Prime Minster of England ordered for them to search the whole of India for Finn Between

August the 6th 1921 Leeroy's meeting with Mr First

So Leeroy and Blunt got escorted into a room with many books all over the place, and a table and a mirror on the wall, and a window which could see the sea one side, and forest where X-Ham and Finn went into.

Blunt said, "So this is what the Mansion looks like?"

"Yes."

Leeroy said, "No to be rude, but where is Roman James the First?"

"Here."

Leeroy laughed and replies, "No, I mean where is he right now?"

"Standing in front of you?"

Blunt replies, "Impossible, you're like twenty two."

Leeroy replies, "You did a piece on Egypt, seven years ago."

Roman replied, "Yeah when I was thirteen."

Blunt replies, "So you're twenty?"

Roman replied, "Yes."

Leeroy replies, "You're kidding with us right?"

Blunt was still amused on how well built the Mansion was, "This would make a great Sanctuary one day."

Roman, "You could say that Mr…

"Just call me Blunt."

"How do you know so much about us, Mr First?"

Roman replies, "Just like how I would know, that the MI6 recruited Blunt, when you were fifteen, right after you're father and mother were murdered by German soldiers, and that you, your name is Leeroy Tyrone Blair hmmm yes I feel royalty runs through your bloodline."

Leeroy replied, "Royalty."

"I've talked too much on one subject, let's move on."

"What's the deal with you really?" asked Blunt.

Roman replies, 'since my illness almost six years ago, I've been having dreams about the future, about people and events to come."

Leeroy replied, "Awesome, please tell us more."

"In that case please sit, we have a lot to talk about."

Blunt replies, "Didn't you catch the part, about his illness?"

Leeroy replies, "I guess that's not so awesome after all."

Roman said, "My scientists, say I won't live pass seventh."

Leeroy replies, "Well you know why we are here?"

Roman replied, "Yes and no, things have become cloudy lately."

Blunt replies, "Let me explain……

Roman replied, "You don't have to explain anything."

Leeroy asked, "Was all this really inherited to you?"

Roman replied, 'there are so many stories behind it, I like to keep to the simple ones al."

Sometime mid 2011 location Mesink, Mountain heavies

The scene changes to the moment a teenage boy dying in what it seemed like his father's arms, the boy was laying in his father arm in a cave, with another man standing across from them.

"Princess the Destroyer's true soul said to me, that a war will come, you fighting alongside with a group called T.O.R.E.O.A.Ds. That will be you're greatest failure, you will be defeated."

As the teenage boy vanished away into thin air, everything went to a bright white place, as the teenage boy walked forward in white clothing bare footed.

"We are giving you a second chance to live."

"Where am I?"

"You are between times, in a place of nowhere, Pasture."

"Why give me a second chance?"

"So that he can live, and become what he's meant to become, he will save us all or doom us."

"My father you mean, but how can I help him?"

"We're sending you back just before world war one, with a gift of pure knowledge, if he comes to you then we are truly winning."

The teenage boy woke up but not as himself but as Roman James the First, as a kid runs in, shouting his name, "Roman, Roman woke up."

"What it is?"

"They've found the scrolls?"

"It seems like the army of dead is not a myth."

6th of August 1921 The Meeting continues

Blunt replies, "We're getting side-tracked here."

Roman replied, "So you want to know about this war, and what your enemies are planning?"

Leeroy replies, "Yes."

Blunt replied, "Wait, you said enemies?"

Roman replies, "Yes, because you will be fighting against three."

Blunt replied, "What do you mean three?"

Roman replies, "Hudson is just a distraction, someone which isn't so much important, lost in his own doom may I say."

Leeroy replied, "Isn't important, he holds the world's largest and powerful Empire, He's basically taken half of Europe, and He's not so important."

Blunt replies, "Let's hear him out, because we throw options everywhere like they truly matter."

Roman replied, "Hudson isn't the worse to come, but as we are talking about him, let's stay talking about him."

Blunt replies, "That doesn't make sense?"

Roman replied, "He will open up all of your eyes."

Leeroy replies, "I'm lost."

Blunt replied, "Tell me about it."

Roman said, "Fine, let's me tell you, that the war will be won."

Leeroy replied, "How do…

Roman replies quickly, "How do I know this fact, because I've dreamt it before, this war will be won but at a cost."

Blunt replied, "What cost?"

Roman replies, "A new enemy merges, yes I see it so clearly now."

Leeroy replied, "This is like talking to a wizard or something."

Roman replies, "One which will be you're hardest, people will start to die, just like a hit list."

Blunt replied, "I just can't imagine that, like the same with winning this war."

Roman replies, "You're focusing on the wrong things."

Leeroy replied, "Do you mean Africa?"

Roman replies, "Yes and no, that future was foretold, Hudson will not find an Army of Dead, because that Army of Dead was a vision of someone else's which left instruction on the scrolls."

Blunt said, "You really do puzzle me."

Roman replied, "Well I should."

Leeroy replies, Should we know anything else."

Roman replied, "Yes, Hudson plans on making allies with Japan, if he does, that means the Chinese will fear him."

Blunt replies, "So what do you want us to do?"

Roman said, "Wrong question."

Blunt replied, "So what should we do?"

Roman replies, "That's simple…

Leeroy said, "Make allies with China."

Roman replies, "China plays a massive role in the next world war."

Blunt replied, "A world war II, impossible."

Roman replies, "Impossible, but yet you are here."

Blunt replied, "I don't know if you're just a kid, with a great imagination."

Roman said, "If you don't take me serious, you're enemies sure won't take you serious either."

Leeroy replied, "I believe in what you are saying."

Roman replies, "Thanks, but that means nothing to me."

Blunt replied, "We must leave now, and act before it's too late."

As Blunt and Leeroy was about to leave the Sanctuary and get into a Motor-Vehicle, Roman James the First came running towards them.

Roman said, "A few months back I had a dream or a vision whatever you want to name it, and I told my scientists to create this sword for you, they've managed to increase its element, you will need to use it against a new but yet old friend when the time comes."

Blunt replied, "I guess I should say thank you."

"X-Ham has one like it," said Leeroy.

"This is an upgrade; it has Dragon blood merged into the blade."

"Isn't dragon blood, basically a form of gold?"

"You are very wise, Leeroy."

"No, I just listened to my history lessons."

"Thanks, Roman, and do get some rest," Said Blunt.

Chapter Nineteen

To kill an Emperor

18th of November 1921 location Japan

Emperor Hudson and his forces travelled to Japan, as chaos was
spreading throughout an Island near Japan, with the Chinese warring
against the Japanese trying to claim this small Island, this was
perfect for Emperor Hudson to intervene, as the Japanese imperial
Army was losing this Island to the Chinese Army. Emperor Hudson was
in a Hover-Jet entering Tokyo's headquarters, as the Imperial army
saw this flying machine for the first time; they did not know what
to do. So the Jet landed down Husdon came of it with a few of his
soldiers and a few Imperial troops came running towards Hudson as
they did, three of Hudson's soldiers moved in front of him, and
started blasting the hell out of the troops. Commander Okuma walked
out to see Emperor Hudson with a handful of soldiers by his side,
one of Okuma's troops came up to him.

Commander Okuma said, "What are you doing, stop him?"

"Commander Okuma, his forces are, too strong."

Okuma pulled out his samurai slicing the troop in half, and then
looking at his other troops, his troops moved off towards Hudson. As
that was happening Finn came off the Hover-Jet, as more troops moved
forward, Finn went of attacking them all" all Okuma could do is
watch and see all of his troops died. Emperor Hudson moved towards
where Okuma was standing while Imperial troops were still trying to
attack him, but getting nowhere as Finn and his soldiers were
protecting him. As Emperor Hudson stepped onto Okuma floor, Okuma
moved forward but before he could imagine getting any close to
Hudson, Finn already moved forward punching the side of his neck and
trapping him to the floor pinning him.

Emperor Hudson said, 'stop."

Finn moved his blade from Okuma's throat, leaving a slice mark with
a little bit of blood coming out from it; Finn got up and moved over
to Hudson.

Commander Okuma said, "Kill me already."

Emperor Hudson replied, "How about you join me?"

Commander Okuma replies, 'so you are not here to kill me?"

Emperor Hudson replied, "I can help you win against China."

Commander Okuma replies, "Why would I let you help me?"

Emperor Hudson replied, 'the Chinese fear my Empire."

Hudson moved forward placing out his hand lifting Okuma upwards onto his feet.

Commander Okuma said, "In return what do you want?"

Emperor Hudson replied, "Just an alley."

Commander Okuma placed out his hand and Emperor Hudson did as well, and they shock hands together.

The Chinese moved back the Japanese imperial army making them retreat back to their ships, until these flying machine came flying in. the Chinese forces was not ready for this as they got whipped out, in seconds, word got back to China that Commander Okuma was now Emperor Hudson's general.

24th of November 1921 China, Hong Kong

Blunt landed down in Hong Kong he was surrounded as soon as he stepped off the Hover-Jet, While Leeroy was back in London. As Blunt moved forward one of the guards knocked him down to the floor, a while later Blunt woke up chained to a chair, with three men suited and someone seating behind them.

"你是谁？"

Blunt replied, "I don't understand."

"你是谁？"

Blunt Replied, "I don't understand."

"Cantonese?"

Blunt replies but speaking in Cantonese, "How would you know I speak Cantonese?"

"Who are you?"

"My name is Blunt, I am a British MI6 Agent."

"I am General Liang Shiyi, and I welcome you here."

Blunt replied, "What was that all about before?"

General Liang Shiyi replies, "These are dark hours, we have to be safe, the Prussia forces grow every day."

Blunt replied, "Well on behalf of Britain and America, we are pleased to assist you."

General Liang Shiyi replies, "The Japanese with the support of the Prussia forces took back Taiwan."

Blunt replied, "Why is Taiwan so important?"

General Liang Shiyi replies, "It was home to the infamous red dragon, on the land there are materials, medications, and much more."

Blunt replied, "Dragons have been extinct for more than hundreds of years."

"Taiwan was the only place the red dragon would nest."

Blunt replied, "So what's your next plan?"

General Liang Shiyi replies, "It's madness over here, a civil war has broken out, the country is in pure chaos." As Blunt walked into a room where to be more Generals, members of the council, and the President sitting there, they all started to talk Blunt couldn't understand again.

Blunt said, "What language are they saying?"

General Liang Shiyi replies, "Mandarin."

"Mandarin, that's interesting, what are they talking about?"

"They are talking about you, they are disappointed."

Blunt replied, "What a nice feeling?"

General Liang Shiyi replied, "Walk forward then."

Blunt replies, "Who is that man?"

General Liang Shiyi replied, "Emperor Chan."

Blunt moved forward as he did he moved his hand upwards and forward, refilling a hidden knife which went flying into the Emperor's back, just afterwards he killed the President.

General Liang Shiyi said, "What are you doing?"

Blunt replied, "He's working for Hudson."

Suddenly Blunt was surrounded by rebel forces, and other rebel soldiers were pointing their weapons at the Emperor on the floor.

"谁做你的工作吗？"

"谁送你？"

"你为什么要刺杀总统?"

Blunt moved forward as he did the Emperor open up his shirt refilling a bomb, as Blunt got closer the soldiers moved back, as the bomb went off forcing Blunt to go through a window also blowing half of the room to pieces killing a few Generals. Blunt flew downwards onto the ground crashing into it breaking his arm, as he lift his head up he saw a massive army heading his way, as General Liang Shiyi came down to the ground helping Blunt up onto his feet again he saw the massive army as well.

Blunt said, "How long?"

General Liang Shiyi replied, "Twenty minutes."

Blunt replies, "I need to get you out of here."

General Liang Shiyi replied, "No you don't, I'm staying here with my family, I'll get you back to your flying machine."

As Blunt got onto the Hover-Jet looking down at General Liang Shiyi a gun sound went off, and Shiyi moved forward onto the ground, Shiyi looked up towards Blunt.

"Get out of here."

Bullets after bullets started hitting the Hover-Jet Blunt got backwards sitting in his seat, as the Hover-Jet flew off, Blunt looked backwards through the protected glass window and saw a flew Hover-Jets flying after him.

"Sir, Sir, we won't make it, we're low on fuel."

Blunt replied, "Push it."

The Hover-Jet got hit to many times started to lose power on the edge of Mother Russia, Blunt grabbed his sword attaching it to his back, grabbed his machine gun, and some grenades. The Hover-Jet surrounded the Hover-Jet blasting the hell out of it, Blunt got to the edge as he saw the pilot turn around aiming towards him, Blunt quickly jumped back into the Hover-Jet as the blast blew of the door of the Hover-Jet.

"Sir, go, go now."

Blunt opened a trap door slipping down through the Hover-Jet, and out of it while the pilot crashed into one of the Hover-Jet the explosion forces a few other Hover-Jets to lose control. Blunt landed down somewhere in Mother Russia as he did he saw a group of Prussia soldiers patrolling the area, Blunt quickly went into cover.

"Soldier what are you looking at?"

"I thought I saw someone head into the shadow."

"You, you, and you follow me, it must be him."

As those few soldiers cut off from the rest heading into the shadow, Blunt jumped down from above them, slicing out their necks, and rolling to the ground. Blunt changed into their uniform regrouping with the rest of the Prussia soldiers, as the first commander instructed them to march back to the palace.

Chapter Twenty

Blunt's aim

24th of November 1921 Location Emperor Hudson Palace Mother Russia

Hudson stormed into his Throne room hitting his fist onto the table, Finn moved forward Hudson hold out his hand and Finn stopped.

Emperor Hudson said to one of his advisor, "Where are the soldiers at the south wall?"

"They should have been there already."

Emperor Hudson replies, "If you don't correct this, I will correct you."

As the Advisor was walking out Emperor Hudson turned around calling back his Advisor, the Advisor turned around to Hudson.

Emperor Hudson said, "In fact let me correct it now, so the rest of you, don't need to make the same mistake as this one."

Hudson aimed his golden gun firing it off turning his Advisor into dust, and then turning back at his other Advisors and Generals.

"What's the next move Emperor?"

Hudson replied, "I thought you were my Advisors and Generals?"

"Emperor Hudson, I think we should return to Germany."

Emperor Hudson replied, "What are you telling me?"

"Emperor, you've made a lot of enemies, we believe there's a secret plot to eliminate you."

Emperor Hudson replied, "Why didn't you come to me with this before?"

"Emperor we thought it were a myth."

Emperor Hudson replied, "Myth, if someone threatens the Emperor you take it seriously, and put up measures to ensure I am safe."

"A group of the world's greatest scientists, hidden within this country, were building a cyber-machine, which purpose was to whip out us."

Emperor Hudson replied, "What do you mean were building?"

"Emperor we believe they have built it, with the aid of an outsider, meaning possibly an Alien."

Emperor Hudson replied, "We leave to Germany right now."

As Emperor Hudson said that his Prussia forces from the south wall came into his Throne room, Hudson looked at them walking forward towards them.

Emperor Hudson said, "About time."

As Hudson said that Blunt pulled out his blade slicing into a soldier's throat, then slicing another soldier's throat. Stabbing into another soldier's neck, and cutting into another soldier's chest also kicking down the last soldier and blasting his head off. Finn went to move forward but Hudson stopped him as Blunt raced off towards Hudson, Hudson gave Finn the order and as Blunt force down his arm racing the blade towards Hudson chest Finn power-kick Blunt downwards making his blade fly out of his hand. Hudson's Advisors and Generals quickly left the room with Hudson; Hudson turned back and shouted towards Finn.

Emperor Hudson said, "Kill him, no, bring him back to the head-quarters."

Blunt slide down to the ground grabbing his blade, and then turned back at Finn throwing it towards him, Finn dodge around it grabbing it. Finn then force slide over to Blunt punching him up into the air, and also slicing his side, and kicking him to the floor. Blunt roll over onto his back while Finn flipped upwards, and then on top of him, Finn was holding Blunt's blade against Blunt's throat.

Blunt said, "What has happened to you?"

Finn just stared into Blunt's eye nothing was said, and Blunt noticed a golden lock around Finn's neck, like Hudson had tamed him by making him wear it. Blunt tried to reach up to it but Finn knock his hand down, and also punched him in the chest; Finn grabbed Blunt throwing him on top of the table. As Blunt hit the table Blunt quickly pulled out a golden sword Finn quickly moved backwards, Blunt jumps up onto his feet and Finn took out his sword as well. Blunt flew forward towards Finn" Finn flip sideways and pass Blunt, Blunt move his feet around facing Finn, as Finn drive forward Blunt rise up the golden sword. Finn attack was weakening by the sword, in fact Finn's hand started to shake from it.

Blunt said, "I guess this has changed what the outcome could have been."

Finn dropped to his knee as he did Blunt move downwards to Finn moving his sword towards Finn, but Finn rolled sideways.

Emperor Hudson said, "Where is he?"

"Emperor, I will go back, we will meet you in the head-Quarters."

As Emperor Hudson stepped onto his Hover-Jet a large noise happened, as he looked pass his Hover-Jet through the protected glass, he saw this shiny silver metal man standing by to the side of a female.

Emperor Hudson said, "Who the hell are they?"

"That's the thing we were talking about, the Cyber-Machine."

Emperor Hudson replies, "Impossible."

Hudson witness his forces move in on the female and her machine, but he also witnesses the female and her Machine destroying his forces like nothing.

"Emperor, their heading here."

"We must leave."

"What about Finn, and Blunt?"

Emperor Hudson said, "He'll find his way."

The Hover-Jet started moving upwards into the sky as he did, Eight ordered her robot to destroy Hudson, so her robot move forward and then fire came down from the Robot's legs and back also back of shoulder.

Emperor Hudson shouted, "Destroy the Machine."

As missals after missals came shooting out of the Hover-Jet towards the Cyber-Machine, the Machine placed up two force fields from its hands. The missals impacted in the flames spread around the outside of the force field, the Cyber-Machine started walking forward looking up at Hudson. As the Machine forced jump from the ground heading face on with Hudson, Finn trickle the Machine while in mid-air, hitting it back down to the ground, Hudson turned to one of his Generals.

"Press the button now."

"Are you sure?"

"Mother Russia has no use for us anymore."

While that was happening Blunt crawl out of the palace as he did the female stepped forward, Blunt only saw her boots, until he lift his head upwards.

Blunt said, "Who are you?"

The female looked passed Blunt as this device came up through the ground, and started counting down from ten, "My name is Eight," Eight turned around ordering her Cyber-Machine to her. The Machine sliced Finn's throat breaking the golden lock around his neck, and then the Machine fly backwards grabbing Eight and flying upwards and away. Blunt looked back at the device it was counting down from five, Blunt tried to get out, but he passed out, as he did everything around him blew to pieces.

14th of June 1924 location England, London King Cross Hospital

Blunt woke up to feel a person standing there with his back to him. Blunt struggles to say something and that person turned around, it was no other than Finn, Blunt vision came back to him.

Blunt said, "Finn."

Finn replied, "I failed."

Finn removed his arm from his side Blunt could see a golden blade wedge into him, and his left hand sliced off.

Blunt said, "Finn…

Finn replied, "You must get help, my brother is in danger, Hudson plans to execute him."

Finn drops down to his knees as he raises his head upwards at Blunt, Blunt saw blood running out of his eyes, and then cracks started to appear all over Finn. Blunt reach out his hand and this blue portal open up forcing Blunt back out walked a being quickly moving over to Finn touching Finn's head with his hand, this stopped Finn from being deleted from all history.

Blunt said, "Who are you?"

"A friend."

Both the stranger and Finn disappeared into the blue portal this blinded Blunt for a few seconds, and then the British soldiers came marching in.

"Look it's Blunt."

"Blunt, it's good to have you back."

Blunt replied, "Where is Finn?"

"Sir, who are you talking about?"

"Never mind, any luck on X-Ham where abouts?"

"The palace Sir, Buckingham Palace."

Blunt replied, "I need you to take me there."

Chapter Twenty one

Death of Asquith

03ʳᵈ of June 1924 Location Germany Emperor Hudson Headquarters

These four armed men walked down some stairs which led to a blank brick wall, one of the armed men placed out his hand, and this device scanned his hand. The wall opened up leading into a prison, as the men got to a cell, the prisoner inside had his back turned to them.

"Turn around slowly."

As the person turned around it was no other than Asquith.

"Walk forward slowly."

Asquith walked forward."

"Place your hands through here."

Asquith placed his hands through a gap, and the armed men placed golden cuffs onto him.

"Unlock the door."

As Asquith walked out of the cell he quickly got his face covered, and then escorted out of the hidden prison, and into a van. Moments later the van turned into a private runway, and pulled out close to a Hover-Jet, Asquith got moved out of the van and into the Hover-Jet.

Asquith said, "Where are you taking me?"

The armoured man hit Asquith" Asquith felt it like a Science being would, he now knew his abilities were nearly gone, Asquith got hit again by the same armoured man, leaning forward off his seat to his knees, the rest of the armoured men lift him back up onto his feet, and the Hover-Jet took off into the sky.

As Emperor Hudson came into a room his daughter the Queen of England got up running towards him, and jumping up into his arms, Emperor Hudson placed her back down. Hudson said, "Listen to me darling, you will go back to England, reclaim your throne. As you are the only air left, once you are old enough instructions will follow, do you understand?"

Princess Elizabeth replied, "I want to stay here, I want to stay with you."

Hudson replies, "You must do this for me, so I may have a future."

14th of June 1924 location England Buckingham Palace

As Blunt got to Buckingham Palace he looked outside of the window, seeing a Hover-Jet flying away, Blunt looked at the guards which took him to X-Hamstring. Blunt walked into the room where X-Hamstring and Leeroy were; as he did he quickly took out the guards.

X-Hamstring said, "What are you doing?"

Blunt replied, "Are you two blind?"

Leeroy replies, "No."

X-Hamstring replied, "Why?"

Blunt replies, "There are Prussia forces within our walls."

X-Hamstring replied, "You've been in a coma for almost three years."

Blunt replied, "Three years, it's only felt like yesterday."

Leeroy said, "That's what comas be doing."

X-Hamstring, "In the last three years, we've had a massive clean-up crew, so that's impossible?"

Blunt replies, "For now we must kill Hudson."

Leeroy said, "What do you want me to do?"

Blunt replies, "Go back to America, and live your life."

X-Hamstring replied, "How will we get to Mother Russia?"

Blunt replies, "Mother Russia has been destroyed, Hudson is back in Germany, also with not a lot of forces left."

X-Hamstring replied, "We only have two Hover-Jets left?"

Blunt replies, "That will have to do."

Leeroy said, "Wait, come here, look."

Blunt replied, "Princess Elizabeth?"

As Princess Elizabeth started walking from a Hover-Jet, and started heading into the Palace, X-Ham, Blunt and Leeroy raced down towards her.

Blunt said, "Princess?"

Elizabeth turned around and replied, "Who is he?"

Blunt replies, "You're alive?"

Princess Elizabeth replied, "Emperor Hudson let me go, to insure that we do not attack him."

Blunt replies, "You've grown up so quickly, it's been years since I last saw you."

X-Hamstring said, "Blunt, did you not hear, the Princess?"

Blunt replied, "Huh."

Leeroy said, "We cannot attack Hudson, she's made an agreement, with him."

Blunt replied, "What agreement?"

X-Ham replies, "By him letting her come back here, is to insure we do not attack."

Blunt moved X-Hamstring and Leeroy into a room.

Blunt said, "This will stay between us, we take one Hover-Jet, with a handful of soldiers and we end him for good."

Leeroy replied, "He's right X-Ham, Hudson alive, is just too dangerous."

X-Hamstring replies, "I understand that, but what about the Princess, what about the agreement?"

Blunt replied, "Too hell with the agreement, we have a chance to end this madness."

X-Hamstring replies, "Fine, we leave after sunset."

Blunt replied, "Good."

X-Hamstring said to Leeroy, "If what Blunt said, about the Prussia forces, you will be a lot safer in America. So take one of the other Hover-Jets, and go."

Leeroy replied, "Good luck."

X-Hamstring replies, "I'll need something more than just luck."

6th June 1924 Emperor Hudson first Head-Quarters Germany

Emperor Hudson sitting in his chair, as he did the same armoured men removed the cover from Asquith face, throwing him down to the ground, Hudson moved upwards onto his feet pulling out his golden gun.

Emperor Hudson said, "It looks like the end of the road for you."

Hudson raises his arm aiming his golden gun towards Asquith, Asquith lifted his head up, and as he did Asquith leaped forward.

Asquith replied, "Not now not ever."

Hudson fire off the golden gun golden bullets were rushing towards Asquith, Asquith twisted and dodged the bullets as it went pass him, and into two of the armoured men. As Asquith came up close to Emperor Hudson, Hudson moved backwards slightly, and then Asquith got kicked backwards along the ground to the other two armoured men, which quickly held him in place.

Emperor Hudson said, "Look who it isn't."

Asquith said, "Brother it's me, what are you doing, it's me."

Hudson noticed Finn didn't have the golden chain around his neck, but he carried on as if Finn was still his loyal soldier.

Finn replied, "Brother, I have no brother."

Asquith replies, "What have you done to him?"

Hudson replied, "All that time while you were locked away, my scientist done experiments on you, and they found something very interesting. The formula so that I could control let's just say, another Being with your same blueprints."

Asquith replies, "Fine, take me as well."

Hudson replied, "I would if I could, Finn kill him."

Asquith forced the armoured men off him quickly moving back towards them, killing them, and removing their machine guns. As Finn came in Asquith fired off the guns, Finn merged through all of the bullets, until the guns were empty, and he was up close and personal with Asquith.

Asquith said, "Brother, don't do this, you're stronger than the will."

Finn replied, "Brother, what, what did you just call me?"

Hudson shouted, "Finn, destroy him."

Asquith said, "You're my brother."

Finn looked back at Hudson shouting at him and Finn moved forward grabbing Asquith and forcing him into the ground, breaking it appear. Finn then grabbed Asquith around his neck lifting him up, choking Asquith out, Asquith's vision started to become blurry. Finn dropped Asquith to the ground Asquith landed on his knees, with Finn turning his back to him, and then back kicking Asquith along the floor.

Emperor Hudson moved forward saying, "Well done Finn, well done."

Finn turned around to Hudson as he did, Emperor Hudson fire of his golden gun, and a bullet went into Finn chest and leg, Finn dropped to the floor Hudson moved over to Finn drawing out a bladed sword made from gold slicing Finn's hand off and also stabbing Finn into his side. Finn moved backwards next to his brother, lying there dying Asquith struggling to get these few words out, "Finn, my brother, brother……

Emperor Hudson moved closer to Asquith, and said, "Goodnight."

Hudson fire of his gun and the golden bullets went into Asquith's forehead, and then starting to walk away.

"Stop."

Emperor Hudson replied, "Impossible."

Finn replies, "You fooled me in believing so many things, that I lost my way, I may be gone but I curse you forever."

Emperor Hudson witness as Finn teleported away sending a harmful blast towards causing him to drop backwards, onto his chair and Asquith body burst to pieces vanishing away into thin air.

Name: Herbert Henry Asquith better known as Asquith Between

Prime Mister of England Term served: 1912-1920

Gender: Male

Height: five foot ten

Build: Medium-slim

Features: black and grey hair, black eyes

Nationality: unknown

D.O.B: 12/11/1872

Died: 06/06/1924

15th of June 1924 Blunt and X-Hamstring failed attack

"Emperor, Emperor."

Emperor Hudson replied, "What is it?"

"A Hover-Jet is heading this way."

Hudson replied, "How long?"

"Within minutes."

Hudson replied, "Shoot it down."

So as Blunt and X-Hamstring with a handful of British soldiers were flying in the Hover-Jet, heading towards Emperor Hudson's headquarters in Germany, one of the soldiers pulled out his pistol firing it towards X-Hamstring shooting him in his upper-body. Blunt moved forward but two soldiers kicked him backwards to the floor, Blunt tried moving up, but they held their weapons at him. X-Hamstring was bleeding out but he started to heal back, Blunt looked pass the soldiers at a dozen Hover-Jets heading towards them.

Blunt said, "Watch your Backs."

"Like we are going to fool for that."

Blunt replies pointing pass them at the other Hover-Jets, "No, really."

As the soldiers turned around many missals came in on them, blasting the Hover-Jet to pieces, all you could see is two objects falling from the sky landing somewhere in Germany. Reports quickly got back to Emperor Hudson' Hudson was pleased to hear that, the Hover-Jet had been destroyed.

"Emperor, the Jewish have started to catcher, Germany people, you should be thinking about attacking them?"

Emperor Hudson replied, "The Jewish are not my enemy, and those people are not my people, rebuilding Mother Russia is my main focus."

Chapter Twenty two

Eight's Cyber-Plus

18th of June 1924 location Emperor Hudson's German headquarters

A few nights and days after the Hover-Jet Blunt and X-Hamstring was in which got destroyed, Emperor Hudson was planning on his mission, as he pulled back all of his forces from Africa, giving him an enough labour to start to rebuild Mother Russia. Hudson was not depending on this next action to happen, as he saw three of his Advisor turn to ash, and five of his Generals turn to dust.

Emperor Hudson looked left to him and said, "It's you."

Eight replied, "Yes it's me."

Emperor Hudson replies, "And you're machine."

Eight replied, "Please, call him by his name, Cyber-Plus."

Emperor Hudson replies, "Why, you're about to kill me, any point in me remembering his name?"

Eight replied, "Kill you, why would I waste my time to kill you, you're pathetic like the rest."

Hudson replies, "Why are you here?"

Eight replied, "So that you know Russia is mines."

Emperor Hudson replies, "If you're not here to kill me, and here to tell me that Russia is yours, why don't we join forces."

Eight replied, "I know you're future, it stay the same, and you will always die in every outcome."

Emperor Hudson replies, "I'm kinder counting on that."

As Hudson's Prussia forces came into the room attacking Eight, Cyber-Plus place a shield around her protecting only Eight, Eight started walking towards them; the bullets were bouncing off the shield all over the place, and the Cyber-Plus beam them away with a sonic blast.

Emperor Hudson said, "Truly amazing, what is that machine, I mean Cyber-Plus built from."

Eight replied, "Magbranium, the strongest material known to the Galaxy Sub-Zero, his system are similar to an AI known as Mainstream not as powerful yet."

Emperor Hudson replies, "Wow, all sudden everything has gotten so much more interesting, I've never heard of any of that before."

Eight replied, "You will never hear of it again, as the Galaxy is not in this universe."

Emperor Hudson replies, "Very interesting, I guess I wouldn't want you as an enemy."

Eight replied, "You won't have me as an enemy, as long as you stay away from Russia, do you understand?"

Emperor Hudson replies, "Yes I do."

Cyber-Plus walked forward placing out his arm, and this force came out of it, opening a portal Eight and Cyber-Plus walked into it disappearing.

Emperor Hudson turned around to found Blunt throwing a punch at him, forcing Hudson backwards onto his butt.

Emperor Hudson replied, "What are you doing?"

Blunt replies, "It ends here."

Emperor Hudson moved upwards as he did Blunt sliced off his clothing, and then kick him on his back, forcing him onto the floor again.

X-Hamstring moved forward shouting, "Stop."

Blunt looked back at X-Hamstring, while holding his blade at the back of, Hudson's neck.

Blunt said, "What is it?"

X-Hamstring replied, "Look on his chest."

Hudson turned around and there was a device, which looked like it was pumping green and blue liquid through his chest, and around his body.

Blunt said, "What in hells name is that?"

Hudson replied, "My insurance."

X-Hamstring replies, "What Insurance?"

Hudson replied, "If you kill me, you destroy England."

Blunt replies, "What have you done?"

Hudson replied, "Isn't it simple, I've planted bombs under the whole of England, in every city if I die England skinks."

Blunt replies, "You sick bastard."

X-Hamstring replied, "Dammit."

Blunt said, "The same thing you did to Mother Russia?"

Hudson replied, "Not quite as Mother Russia, can be rebuilt, but for England it will be lost forever, known as a myth."

X-Hamstring replies, "Blunt think fast, I can see a hellah Prussia forces, coming our way."

Emperor Hudson said, "Take that Hover-Jet, go back to England, you may be able to safe it after all.

X-Hamstring said, "We must leave now."

Blunt replied, "This won't be our last meeting, but sure that I will see you again, and when I do……

X-Hamstring grabbed Blunt moving him out to the ledge of the Head-Quarters, onto the Hover-Jet.

Emperor Hudson replied, "No, in fact it will be."

As Blunt and X-Hamstring were flying up into the sky, X-Hamstring looked backwards at a device counting numbers down from ten, X-Hamstring moved backwards touching Blunt" Blunt looked back at the Device as well.

Blunt said, "That bastard."

X-Hamstring opened the Hover-Jet door as he did the Hover-Jet blew to pieces, forcing both X-Hamstring and Blunt out of it, they both were falling. Emperor Hudson looked up into the sky to see the explosion from the Hover-Jet, Emperor Hudson moved backwards dropping to one of his knees.

"Emperor, Emperor, what's wrong?"

Emperor Hudson replied, "It's time I took this off, it's killing me."

22nd of June 1924 Boarder of France

Name: Blunt Supreme

Gender: Male

Height: Five foot elven

Build: Medium toned

Features: Black hair, blue eyes

Nationality: English

D.O.B 02/05/1897

MI6 agent: Mother's intelligence unit 6

Weapons: Handgun, combat knife, Machine gun

Status: M.I.A

Blunt and X-Hamstring both climbed up onto a mountain overlooking France.

X-Hamstring said, "What now?"

Blunt replied, "Go back home."

X-Hamstring shouted, "Watch out."

As a few missiles hit the side of the mountain where Blunt and X-Hamstring were standing, it all crumbled around them, making them slip through the ground.

While that was happening Eight and Cyber-Plus came walking out of the portal in Russia looking at the city which got destroyed by Hudson, Eight nudged at Cyber-Plus which started to build back the city, but this time around a more advance city. Word got back to Okuma that Hudson had a small amount of forces left; Okuma did not like this, so he started to plan his attack on America.

Emperor Okuma said, "Give them the blue-prints, we will build our own flying crafts." So while that was happening the Prussia forces scanned the whole area of the mountain, but they were no signs of Blunt or X-Hamstring.

"Emperor, Emperor."

Hudson replied, "Yes."

"We have killed them."

Hudson replied, "How sure are you?"

"There are no bodies."

Hudson replied, "That can sometimes be a bad thing."

"Should we check for the twentieth time?"

Hudson replied, "That's a good idea."

5th of July 1924 America, Washington DC White house

Leeroy was back in America, he headed straight to the new White House, marched inside the White House.

"Mr Blair am I right?"

Leeroy replied, "I prefer Leeroy "Sir, but yes who are you?"

"That does not concern you."

Leeroy walked pass this guy with an eye pouch on, he felt a weird feeling towards him, but carried onto the President.

"Sir, Leeroy is here."

"Leeroy, come in, he will see you now."

"Talk."

Leeroy replied, "Mr President."

"Please call me Z, short for Zero," that's right Zero is back he became a true Master of Time, he knew he could say his real name as no one knew who he was from this time, he thought to believe.

Names: Zindus, Zero, President Z, White Assassin

Gender: Male

Height: Six foot one

Build: Slim toned

Features: Bold head

Nationality: Unknown

D.O.B: Unknown

Weapons: Sword, Diamond Machete, Handguns, knives

Abilities: Shapeshifting, healing abilities, supreme intelligence, advance swordplay, advance strength

Leeroy replied, "Z, X-Hamstring……

President Z replies, "I heard they are dead."

Leeroy replied, "Dead?"

Chapter Twenty Three

Secrets and Lies

13th of May 1925 location America, New York inside a bar

Leeroy was drinking his problems away, drink after drink he knocks back; the bar-man looked at the young boy.

"Slow down kid."

Leeroy replied, "Why, all my true friends are gone."

"Let me tell you a secret."

Leeroy replied, "As long as it doesn't end with a lie."

"Friends come and go, I'm sure they will be back."

Leeroy replied, "I'm afraid this time they won't be."

"Have this one on the house."

"Hey, you nigger, what you doing in here drinking, putting them black lips on them glasses right there."

"Easy now."

"Easy who."

The stranger grabbed the Bar-man's head smashing it off the bar, Leeroy moved upwards and backwards into another stranger, that stranger pushes Leeroy downwards.

"Why ain't this nigger, in the field, working like the rest of them?"

"Bucky, he had to one of the lucky ones, he must have escape."

"What are you doing to that young man?"

"Oh don't worry, he's our friend, can't you see." While squeezing on Leeroy's head.

Leeroy replied, "No, I'm not, let go off me."

One of the stranger's kicks Leeroy downwards, the other grabbed a bottle, and went to smash it on top of Leeroy's head, but an unknown person smashed a chair on the stranger side, forcing him down.

"What are you doing, that nigger right there, he's our friend."

"I don't think he is?"

Leeroy looked upwards and said, "X-Ham."

"Oh, so two niggers want to play."

"Get him Billy, hurt him real bad Billy, show them who the man is."

The stranger tried to throw a punch but X-Ham caught it twisting up his arm, and then punching him, forcing him back into the bar.

"This nigger got some kind of strength, Bucky."

"Billy I get him don't you worry, I'll show this nigger, what it means to be a true American."

Bucky moved forward kicking out his leg but X-Ham moved around his leg, kicking Billy's leg trapping him to the ground.

"I got him Billy, I got him."

X-Ham twists up in the air kicking Bucky backwards, while grabbing Billy's head, and smashing it down to the ground.

"Ok, let's get out of here."

Leeroy gets up moving over to X-Ham, "hold on X-Ham." Leeroy grabs a bottle and smashes it on one of the guy's head. Leeroy then said, "They said that you were dead, in fact you and Blunt?" while leaving the bar and walking down the street.

X-Hamstring replied, "I'm not sure about Blunt, I saw flames cover him, I doubt he made it."

Leeroy replies, "It's good to have you back."

X-Ham replied, "So it looks like you been getting into a lot of fights it seems?"

Leeroy replies, "Yeah a few, I guess the land of the free, isn't so free as it seems."

X-Ham replied, "Won any or should I need to ask?"

Leeroy replies, "This whole year, since you both were gone, has been hell for me."

X-Ham replied, "Well, I'm back and I'll teach you how to fight."

The barman came running behind X-Ham, "Sir, "Sir." X-Ham stopped and looked back.

"You saved all of us."

"I guess."

"What's your name?"

"Call me X-Hamstring."

"Where are you from "Sir?"

"The mother land."

"The mother land?"

"He means Africa."

"Well, you're a true hero."

"More like a superhero."

"Well thanks, and Leeroy let's get going."

19th of June 1925 location England, MI6 base

X-Hamstring and Leeroy back in England walking into this underground hidden base, where a lot of people were rushing around Leeroy looked around.

Leeroy said, "What is this place?"

X-Hamstring replied, "A place full of Secrets."

Leeroy replies, "If it has secrets than it must have lies?"

X-Hamstring replied, "No, that's what it's called, Secrets."

Leeroy replies, "So they are no lies down here?"

X-Hamstring replied, 'the only lie down here is me."

Leeroy replies, "What do you mean?"

X-Hamstring replied, "Hudson, Okuma, they believe me to be dead, and we want it to stay that way."

Leeroy replies, "How do you know you can trust any of these people, to keep you're lies?"

X-Hamstring replied, "Most or a lot of these people, are my people from my hometown."

Leeroy replies, "Awesome."

"Hello, Mr Blair."

Leeroy replied, "Mr Blair."

'sorry, what would you prefer to be called?"

Leeroy replied, "Leeroy is nice, but LJ is better."

"Ok, LJ it is."

Leeroy said, 'so why have you brought me here?"

X-Hamstring replied, "I believe you can build the first real aircraft."

Leeroy replies, "That's a bit silly, isn't it, there's Hover-Jets out there."

X-Hamstring replied, "There's only two left in the world, and Hudson has both of them."

Leeroy replies, "How am I meant to build these aircrafts."

X-Hamstring opened up a door leading into a massive warehouse, with many scientists and blueprints, from the aid of Roman."

Leeroy replied, "Mr Frist."

"Mr Blair."

"Leeroy, he here to help you build aircrafts for us."

"I don't need scientist I need engineers and mechanics, find me some of those skilled people and then we can talk."

"Where do we find them?"

"That's simple; this is my hometown in the Bronx, New York. Once you get there tell them LJ sent you."

"Alright guys, you heard the man."

As Leeroy walked around with X-Hamstring and Roman James the First, he noticed something, "What is material here?"

"Leeroy, that's from my home in Africa, the strongest metal on Earth. As you can see you have an unlimited supply with gold and copper, you even have diamonds over there."

"Damn, we definitely are about to advance, way ahead of our times."

'That's the whole point."

"Alright, I'll let you guys get on with it."

"Thanks X-Hamstring."

26th of February 1927 the Hover-Jet was redesign as the Hover-Craft

Inventors: Leeroy Blair and Roman James the First

Use only for: MI6, C.I.A and Special Forces

Chapter Twenty Four

Future FORETOLD Part 1

Mid 1926 location Germany Hudson's headquarter

Hudson was no longer an Emperor, he had less than five hundred soldiers left, but he was about to find out his true density. As Hudson walked back into his throne room standing there was no other than Roman James the First, Hudson held out his Golden pistol.

Hudson said, "Who may you be?"

Roman replied, "Shouldn't I be asking you that?"

Hudson's General said, "We have recovered true information from our British spies, this man here, he holds true knowledge of the future to come."

Hudson replied, "We really are getting carried away aren't we, kidnapping a kid."

Roman said, "I know you're Hudson, but everyone knows that, but do they know you're father's true name?"

Hudson replied, "No one knows my father's true name, not even me until, a few years back."

Roman replies, "Erich Huston Bergmann, the only truth you kept, was Huston just removing the t and replacing it with a d."

Hudson replied, "No one knows that information, not even the world's best spies, who are you really?"

"Before you do anything crazy "Sir, please hear him out, we used a lot of our resources to bring him here."

Hudson replied, "Fine, talk."

Roman James the First replies, "Talk about what, I am you're guess am I not?"

Hudson then says, "The way you stand with no fear, means a lot about your character, if you hold all this knowledge like my advisor is telling me. Tell us of the Future, what we should prepare for?"

Roman James the First replied, "That's simple, the Jewish will over-throne you, but yet you won't be killed by a Jew."

Hudson leaned forward and replies "Carry on."

Roman James the First replied, "A person who means nothing to you, but you mean a lot to him, will kill you."

Hudson replies, "Who is this person?"

Roman James The First replied, "Mr Hitler."

Hudson replies, "That's a German name?"

Roman James the First replied, "Yes it is, he will seek revenge after the death of his father and brother, this revenge will be driven because you never help the German people."

Hudson replies, "Why should I care?"

Roman James the First replied, "I'm not saying you should, but if you want to live, and regain Mother Russia from Eight and Cyber-Plus, then you should care."

Hudson replies, "Regain Mother Russia, but how?"

Roman James the First replied, "By seeking help from a Being, which floats between neither sides."

Hudson replies, "He talks some much nonsense, how can I seek a person, which intention doesn't match mines?"

Roman James the First replied, "That is the only Being, which could possibly kill Cyber-Plus."

Hudson replies, "My second thought, which stands highly with me, is asking why you are giving me this information, do you not know who I am?"

Roman James the First replied, "I'm not here to judge, I'm just here off my own will, I am just telling you what should be so clear already."

Hudson replies, 'that's what I mean."

Roman James the First replied, 'the right outcome will always be the outcome, whatever way it goes."

Hudson replies, "Me dying right?"

Roman James the First replied, "You're a small prawn in this part of history."

Hudson replies, "Fine, what's to say I believe you, how will I ever find this Being?"

Roman James the First replied, "That's simple, the Mountains of Heavies."

Hudson replies, "Mesink."

Roman James the First replied, "Yes my home Island."

Hudson said, "Thank you my advisor, you've brought me something, worth everything."

Roman James the First replies, "Am I free to go?"

Hudson replied, "Yes, we be leaving together."

Hudson looks back at Roman sitting down in the Hover-Jet, Hudson moves over to him.

Roman James The First said, "I know you want to ask me something more?"

Hudson replied, "In fact I do."

Roman James the First replies, "No thank you."

Hudson replied, "How……

Roman replies, "I have dreams, maybe vision, off the near and far future."

Hudson replied, "If you did………

Roman replies, "But I don't, I am not built that way."

Hudson replied, "At least let me protect you, get some people to watch over you."

Roman replies, "You know that won't be possible."

Hudson replied, "Explain to me why?"

Roman replies. "Only two others know what I can do."

Hudson replied, "What you can do is more than amazing."

Roman replies, "It's killing me."

Hudson replied, "If you know anything, you know I have great scientists."

Roman replies, "I know a lot, maybe not everything, but a lot sometimes too much."

Hudson replied, "If you ever change your……………

Roman replies, "I won't."

Hudson stared at Roman for a long time as the pilot looked back at Hudson, Roman looked away.

"We are very close."

Hudson replied, "Push it."

Introducing Grandmaster Castro

Mid 1926

As Hudson dropped Roman James the First back to his Mansion, Hudson flew over to Mountain Heavies, the Hover-Jet landed down at the peak, where he saw a cave entrances. Hudson walked out of the Jet with more than a dozen of his forces, heading straight into the Mountain. Hudson and his forces were inside the Mountain, moments later they came to an opening through the top, with lights shining down inside it.

"Sir, over there, look."

As Hudson turned his head looking across from him, he saw a person floating with his legs crossed in mid-air.

Hudson said, "Hello."

The Being's eyes opened up then the Being disappeared, reappearing behind Hudson forces, Hudson turned around to witness the Being killing his forces like nothing.

Hudson said, "I'm not here……."

"Why are you here?"

Hudson replies, "I need your help."

"Your full of anger, I cannot help a Science creature, like you."

Hudson replied, "Please help me, please."

"I will do one thing for you."

Hudson replied, "Yes, please."

"I will let you walk out here alive."

Hudson replied, "No, no, no."

"Fine, I guess, it shall be."

Hudson replied, "Wait, ok, I will leave."

As Hudson was walking out he turned around.

Hudson said, "What is your name?"

"Grandmaster Castro."

Hudson replies, "Well Grandmaster Castro, I'm sure we will meet again."

Grandmaster Castro replied, "If we do, it won't be under good terms."

Hudson walked back to his Hover-Jet.

"So."

Hudson replied, "As you can see it didn't work."

"Plan B?"

Hudson replied, "Ahaha, yes of course."

As Hudson boarded his Hover-Jet dozen more appeared, "And they believe me to only have two left."

Hudson replies "Blow the Mountain to pieces."

Grandmaster Castro eyes opened again and he teleported away, the mountain blew to pieces, and Grandmaster Castro appeared in Mid-air, "I must find a new home."

"What the fuck, destroy him, I'm getting sick of these beings with abilities."

Bullets and missals came flying towards Grandmaster Castro knocking him down to the ground, as that happened the Mountain crumbled all over him, and Hudson forces kept on firing until they ran out of ammo.

"Sir, behind you."

A Hover-Jet came in blowing one Hover-Jet to pieces, and then something shot out from the ground destroying three more Hover-Jet.

Hudson said, "Get us the hell out of here."

Grandmaster Castro holding a Staff came flying towards Hudson, but three more Hover-Jet blasting him out of the sky, and into the front part of the Hover-Jet.

X-Hamstring said, "Grandmaster, are you ok?"

Grandmaster Castro replied, "Yes."

Grandmaster Castro power jumped out of the Hover-Jet, and on top of the Hover-Jet Hudson was in, breaking through the top part, climbing inside of it. Hudson was standing away from Grandmaster Castro, Hudson started firing his Golden Gun of at Grandmaster Castro, the bullets flipped of Grandmaster's Staff and down next to Hudson's feet.

Grandmaster Castro moved forward as Hudson soldiers move in on him, Grandmaster Castro quickly forces them to the floor, and then turned his Staff into a large blade, slicing the Hover-Jet. Hudson went flying back into the controls, as Grandmaster Castro turned his Staff into a large blaster, Cyber-Plus appeared in front of Hudson, shielding them both from the blast and transporting him out of the Hover-Jet as it crashes into the side of the Mountain.

Cyber-Plus appeared holding Hudson in mid-air, on the ground next to Eight, Cyber-Plus dropped Hudson to the floor.

Hudson said, "Why are you helping me?"

Eight replied, "We now have another common enemy."

Hudson replies, "Grandmaster?"

Eight replied, "Yes, I watched his son, kill my father."

As Grandmaster Castro teleported near to Eight, he looked pass her and at Cyber-Plus.

"Yemini, you stole her chip, with Mainstream AI porotype on it."

Eight said, "Get Hudson out of here, Grandmaster Castro is mine."

Cyber-Plus transported Hudson back to his Head-Quarters in Germany.

As X-Hamstring was flying in a Hover-Jet, he noticed Grandmaster Castro, standing away from un-known person.

X-Hamstring said, "Roman, I'm going to need your help here."

Roman James the First replied, "The person is known as Eight, which is Zero's daughter, impossible Zero."

Names: Octadic, Eight, Ella Grey

Gender: Female

Height: five foot ten

Build: medium toned

Features: Brown hair and blonde strips, white eyes

Species: unknown

D.O.B: unknown

Abilities: Speed, time shifter, advance combat defence, supreme intelligence and advance healing

Creator of Cyber-Plus new advance AI Android

X-Hamstring replies, "Wait, Zero as in President Z?"

Roman James The First replied, "I believe so, he has travelled from the future, but I wasn't aware of this. That's why there is a new strain in the timeline."

"Timeline, new strain, what are you talking about?"

"Not now X-Hamstring, watch out."

X-Hamstring got smashed into the side of the inside of the Hover-Jet by Cyber-Plus, Cyber-Plus picked X-Ham up and kicked him backwards, Cyber-Plus placed out his arm while a mini sonic gun was formed out of it. While moving towards X-Hamstring aiming it down at him, X-Hamstring pulled out his Machete, and as Cyber-Plus fire of his Mini Sonic Gun, it broke the machete in half also forcing X-Hamstring out of the Hover-Jet falling form the sky.

Eight moved forward firing of her guns the bullets came towards Grandmaster Castro, forcing him backwards. Eight kicked, punched, kneed and shot Grandmaster Castro down to the ground. Grandmaster Castro went to move away from Eight's blade, but his cheek got sliced slightly, and then Eight power kick Grandmaster Castro backwards off his feet onto his front.

Cyber-Plus appeared behind Eight Cyber-Plus back slightly opened, and he pulled out two mini blade, Grandmaster Castro twisted upwards towards Eight, but Cyber-Plus shielded Eight knocking Grandmaster Castro back down.

Eight said, "Finish him."

As Cyber-Plus went in for his final strike, X-Hamstring through his sword which went inside of Cyber-Plus chest, Grandmaster Castro quickly moved upwards twisting the sword pulling the sword out, also turning his Staff into a sword slicing off both Cyber-Plus arms. Cyber-Plus moved backwards but suddenly his arm started to merge back, "Regeneration, she must have stolen that from the Worth Centre X" Cyber-Plus then started firing at Grandmaster Castro, but he turned his Staff into a force field protecting him from the blast.

Eight said, "Let's go."

Cyber-Plus opened a portal and they escape through it, X-Hamstring came sliding over to Grandmaster Castro.

X-Hamstring said, "How are you doing?"

Grandmaster Castro replied, "Will you stop asking me that."

X-Hamstring replies, "We need to get to the White House."

Grandmaster Castro replied, "The White House."

X-Hamstring replies, "The person whom your son killed, is acting as the President."

Grandmaster Castro replied, "Zindus, his species conquered Sub-Zero the Galaxy."

Grandmaster Castro touched X-Hamstring teleporting them inside of the White House, in fact in front of President Z, President Z move upwards.

President Zero said, "Thought this day would never come."

Grandmaster Castro replied, "Zero or Zindus?"

X-Hamstring said, "Who's that guy?"

Grandmaster Castro replies, "A Shadow-Walker, they personal have no names."

Shadow-Walker said, "Hello old friend."

Grandmaster Castro replied, "How can you be working for him, after what his species done to the Galaxy."

Shadow-Walker replies, "He promised me your life."

X-Hamstring said, "So you're Eight's father?"

Zero replies, "You say that like you've met her?"

Zero dashes over to X-Ham grabbing him, and forcing him onto the wall, punching his throat blocking his air supply, X-Hamstring dropped to the ground.

Zero said, "I will look into your mind."

Grandmaster Castro through his Staff at Zero knocking him away through the wall, and then Shadow-Walker moved forward, merging into Grandmaster Castro and then out of him behind him.

Grandmaster Castro said, "Why are you here?"

Shadow-Walker replied, "For your Staff of course."

Weapon Staff: Powers to form into any weapon the mind can imagine, key to unlocking all Dimension

Owners in order: Great Grandmaster Castro aka Grandfather Castro, his son Master Castro, Touch and Switch

Grandmaster Castro replies, "No one which is not pure, should not will it, especially something that function outside of gravity."

Shadow-Walker replied, "I'm not here to will it, I'm here to give it to Switch."

Grandmaster Castro replies, "Switch."

Shadow-Walker replied, "Can't you see."

Grandmaster Castro replies, "You're not from any timeline, you're from a whole new dimension, that's why we are equals at the most."

Shadow-Walker replied, "Imagine that a Dimension where I have the edge over you."

Shadow-Walker held out his hand, and the Staff from Grandmaster Castro's back, came into it. Shadow-Walker threw down a ball which rolled to the window, exploding but also creating a gateway into the Dimension pull.

Shadow-Walker said, "Follow us if you dare."

Grandmaster was frozen in place as Zero was linked to X-Hamstring seeing into his brain while Shadow-Walker says, "I have the Staff Zindus, and we must leave while we can."

X-Hamstring got back up after Zindus free his mind X-Ham looked over at Grandmaster Castro, which he noticed he couldn't move, X-Hamstring moved towards Zero, but Zero forced x-Hamstring backwards with the Diamond Machete into a book shelve.

X-Hamstring said, "The Diamond Machete."

Weapon Diamond Machete: Powers of magic, time travel via all dimensions, granted immortality and immune to electrical beings

Rightful owners: Righteous, Zindus, X-Hamstring, Blood Warrior, Lord Warrior

Zero replied, "Is mines." Zero then went into the Gateway after Shadow-Walker.

The secret service came into the room seeing that the President was gone, they quickly surrounded X-Hamstring, and then Grandmaster Castro was release from the force which was holding him in place.

"Where is the President?"

X-Hamstring replied, "He wasn't the President, he was pretending to be the President."

"Take them away."

Grandmaster Castro made this light appear which blinded the Secret Service, allowing them enough time to teleport, appearing on a building not so far from the White House.

Grandmaster Castro said, "Where can we go which is safe?"

X-Hamstring replied, "I know someone in Canada."

Sometime in 2100's

"Switch."

"Shadow-Walker."

"It was a success."

"Of course it would be, my great Grandfather shouldn't have been an match for any of you too, through that dimension."

"However Switch, there were other heroes there, I thought history told us, that there was no heroes until the great battle."

"A new strain in the Timeline has been created, we are winning meaning, he is changing the outcome, meaning if he succeeds he will have no reason to end it all."

"Lord Warrior Or"

"Lord Warrior."

"You mean B… Warrior?"

"He has his father's title now, he wills more power than his father ever could, we are far from defeating the Warrior's bloodline."

"I am still amused how you survive the Mind-Wavers."

"I am not one of the chosen ones that will force he who is known as…..

Mid 1926 location Canada, Toronto Leeroy's apartment

As the door knocks Leeroy opens it, Leeroy said, "X-Ham and a friend I guess."

As Grandmaster Castro walked passes Leeroy, Leeroy had a vision off a forgotten future past.

"Your Kenroy's grandfather."

Leeroy replied, "I don't even have kids, for my kids to have kids."

X-Ham replies, "Don't mind him, He's not from around here."

Leeroy replied, "Yeah I notice that, could tell from his clothing."

X-Ham said, "I need to ask you something."

Leeroy replied, "Anything."

X-Ham replies, "I'm out of friends, except you."

Leeroy replied, "What's wrong?"

X-Ham replies, "I need to stay here for a while."

Leeroy replied, "Yes of course."

Grandmaster replies, "You people are good people."

Leeroy replied, "What's wrong with him?"

X-Ham replies, "I'm not sure, but I know it's to do with that Shadow Being."

Leeroy replied, "Shadow-Walker?"

X-Ham replies, "Yeah it seems like the Shadow-Walker is from the same Galaxy as his."

Grandmaster Castro replied, "Shadow-Walker, Switch, my Staff."

Leeroy said, "I think there's a battle going on in the future, that will affect everything."

Grandmaster Castro replied, "It is true about you."

Leeroy replies, "What is he talking about X-Ham."

X-Ham replied, "I'm not sure."

Grandmaster Castro replies, "Leeroy, you may not realise yet, but you have abilities inside you, one day it will save us all."

X-Ham replies, "On that note, next chapter please."

Grandmaster Castro replied, "It's not that easy X-Ham, but with the power you have inside you, use it to protect this young man, that is you're new duty."

Leeroy replies, "Protect me because I had a vision."

Grandmaster Castro replied, "It wasn't only a vision, it's more than a vision, and with X-Ham's gifts or curse he can watch over your whole family, for the next hundred and so years."

X-Ham replies, "It would be an honour to watch over you Leeroy, especially with what you have said, and Grandmaster also."

Leeroy replied, "So what do we do now?

Chapter Twenty six

The Road to World War II

9th of March 1940 Location England, London

There was a new Prime Minster of England, in his office he was sitting down, as someone placed down a folder, with the words written on it. Classified documents, the Prime Minster opened it up.

"Prime Minster Churchill, it's been almost fourteen years, you must sign the form."

Prime Minster Churchill replied, "If He's alive, he will find his way back."

Prime Minster Churchill stamp the folder with the letters mark on it, M.I.A.

Churchill replied, "Blunt Supreme will be class as Missing in Action, until the evidences we have are no longer useful."

Churchill got up out of his chair moving over to the window, as he did X-Hamstring came walking into his office.

Churchill said, "X-Ham."

X-Ham replied, "How did you know?"

Churchill replies, "Do you need to ask?"

X-Hamstring replied, "I'm sorry about your brothers, Finn and Asquith Between."

Churchill replies, "Let's make sure that the past stays in the past, and focus on catching or even more defeating Hitler, and Empress Eight."

X-Hamstring replied, "Oh, so you did hear?"

Churchill replies, "No, but I just did."

21st of June 1936 location Germany Head-Quarters

Hudson was on his throne in his Germany Head-Quarters, Hudson heard a weird sound, and then sudden two guards dropped from the outside of the throne doors.

Hudson said, "Who is there?"

The Prime Mister walks in.

Hudson replied, "What is it Prime Mister Berger?"

"Please call me Mr Hitler."

Eight and Cyber-Plus was over-looking the whole situation, Cyber-Plus looked at Eight, Eight turned her head.

Eight replied, "Yes, his time has come, we must not intervene."

Hudson replies, "So it's true, this is you're rise to power."

Hudson draws for his golden gun, but Hitler fired it out of his hands, and shot him in his chest making him fly backwards.

Hudson said, "I wouldn't believe this is how it ends for me, but I guess it does."

Hitler replied, "Behind your wonderful walls, my rise to power, happened years back, when the members of the Nazi party stormed into the Jewish Prison camp."

Hudson replies, "I don't see Light or Dark, but I do feel cold."

While Hitler was moving forward towards Hudson" Hudson looked outwards towards a building where he could see, Eight and Cyber-Plus standing. "All you had to do is send in a group of your forces, if you did my father and brother, wouldn't have been murdered. I and you would be working together, building back a better and more powerful army."

Hudson said, "I can't see nothing, everything is blurry, everything is so far away."

Hitler kicked Hudson to his side, moving him onto his butt, while aiming his handgun downwards towards Hudson.

Hitler said, "As much as I hate you, I have pure hatred for the Jews, but that doesn't mean I shall let you live."

Hudson replied, "You are and always will be…………

Hitler shot Hudson five times in his chest, Hitler then quickly turned around firing his gun off, but Cyber-Plus blocked the bullets.

Name: Emperor Hudson better known as Robert Hutson

Gender: Male

Height: Five eleven

Build: heavy but toned

Features: Grey beard, blonde hair, blue eyes

Nationality: German and Russian

D.O.B: 17/04/1886

Died: 21/06/1934

Cause of death: Five bullets to his chest

Killed by: Hitler

Hitler said, "What I saw was right, I guess you are here to kill me."

Eight replied, "We come as friends."

Hitler replies, "Hitler doesn't need friends."

Hitler fire of his gun again but Cyber-Plus moved forward in front of Eight, catching the bullets crushing them in his hand, dropping the bullets to the ground as they bounce of it.

Hitler said, "I like him."

Eight replied, "Cyber-Plus and I, are not here to kill you, in fact do you accept us as allies?"

Hitler replies, "So he's called Cyber-Plus?"

Eight replied, "You're eyeing up my machine."

Hitler replies, "I'm only fascinated by its appearance, so human like."

Eight replied, "I guess we are on board."

Hitler replies, "The Cyber-Plus could become useful."

Eight replied, "He only follows orders from me."

Hitler replies, "Then I welcome both of you, with open arms."

As Eight went to move forward a group of German soldiers surrounded her, Hitler moved backwards sitting down onto the throne.

Eight said to Hitler starring him in the eyes, "Think wisely off your next actions."

Hitler replied, "Oh, but I have."

His German soldiers placed down their weapons, Cyber-Plus placed out his arm creating a gateway, "Wait, we are allies right?" said Hitler.

Eight looked at Hitler winking at him and then disappearing into the gateway along with Cyber-Plus.

Adolf Hitler said, "He alone, who owns the youth, gains the future."

Chapter Twenty Seven

Unlikely Events

7th of December 1919 location Germany

A group of armed men were marching in a large group of German people
into this camp, on the side of the vents, were some writing which
stated that it was a Jewish Prison Camp for German people involved
with the N.A.Z.I.

One of the prisoners which was Marching into the Prison camp dropped
to the floor, and an armed man walk slowly over to the prisoner, the
armed man looked down at the man.

"Get up onto your feet."

"I cannot go any further."

The armed man got onto one of his knees, leaning in close to the
prisoner, quickly drawing out his pistol, holding the pistol to the
prisoner's head.

"Get up now."

The prisoner struggles to get up dropping back down to the floor,
one of the other prisoners moved out of the line, going to help that
prisoner get up, but the armed man fire of his pistol killing both
the prisoners.

"Anyone else want to take a break?"

The armed man looked around at all the German prisoners.

"I thought so."

One of the German prisoner started talking quietly to another one.

"Emperor Hudson, will do something about this."

"Father."

"Adolf not now."

Another armed man moved to the side of Adolf's father, taking his
rifle and hitting him in the stomach, Adolf's father dropped to the
ground.

"Take him in there."

"FATHER!"

The armed man watched as this other young man moved in front of the young man, and then the armed man smacked the feeling out of Adolf face.

"Your father will be punished for his actions."

Adolf spitted at the armed man hitting his face cheek, the armed man pulled out his pistol, pointing it on Adolf forehead.

"Brother."

"STOP."

"General…………

"There's a better punish than death for this one."

The armed man smacks Adolf to the ground and some other armed men dragged Adolf into a building.

22th of May 1920 the Jewish prisoner camp

"I told you, Emperor Hudson, do not care for us."

Adolf replied, "Brother, I promise we will get out of here."

As Adolf said that a group of armed men rushed into the room, where his brother and a few other German men were being hold, Adolf got up as he did one of the armed men hit Adolf around the face with the bottom of his rifle.

'Take him, it's time."

Adolf said, "Where are you taking him?"

'Strict him off his clothes, bring that one as well, he should watch this."

As Adolf brother got pulled out of the room naked, and bleeding. Adolf saw his father tied to a wooden pole, and then the armed men tied his naked brother to another next to his father.

Adolf also saw other people who were his friends he had made, while being in the Jewish Prison camp, one of the armed men knee Adolf to the back of his head.

"So you are called Adolf Hitler, I am I right?"

Adolf replied, "Yes, why should that matter to you?"

"You German people make me sick."

Adolf replied, "And you Jewish………

Adolf got shot in his leg Adolf screamed out; his father lifted his head up, looking straight at his Adolf.

"Son........."

"Quite him now."

"Be brave."

Adolf reached out his arms towards his father, as he witness one of the Jewish armed men, killing his father instantly, Adolf screamed out.

"NOOOOOOOOOOOOOOOOOO!"

Adolf got hit again to the back of his head, making his vision blurry, as he could barely see, but what he saw were another man killing his brother and his friends too.

Tears after tears came running out of Adolf eyes, Adolf then tried to get up but couldn't, as he was bleeding out.

"Death would be to kind for you, instead you will live out you're remaining years here."

"Fuck you."

"Nazi will never rise."

Mid 1925's the same Jewish Camp

Adolf was doing some field work as another German prisoner started talking to him, one of the Jewish armed men, shot the prisoner to death.

Adolf dropped backwards as he did the Jewish armed man, moved over to him.

"Get up, get back to work."

Adolf replied, "Why are you doing this?"

The Jewish armed man smack Adolf head with the bottom of his rifle, Adolf went flying down the hill, into the dirt.

"What are you doing?" asked the General of this small Rebel Jewish group.

"He's one of the members of the N.A.Z.I."

"Yes I know, bring him to my office."

Moments later Adolf got dragged into the Jewish General's office, blood running down the side of his head, his face covered in dirt and hands a mess, clothes tare.

"You must be wondering, why we are doing this, what we are doing?"

Adolf lifted his head slightly upwards, and replied, "You are Russian?"

"No, I am half Russian and half Jewish, but more so I am Russian."

"Enlightening me a little."

The Aftermath of most of Emperor Hudson's army moved into my Mother Russia, leaving Germany in pure chaos, the government started to turn dark. As my Jewish people didn't agree with the Nazi Party, you're plans, plus with the aid of Emperor Hudson. Only leaving a few hundred Prussia forces to, rape, kill and abuse their family, yes their family those men outside there. I helped them to overpower the Prussian forces, saving other families."

Adolf replied, "Even so, it's fine for you to torcher German people?"

"Let's not pretend here, if that Nazi Party got into power, you would have done the same to my people."

Adolf replied, "No, but now, if I get free yes."

"We want to be free people, within this country."

Adolf replied, "What we believe in is the way forward."

"We know there are more of you out there; we will catcher the rest of you Nazis."

Adolf replied, "What do you want from me?"

"Tell me where they are, and I'll make sure no harm comes to you."

Adolf replied, "You took me away, I know nothing off their were abouts, I guess I am no use to you, kill me already I have nothing left."

"We are not like you Nazis, we are not weak."

Adolf replied, "I never said that, or thought that, but my opinion has changed."

"So you being here have changed your opinion?"

Adolf replied, "No, when my first wife, which was Jewish died by another Jewish person which was her brother. Which they tried killing my family, and the only people who were there to help, was the members of the……"

"The National Socialist German Workers" Party, what a great way to cover, you're true meaning."

Adolf replied, "I was leading up to becoming the next Prime Minster of Germany, but you stopped me, don't you see the world needs someone like me."

"The world needs not you, but truth to balance it."

Adolf Hitler replied, "It is not truth that matters, but victory."

"Look at this country, it's in chaos, the Prussia forces the Emperor. He doesn't even care about the German people, and you want to be their Prime Mister, there's not even a system in this country for that to work."

Adolf replied, "If I ever get out of this Prison, I will build a new system, and kill the Emperor Mark my words."

"So is it true, there are more of you out there, more members of the Nazi Party."

Adolf replied, "Even if that was true, there is nothing you could do about it."

"Poor Mr Hitler you've already said too much."

Adolf replied, "No General, I said just enough."

"Take him away."

"General, we searched South, East and West, nothing."

"Search North."

Early 1929 Hitler's escape

All of the Jewish armed men retreat from the Prison camp, as this unknown force destroyed more than third quarters of them. Adolf looked out of the window all he saw was an object shining in the sky, moving away. Adolf stood up looking at his people, and then walking over to the door, using the tools his built to open it.

"Adolf, what about the guards?"

Adolf replied, "Didn't you hear that."

Adolf opened up the door flames were everywhere Adolf walked out of the prison room, dropping to his knees, as Adolf looked up he saw a large group of armed men marching into the camp.

"Adolf, down here, over here."

Adolf replied, "No, it's ok, it's the Nazis."

"Adolf Hitler, it is great seeing you again."

Adolf looked back at the other prisoner getting up off his knees, walking over to the armed man, reaching out their hands shaking their hands.

Adolf Hitler said, "The world will be mines."

"After we've cleaned you up, the new Government is ready to be in place, also Hudson has little amount of forces left."

Adolf Hitler replies, "Those who want to live, let them fight, and those who do not want to fight in this world of eternal struggle do not deserve to live."

"Sir, what did you say?"

Hitler replies, "After I've killed him, I then will kill every single Jewish person, whipping them from this world."

22nd of August 1934 location German's House of Minsters

"So that how you did it?"

"Things have changed she doesn't even know I'm her father."

"When should we bring her here?"

"We wait."

"You will make a great Prime Minster sir Hitler."

"For now we move in silence, they won't see us coming this time."

Chapter Twenty Eight

London is burning

Mid 1940

Hitler has been the Prime Minster of Germany, for the past four years, and his army has grown three times larger than Hudson's army did when Hudson was the emperor. Making him a true threat to the rest of the world, as Emperor Hudson was no more, Japan was in chaos having an endless war against the Chinese's forces.

In the main time Hitler was in front of his advisors.

"Mr Hitler, we have upgraded the Arado Ar 240 aircrafts, with the help of what little information we had off their ones, the aircrafts are ready."

Prime Minster Hitler replied, "We bomb England tonight, London will burn."

"Excellent."

Word travelled back to the Prime Minster of England Mr Churchill, as it did he alerted the Queen of England, she got escorted underground for her protection.

"Mr Churchill, the Chinese have finished, building the weapons on the roof tops."

Prime Minster Churchill replied, "What about the underground warehouses?"

"There are still over sixty million people, which there are no spaces for."

Churchill replied, "Inform them to take the children to the country side, and those we are able to fight, get them to the base."

"How will that benefit them?"

Churchill replied, "Hitler's airstrike will not hit the country side, there's nothing there."

"If that is true we could have send the others…..

Prime Minster Churchill replied, "The defences on the roof tops will barely hold back, the German air-strike."

"We greatly advise you to get underground as well."

Churchill replied, "I am the Prime Mister."

"That's why we advise you too."

X-Hamstring was at the bottom of the stairs as the Prime Minster was walking down it, X-Hamstring cut the Prime Minster off.

X-Ham said, "What are you doing?"

Churchill replied, "What do you think, I've been advise too, get underground."

X-Ham replies, "England won't survive the bombing."

Churchill replied, "The Chinese………"

X-Ham replies, "The defence they've built, will not work."

Churchill replied, "What do you want me to do about that?"

X-Ham leaned forward to Churchill and replies, "Can't you fly like you're brothers, create forces and knock the crafts out of the air?"

Churchill replied, "Since last year when I got shot, I last a few of my other powers, I can no longer fly, merge through things, read minds, move all objects. All I have left is my teleportation, super strength, healing abilities and controlling all liquids."

X-Hamstring replies, "The controlling liquids, when the aircrafts bomb London, the buildings will be on fire."

Churchill replied, "Are you saying, what I think you are?"

X-Hamstring replies, "I hope we are on the same mind wave right now."

Churchill looked to his advisor and said, "Get all the labour we have, and insure that the water towers are ready."

"Indeed Prime Mister."

X-Hamstring moved to the side of Churchill, and blocked an attack, X-Ham draw out his machete trapping the unknown person to the ground and holding his blade against their throat.

X-Ham said, "Who do you work for? Hitler!"

Churchill said, "Look, on the side of his neck."

X-Ham replies, "Impossible."

Churchill replied, "Really?"

X-Ham replies, "I guess not."

Churchill's body guards moved forward lifting the unknown person up onto his feet, locking his arms up in place.

Churchill said, "America is not my enemy, so who do you work for?"

"Hitler has America around his little fingers, by him having America around his fingers, that means he has………

X-Ham said, "Great Britain as well?"

"You said it, you said it right."

Churchill said, "Kill him."

"Prime Minster……

X-Hamstring sliced opened the assassin's throat.

"Prime Minster, we don't do things that way."

Churchill replied, "No we didn't, but we do now."

X-Hamstring said, "The Queen?"

Churchill replies, "Get after her, she could be in danger."

"Prime Minster, if you would, this way quickly."

A few hours later a massive group of aircrafts had just flown pass France, you could see on the side of the aircrafts, who they belonged too.

The scene changes to X-Hamstring walking down a flight of stairs opening a door, which led to other door, which led to some more stairs. X-Hamstring then came to a wall X-Ham looked around it, as he saw dust and dirt on the ground near a brick, he pushed the brick in. Seconds later the wall opened up and he walked into a room with a dozen guards, and saw the Queen talking to a guy with the same mark as the assassin also holding his hand around his sword handle.

X-Ham said, "Queen Elizabeth, move from him."

Queen Elizabeth looked to the side of herself at X-Ham moving towards her, Queen Elizabeth said, "Poor fool, kill him."

Four guards moved in front of him firing their rifles at him, X-Hamstring went flying backwards taking cover.

X-Ham thought to himself, "What the heck was going on?"

As he peak around the cover seeing two guards holding Queen Elizabeth, looking like they were forcing her to move, X-Hamstring pulled out his handgun. X-Ham jumped out shooting the four guards down, and some more started firing towards him. X-Hamstring took two or three bullets, to his side forcing him side wards, to the ground. The guards moved in on him but X-Hamstring wasn't there no more, in fact he was behind them, as they turned around X-Hamstring moved forward slicing them to pieces. X-Hamstring moved back slightly lifting up his clothing, looking at the bullet wounds, as he did the bullets slowly started to move out of the wound, and then he started to heal. X-Hamstring thought to himself that his never healed this fast, X-Hamstring then stormed through a hidden door, and then up some stairs, until he came to the outside of the underground safe house. Queen Elizabeth whisper into one of her guard's ear, "Him again, kill him already."

Queen Elizabeth got into a vehicle which drives away as it did, the two guards fire of their guns, which were shotguns, blasting X-Hamstring backwards down to the ground.

"No way he could survive that?"

"I wouldn't be surprise; He's a super-human isn't he."

As the guards got close to X-Hamstring one of them kicked him slightly, but X-Hamstring did nothing, the other guard looked at the other one.

'told you he wouldn't survive that."

"Come on then let's go."

X-Hamstring said, "Actually I did."

The two guards turned around as X-Hamstring flew at them dodging the bullets, and stabbing them, as he and they dropped to the ground together X-Ham rolled forward and upwards stopping himself.

X-Hamstring looked into the sky about half a mile away he saw the aircrafts, X-Hamstring quickly got into a vehicle and drives offv after the Queen.

"Prime Minster Churchill, we have reports, the German aircrafts will be striking London, and you need to get to the underground safe bunker."

Churchill replied, "What for the people?"

"They've arrived in the countrysides, they are safe for now."

Churchill replied, "Good."

"Prime Minster, we really do advise you……

Churchill replied, "Hold your advice."

"The Prime Minster is really crazy."

"What is he going to do with the water towers?"

"I'm not sure."

"I think he's brave, braver than any of us."

"Why have us if we can't stop him from his own death."

X-Hamstring looked back at central London as the aircrafts started to bomb the city, while he witness that he could see ahead, the Queen in the car.

"Elizabeth."

Queen Elizabeth said, "Why can't he just leave me alone?"

Churchill was standing on a tower in the middle of all the other buildings which the water tubes were place, as the other buildings got destroyed, and fire started to spread. Churchill lifted up his arms controlling the water, making it hit the buildings, putting out the flames. Churchill then made large water bullets, and started shooting them at the aircrafts, while that was happening.

The vehicle the Queen was in turned back around heading into Central London, X-Hamstring spin his vehicle around, X-Ham thought to himself, 'their trying to bring the Queen to her death."

The Vehicle the Queen was in drive through the city, as bombs hit the buildings, and the ground around her, X-Hamstring was right behind her.

Churchill could see two cars racing through the city, he didn't know who were in the cars, but as he looked down towards them. A pilot in one of the aircrafts noticed Churchill on the building, controlling the water, and flew downwards towards them. The pilot dodged the water bullets as he started flying downwards to the ground, the pilot started shooting the car behind the Queen, and bullets came in through the front part of X-Ham's Vehicle missing him by inches. As X-Hamstring looked upwards through the front, the pilot came down into the vehicle he was in, X-Hamstring climb through the front part power jumping onto the Queen's vehicle as the aircrafts crashed into his vehicle blowing it to pieces.

Queen Elizabeth said, "Even an aircraft can't kill this guy."

The driver pulled over near to the river Thames as he did X-Ham went flying of the car along the ground, the Queen and her other guards came out of the car, walking slowly over to X-Hamstring.

X-Hamstring said, "Move from them, their trying to kill you."

Queen Elizabeth replied, "Are you pathetic, they work for me."

X-Hamstring replies, "Work for you, my Queen, they are here to kill you."

The Queen refill the side of her neck to X-Hamstring, he saw that she had the same mark, which the assassin had.

X-Hamstring said, "You're working for the Americans?"

Queen Elizabeth replied, 'think bigger."

X-Hamstring replies, 'the Americans are working for you."

Queen Elizabeth replied, "Yes."

X-Hamstring replies, "What's your aim?"

Queen Elizabeth replied, "Aren't you a super-human, with super-abilities, I'm sure you can figure that out."

X-Hamstring got up onto his feet as he did the guards moved forward kicking him backwards, and punching him down to the ground.

Queen Elizabeth said, "I would have believed you to put up a better fight, but I guess you have done well."

X-Hamstring replied, "You better kill me now, or else…

Queen Elizabeth grabbed her guard's pistol, aiming it at X-Ham as he was saying that, shooting him three times, and then walking forward towards him.

Queen Elizabeth said, "Bullets for some reason are not killing you."

Queen Elizabeth places her hand backwards towards her guard, he walked forward giving her a sword, and Queen Elizabeth moved the sword around placing it onto X-Hamstring throat.

Queen Elizabeth said, 'this should do."

As Queen Elizabeth went to slice X-Hamstring throat, he was covered with water, and as she looked down at him, he was no longer there. Queen Elizabeth looked around quickly, and then looked upwards at a tower, which she could see Churchill standing on looking down at her.

Queen Elizabeth said, "Let's get back to the USA."

Churchill flew off the building using the water to glaze through the air, down to the ground where the Queen stood, Churchill quickly moved to the edge of the river.

X-Hamstring said, "Well are you going to get me out of here?"

Churchill used the water to push X-Hamstring up into the air, moving him gently down to the ground; X-Hamstring started walking forward towards Churchill with his own will.

Churchill said, "We have a lot to do."

X-Hamstring replied, "I looked after her, how did this happen, without my knowledge."

Churchill replies, 'sometimes Science Beings like you are easily blinded, by what is truly taking place around you."

X-Hamstring replied, "I don't know if I should take that as an advice or an insult."

Churchill replies, 'take it how you want, but make sure it has opened you're eyes and ears."

x-Hamstring replied, "Where to now?"

Churchill replies, "Any of them could be corrupted."

X-Hamstring replied, "You think word could have got back to them?"

Churchill replies, "Let's just take the safe path."

X-Hamstring replied, 'there's one person we could possibly trust."

Churchill replies, "Are you sure we can trust him?"

X-hamstring replied, "Are you sure you haven't lost your mind reading abilities?"

Churchill looked at X-Hamstring like he was saying to him really, X-Hamstring moved sideways, and then looking back at him.

Churchill said, "Yes I can feel it as well."

X-Hamstring replied, "Let's move."

Moments later a vehicle pulled up to where Churchill and X-Hamstring were standing, searching the area.

"Sir."

"Yes."

"No signs of Prime Minster Churchill."

"Neither the Queen."

Chapter Twenty Nine

A Corrupted leader

7th of August 1940 who is Queen Elizabeth

"Sir Hitler, Queen Elizabeth has arrived in the USA."

Hitler replied, "That could only mean, Churchill and X-Hamstring, know her true intentions."

"Sir Hitler…"

Hitler pulled out his pistol but before he did anything, his right hand side man, shot the trooper three times for Hitler, Hitler turned around facing him.

Hitler said, "I wanted to do that." Hitler then walked out of the room.

As Queen Elizabeth starting walking on the footpath into the White House, all the secret service, and guards place their hands up in the air.

"Queen Elizabeth."

The Queen stopped walking and then slowly turned around facing the person which said her name; it was only a young girl the parents were beside the young girl. Queen Elizabeth moved closer to her, but also her bodyguard slyly placing her hand on his blade handle, as she went to say something, the President placed his hand on her shoulder, the Queen moved backwards, and then slowly kneel to the young girl and the young girl did the same.

The President leaned forward whispering in Elizabeth's ear saying, "What were you thinking?" the Queen looked back at the President and smiled.

One of the guards said, "Crazy bitch."

8th of August 1940

Leeroy Blair was sitting down on his chair in his office in his own building, one of his workers placed down a newspaper which was called KBRealTv, Leeroy Blair looked at the front part, seeing that the Queen was in America staying at the White House.

Leeroy Blair said, "Who took this photo?"

"Mr Mars."

Leeroy Blair replies, "He's an outstanding journalist, give him $100 dollars ASAP."

"Where are you going, you have meetings all day."

Leeroy Blair replies, "You are my PA aren't you, cancel them or move them to a different date, do whatever you have to do, this is important."

A few hours later Leeroy Blair pulled up to the outside of the White House, where the gates were, three guards moved forward.

"Yes "Sir."

"I am Leeroy Blair, I am here to see the Queen."

"Sorry, but the Queen is not seeing anyone."

"I am not just anyone; here is my identity card, check it now."

One of the guards took the plastic card moving backwards into the security box using the telephone using the codes on the plastic card, seconds later the gates opened up, Leeroy smiled at the guards and started to drive.

President Johnson said, "What does this asshole want?"

Queen Elizabeth replied, "He did watch over me, for a long while."

President Johnson replies, "That's not good, he might see right through you."

Queen Elizabeth replied, "What about you, a German person pretending to be an American."

President Johnson replies, "We really did a number on them all didn't we?"

Queen Elizabeth replied, "Let's not get cocky too soon mate."

President Johnson replies, "Maybe I'm getting it wrong, more like the British have done a number on you."

Moments later a few knocks was heard from the door, the President stood up tall the Queen noticed the mark on the side of his neck, the President spoke out the door started to open. Queen Elizabeth quickly said to the President that she could see the mark on the side of his neck, as Leeroy Blair walked in the President quickly covered it. Queen Elizabeth bell down to Leeroy Blair, as she did Leeroy immediately said for her to stop, and that she didn't need to do so. The President walked forward placing out his hand, Leeroy then placed out his hand, moving both their hands together shaking. President Johnson said, "Welcome to the White House again, I am pleased to finally meet you; Elizabeth has told me so much about you."

Leeroy Blair replied, "Let me cut to the chase, why are you here Beth?"

Queen Elizabeth replies, "The Germans bombed London yesterday, it is not safe there anymore."

Leeroy blair replied, "What about X-Hamstring, and Prime Minster Churchill?"

Queen Elizabeth replies, "X-Hamstring he killed my bodyguards he came after me… Elizabeth moved forward to Leeroy holding onto his hand, Elizabeth carried on saying. "Prime Minster Churchill is not from this world, he has these abilities."

Leeroy Blair replied, "Churchill now it makes sense."

Elizabeth replies, "What makes sense?"

Leeroy Blair replied, "I Thought or I did see him change his whole body, looking like someone else, but I thought it was my meds."

President Johnson replies, "We must move fast."

Leeroy Blair replied, "Move fast, what are you talking about?"

President Johnson replies, "England could be thinking of attacking us."

Leeroy Blair replied, "If you haven't been listening to what Beth said, but London was just bombed, so what makes you think they are going to attack right now."

Queen Elizabeth replies, "Information was passed to me, saying that the USA, is working with Hitler."

Leeroy Blair replied, "Do you believe that?"

Elizabeth replies, "I am here aren't I, if they were, wouldn't they have assassinated me already."

Leeroy Blair stepped backwards looking at both Elizabeth and President Johnson.

Queen Elizabeth said, "What's wrong?"

Leeroy replied, "I must go."

Leeroy moved out of the President's room heading out of the White House, Queen Elizabeth moved over to the President.

President said, "I will send some people to assassinate him."

Queen Elizabeth replied, "No."

"No, why what are you thinking?"

8ᵗʰ of August 1940 22:00pm location Washington DC, Hotel

The door knocked, Leeroy wealked calmly over to it, as he did he
looked through the peekhole. Leeroy saw five guards standing there,
they moved away and Queen Elizabeth was there. Leeroy quickly opened
the door, and they both looked at each other, Queen Elizabeth then
hugged Leeroy, and then she went into his hotel room.

 "What's going on with everything, Queen…

 "Please just call me Beth, I like it when you do, after all we are
more than just associate right?"

 "I've done some research; I don't think you should trust….

 "Ssshhh."

 "Why, what are you doing?"

Elizabeth kissed Leeroy's lips realizing how soft his lips were,
Leeroy stopped her and looked into her eyes. Leeroy thought to
himself how have this friendship between them developed to the stage
were the Queen of England has just kissed him. Elizabeth moved her
head away in disappointment, but Leeroy moved her head so she could
face him and then begun to kiss her. He lay her down onto his bed,
unzipping her dress slowly taking it off her, She had the perfect
body in great shape, Leeroy kissed around her body as he did she
flipped him onto his back, and got on top off him, they both were in
the room for hours and hours. Elizabeth was lying down next to Leroy
looking at him while he slept, deep down Elizabeth had grown some
real feelings for him, but she knew she couldn't keep them. So just
like that she climbed gently out the bed without making any sounds
and went into her bag taking out a knife, while Leeroy was sleeping,
she then climbed back into the bed, having one last look at Leeroy
she then stabbed Leeroy in his chest not just once but six bloody
times, a whole load of blood pour out from his body, covering his
chest, neck and stomach. She washed herself dried herself placed on
new clothes, and her body guards came in, "Stop." Elizabeth turned
around moving behind her body guards, as a strange man stood by the
window with wind blowing behind him.

"Who the hell are you?" demanded Elizabeth.

He looked at Leeroy bleeding out struggling to catch oxygen.

"Well, in fact guards kill him."

"I am Jason Mars."

 "Jason Mars?"

The guards shielded the Queen while she exit the room, they started to fire of their guns, bullets came towards him, all he did was stood there while the bullets stopped in mid-air, the guards pistols jammed, and Jason Mars force them down, and the bullets dropped to the ground. Jason Mars moved over to Leeroy Blair still barely breathing, "Hold in there royalty, your death is not today, you are important to history itself." Jason placed his hand over Leeroy healing him, and as he was doing that more guards came in, but Jason and Leeroy were gone. A while later the Queen was in a private jet landing down in Germany, soldiers awaited her return, leading her into a vehicle, while that happened Leeroy came back to his normal self.

"Mr Mars, who are you?" asked Leeroy.

"I am not an alien there for I am not from Earth, I am from Mars, I was once the Ruler of Mars for one billion six million four hundred thousand nine hundred and eighty seven years. Until they came and whipped out my species and captured me, turning my Kingdom into a arena to test the strengths of the best Warriors universal."

Name: Apollo Thirteen Mars aka Science being name Jason Mars

Gender: Male

Height: Six foot six

Build: very toned

Features: Long black hair, green eyes, facial hair

Nationality: Unknown

D.O.B: Unknown

Abilities: Able to heal others, teleport, advance combat training, advance strength, can use any weapon, and understand all languages

Purpose on Earth: unknown

"You stand here as a human?" asked Leeroy.

"That's because in this universe we are all science beings, we are not consider as humans, like you believe you are here on Earth. However the Magic and Science universe, they are true Paranormal Humans but with the abilities to use magic just like we use our minds, soul and spiritual energy pure or non-pure."

"Many thousands of years ago, we use to able to talk through using only our minds and purely body language, even communicate with Dragons," Said Leeroy.

"I know your history, even though there have been tweaks along the way."

"I thought I was important, but I am just a Science Being like you say?" asked Leeroy.

"Leeroy you are very important, you are the reason why I am here."

"What happened?" asked Leeroy.

"A time which has not come for you but has happened for me, which I once belonged to in which a powerful Warrior saved me because; he was saved himself by no other than Kyoko Blair."

"What Blair, but no one in my family has that name?"

"Kyoko, will be of importance to your bloodline."

"So that's why you saved me."

"Elizabeth is going to give birth to your son, in which she will send him to Jamaica, not for his protections but to keep him away from their bloodline keep it pure. He will grow up there meet his wife in England where your grandson is born, making him an descendants of royalties."

"Decendants of royalties, what do you want me to do?" asked Leeroy.

"You must stay hidden until, this battle has been won."

"What battle?"

"Between Churchhill and Fate?"

"Churchill's brother?"

"Churchill can defeat his brother with their help."

"Who's help?"

Jason Mars started to fade away like he was being erased from history; you could see this grey shadow behind him.

"X-Ham, Blunt, John and so on, twenty old years from now."

"Wait, John who?"

"I am sorry Leeroy, he has found me."

"YOU SHALL NOT HEAR NOMORE," a strong powerful voice spoke out towards Leeroy, forcing him back along the ground, and then this massive flash happened which blinded Leeroy and this sound which made Leeroy's ear bleed out. Jason Mars vanished away, but this grey shadow remained standing in front of him, it was like it was starring right through him, Leeroy moved backwards trapping over, and then looking back but it was gone.

"What the heck is going on?" asked Leeroy to himself.

6TH of December 1941 location Japan, Tokyo Emperor Okuma headquarter:

At 21:25pm X-Hamstring was now across from where Okuma stood, from another building, he was about to make his attack, but on the ground he saw a massive group of people heading into Okuma building.

"What could possibly be happening?" asked X-Ham to himself.

"Emperor Okuma, we have finished the planes."

"Excellent, America will not see it coming; it will look like the British have attacked them."

X-Ham came through the window smashing it to pieces, and three samurai Warriors came towards him, he quickly killed them, and more of Okuma's Warriors came into the room surrounding X-Ham.

"What are you doing X-Hamstring?" asked Emperor Okuma.

"I am here to stop you," replied X-Ham.

"Why?" asked Emperor Okuma."

"You're the bad guy, you want to destroy Great Britain," replies X-Ham.

"X-Ham, you were close but you are far, I plan to strike the Haleiwa air force based in the morning," replied Emperor Okuma.

"What, impossible," replies X-Ham.

"Relax, why would I attack Great Britain, when we have just made agreements six months ago," replied Okuma.

"I got informed by, President Johnson," replies X-Ham.

"My friend he has fooled you," replied Okuma.

"If that is so, show me what they gave you," requested X-Ham."

"You're a mad man; I can't let you see it."

'then draw your swords."

"Why should we draw our swords?"

Emperor Okuma held out his handgun, so did his Warriors X-Ham looked around he was truly outgunned and outnumbered.

"Well X-Hamstring, I believe it is you're move."

X-Ham quickly threw five hidden daggers at Okuma's Warriors, killing them, and then moving in-between the rest while they fired of their guns, X-Ham dodged all the bullets, killing the rest of the Warriors and then moving over to the door locking it so the others couldn't get into.

"Very impressing, but I've been studying you, X-Hamstring."

Okuma threw X-Ham the folder with the finished designs of the flying-crafts Okuma army was going to use to weakling the USA.

"Wait, we are not enemies?" asked X-Ham."

"What a turn of events, so are you on board?" asked Okuma.

X-Ham looked at the blueprints but noticed that the flying-crafts were the new design of the Great Britain crafts, but with a lot of bombs attached to the crafts.

"I don't understand," said X-Ham

"I thought you did?" asked Okuma.

"Why are you using British flying-Crafts?" asked X-Ham.

Before Okuma could reply it came to X-Ham mind, he was going to pretend to be the British air force attacking America. X-Ham tighten his grip around his machete, leaning in towards Okuma, Emperor Okuma took out his Samurai sword.

"Let's dance," said Emperor Okuma.

Chapter Thirty

Attack on Pearl Harbour

7TH of December 1941 U.S State Island Hawaii

"George, it's four am, we've been up all night."

"Hold in there Taylor, I'm about to win."

As everyone around the table stood up as George threw down his cards, and the other man throwing down his, Taylor's face begun to light up in joy as he noticed George not only won but he won the six hundred dollars which was place in the middle of the table from the other men which played the game.

"Come on George, let's get back."

"One more drink."

Both George and Taylor came crashing to the floor of their quarters, Taylor looked over at George, "I believe today will be a great day."

"Get some sleep George."

7th of December 1941 at 08:00am

An explosion sounds came from outside of their quarters, waking them up and others.

"What was that?" asked Taylor.

"Germans," replied George."

"Wait over there, use this."

"Impossible, that's a British aircraft?" asked George.

Taylor quickly dashed on his tuxedo that he ware to the party last night, "George, over here, get in."

"Hold on wait for me."

As they went speeding in Taylor's Buick, hitting speeds of hundred mph, they got to the Haleiwa airfield, looking over they both saw their airplanes ready to fly. Matter of moments they were in the sky, chasing and shooting down the aircrafts, as Taylor looked over his shoulders down to the sea. Looking at all the ships which were destroyed, and soldiers in the water, a bullet came through Taylor's plane through his arm sending shrapnel into his leg. So Taylor had to land his plane, and let George and the rest of the other pilot finish of the British aircrafts, as Taylor looked up he saw as one of the pilots from the British aircrafts jumped out of the plane as it blew to pieces.

"Michael, drive me over there."

As Taylor came flying out of the car looping over to what it seems like a Japanese pilot, Taylor held his gun at the pilot.

"You're Japanese impossible?"

The Japanese pilot laughed and smiled in Taylor's face, Taylor shot him in his leg, and turned to one of his comrades.

"Michael, report this to headquarters."

As he said that Michael got shot from the sky, and the bullets came towards Taylor, which jumped for cover, and the Japanese pilot he was killed by the bullets.

"Damn," said Taylor.

George came in behind that plane and blast it out of the sky, and the rest of them cleared the airspace, flying over the ships George could see flames and warship destroyed all along the coast.

At 08:45am

Word got back to headquarters that the British had just attacked them.

"I want all available aircrafts in the air, by this evening we attack Great Britain."

7th of December 1941 Japan,Tokyo

Emperor Okuma Headquarter, word got back to him, that his plan was an success, and he ready his pilots to attack the whole of the USA, within the next two days, Great Britain was about to be in a position that'll be impossible for them to get out of.

"Bring me X-Ham," Commanded Okuma.

X-Ham came flying to the floor unarmed, and looking like He's been through hell.

"Hello Mr Iwu, Kwame Xavi Iwu."

"Fuck you, you asshole."

"Now, now, let's not be like that, America needs to get whipped out, do you not agree?"

"By pretending to use Great Britain?"

"Who would have thought too?"

"You're sick."

"Right about now, the US airforce will be in the air heading towards Great Britain."

"No."

"Churchill, but you're dead?" asked Okuma."

"No, Okuma you're dead."

Churchill moved swiftly over to Okuma slicing him into half, also throwing five knives at his Warriors killing them. Churchill moved the table, picking up X-Ham's equipment handing it to him.

"Oh yeah X-Ham, I brought this for you."

"What kind of costume is this?"

"It has very tough material, made from Dragon skin by Mr First's scientist, hard for swords to cut into it, also can stop Colt M1911A1 and M1917 Revolver rounds."

"Nice one, but what about Britain?" asked X-Ham.

"Don't worry, I've sent word to Blunt."

7th of December 1941 16:30pm West coast of England

"We did not bomb you're Pearl Harbour," said Prime Minster."

"Are plane are up with the Atomic bomb, Great Britain will be no more."

"Sir."

"Yes."

"Lieutenant Taylor has a message for you."

"Wait, Prime Minster has something to say, can't it wait?"

"General, it's important, something you may want to hear."

The General was having multiple conversations at the same time.

"Prime Minster you will not pass the blame, we know about both you'll agreement, Japan will be next."

"That was not agreed with me, but Queen Elizabeth which has betrayed England."

"What does Lieutenant Taylor need to say so badly, that it can't wait one more minute?"

"I'll put him on the other line for you."

"Yes Lieutenant, what is it?"

"It's information about Pearl Harbour, I know who bombed us."

"Yes, I'm sorting it out now."

"No, it wasn't Great Britain."

"What are you talking about?"

"It was the Japanese, they were pretending to be the British, and they have fooled us."

"Sir the plane is one mile out from the west coast of England."

"Prime Minster is still on the transmission."

"Tell the planes to turn around; we will plan our attack on the Japanese."

As a line of Hover-Crafts were floating in place they saw the U.S aircrafts turn around.

"Prime Minster."

"Yes."

"It's the plane, they've turned around."

"Any word on Churchill?" asked the New Prime Minster.

"He has informed his trusted ones, to wait for the Queen's Return."

"We can't believe she has betrayed us, we must wait."

14th of December 1941 West Indies, Jamaica

"Make sure this baby knows nothing off me, we've paid you extremely well," said Elizabeth."

"Yes no problems."

"President Johnson, I hoped I made the right decision, I can't have my DNA mixed with others, it must still pure," said Elizabeth."

"He being here, no one will ever know He's royalty."

"With England in the chaos it is, I guess I must return."

"What about Leeroy Blair, the boy's father?" asked Johnson.

"I killed him, but that strange being came, I don't know what happened to his body."

"If he's alive he could be a threat."

"Impossible, I stabbed him six times."

"Nothing is impossible in this world anymore."

"I am really starting to believe so."

"My people, they haven't found Churchill or X-Ham."

"They shouldn't be a problem, with everything going on, England needs their Queen."

Chapter Thirty One

Roses are Red

6th *of August 1944*

As the door open in a mansion a man's laying down in a bed with his face covered up, started to move all over the place.

"Calm down Sir, calm down."

Everton kept trying his best to keep the man calm, but he got pushed backwards. The man stopped moving all over the place, placing his head over to Roman, as he walked in.

"Roman, who is this man," said Everton.

"I know you haven't been working here for long, but this I know I can trust you, take the bandages from around his face.

Everton felt a great feeling from this Science Being, so he looked back at Roman James the First.

"Everton, please leave the room."

Everton exit the room closing the doors behind him, Roman moved closer to this unknown Being's bedside.

"Roman, I'm alive."

"When I found you in my fields, almost six months ago, you weren't barley alive, Blunt you haven't even aged a bit, since I last saw you."

22nd of June 1924 Blunt's disappearance

As the missiles hit the mountain, and the ground crumbles beneath him, he dropped through the cracks hitting his side and legs. He watches as X-Ham went through flames, and then a random, person was flying upwards towards him, just like that a flashing light surrounded Blunt.

"Where am I, Who are you?"

"You are on Mountain heavies, on Mesink, a few good years ahead, and well many years ahead."

"Why have you helped me?"

"You are a great importance in the future, you're sons will lead forward a new security of defence to protect Earth."

"My sons, I don't even have a wife?"

"You will in the year nineteen fifty seven, when you are 40 years of age."

"What date is it now?"

"May the ninth, nineteen forty four."

"Impossbile, I've travelled twenty years into the future."

"In this world kid nothing is impossible."

"Who are you, where are you from?"

"My earth name is Jason, but my real name is Apollo thirteen Mars."

"You're an alien?"

"Watch out."

Cyber-Plus appeared blasting towards Blunt, but Jason Mars moved in front of him taking the blast. Eight stepped from behind Cyber-Plus, Blunt moved backwards.

"Looks like we found you."

"What do you want?"

"To kill you so you're sons can never be born."

Jason Mars threw Blunt one of his swords, and Jason Mars floated back onto his feet, Blunt looked at Jason.

"Man, stop looking at me, and fight not only for you but your sons future."

Eight came in slicing Blunt's shoulder making him move backwards, and then stabbing him in his other shoulder, while she sliced his face a little leaving a scar blunt went flipping to the ground.

Jason Mars punched and sliced the Cyber-Plus, but it didn't do anything so he turned to Blunt just before Eight was going to fire of her guns, he sent him flying safely of the mountain landing somewhere in some fields.

The Cyber-plus picked Jason Mars up, and Eight rammed her sword into his chest, and move close to him and kissed him on his lips.

"You've always had soft juicy lips," said Jason Mars.

"It's his double," said Eight.

"Yeah, I'm over here."

"Cyber-Plus."

Jason Mars was gone as he got to the fields, he saw Blunt being carried in by Roman and his personal assist Everton.

Jason Mars thought to himself, "He'll be better off with them for now."

6th of August 1944 Mr Frist's Mansion

"Roses are red."

Blunt moved his legs so they were off the bed, and he sit up.

"Roses are red, what are you on about?"

"You're a solider."

"Roman, blood is coming from your nose."

"So it has begun."

"What has?"

"His side-affects."

"Who's?

"I can't."

"What is wrong?"

"I can't say it."

"Roman, just say it."

"I CANT."

"Roman, look at me, whose effects?"

Roman said the name but his mouth full up with blood, and Blunt didn't hear what he said.

"I couldn't hear you Roman."

"Ultra-Mist!"

Everything went grey, Blunt and the whole room was empty just leaving Roman there on his own, with an mirror in which this grey shadow appeared, Roman found himself floating in the air.

"You dear speak my name, to a powerless Science Being, that I created."

"I am sorry all powerful master."

"I am not you're master, I am you're ender."

"Please let me be, let me finish the path you have me on."

"In this case I do need you're assistant, but this is the second time you have seen me, when you see me for the fourth time, you will be release from this pain."

X Elsewhere Pasture X

Suddenly a book dropped to the ground, in this massive endless library which white throughout.

"Mr. Warrior."

"What happened to me?" asked Mr. Warrior.

"It's good to have you back, but you must still study the book."

"It's him isn't it, it's true, just like Darkness said?" asked Mr. Warrior.

"Through the Force and the Light, no one has one true path, one true identity which belongs to them. He does not have to become the reason for you to betray him."

"Just tell me the truth, I did it didn't I?"

"Read and finish the damn book."

13th of August 1944

A whole week went by, and then Roman eyes opened up, he had Everton and Blunt standing next to his bed.

"Everton, I can't feel my legs."

"The doctors have informed me, you will never walk again."

"Roman, I'm sorry for what has happened to you, but I must leave."

"Blunt be careful, the world has changed."

"If it didn't I would be more worried."

"The Bank of England."

"What are you talking about?" asked Blunt.

"That's the best place to start it off."

"How, but I have only thought it," replies Blunt

"The Sanctuary," Said Everton.

"Everton?" asked Roman.

"That's a good name Everton, thanks for making me remember," replies Blunt.

As Blunt was about to walk out of the Mansion's doors, Everton came up behind him.

"What is it Everton?" asked Blunt.

"I'm sorry about that Blunt, but Roman doesn't know what he's saying, the doctors say he will start to imagine things at an extreme rate."

"Everton he's right, and I will call it the Sanctuary."

"That's what it should be," said Everton under his breathe.

"Did you say something Everton?" asked Blunt.

"It doesn't matter," replied Everton.

Mid 1945 the attack

Blunt was on a train heading from Brussels, Belgium, to Paris, but little did he know Hitler's spies were on the train as well.

"Sir."

"Yes Agent."

Blunt's agents got shot in front of his face, their blood went all over his face, and the Germans flooded the coach room Blunt was in, he was back up against the window, as that was happening elsewhere Elizabeth was sitting across from Hitler which has been Prime Minster of German for almost ten years.

"Elizabeth my daughter."

"You are not my father, you let him die."

"Hudson was a mad man, he made himself believe he was your father, when he knew of your mother and I, he made the Jewish take me and my family away."

"I do not believe you."

"Prime Minster Hitler."

"We will talk, wait one minute, Elizabeth please."

"Prime Minster."

"Yes general."

"The Hover-Craft is in position."

"Tell them to destroy that train, with Blunt dead, England can be yours without fear my daughter."

"Just because we share the same blood, doesn't mean I am your daughter, Hudson was your half-brother after all."

As Blunt floored all of the German troopers, more came in from behind him, bullets came through the window, and Blunt moved out of the way heading to the front of the train, taking down more troopers along the way. Blunt got to the front as he looked outside towards the Hoover-Craft, missals came shooting towards the train, just as the train was half way across the bridge, the missals destroyed the train forcing it off the tracks, the train blew to pieces, and headed into the water.

Later that night word got back to Hitler, he laughed in joy, Blunt was gone no more, he could now plan his move on England, and well that's what he thought.

As a trooper run into his throne room the trooper was killed, Hitler press the alarm, guards came into Elizabeth's room; she looked at her son and grabbed him. Elizabeth got to the Hover-Crafts landing pad, and boarded it, she looked back down through the building seeing her father shooting towards someone but she couldn't see who it was.

"Looks like you've run out of bullets."

"Why are you here?" asked Hitler.

"So you do not take England."

"You don't even want to rule anything, so what's you're aim?"

"To whip out all my father's enemies."

"I'm guessing I am not one."

"No, you are not."

"Then let me have England."

"No, but Queen Elizabeth will, she will take back control over England."

"What about X-Hamstring?"

"Well, both he and Churchill got captured in Tokyo, back three years ago."

"So what do you want with me?"

"That's the thing Hitler, nothing."

Cyber-Plus appeared next to Hitler, controlling his hands placing his own pistol up against his head, "No way," Hitler fired of his pistol killing himself.

"That's what he gets for taking on Mother Russia, Cyber-Plus, destroy the rest of the Nazi."

18TH OF July 1945 Location Germany Hitler's estate

As the special unit formed of Americans, British and Russian forces show up to Hitler's mansion, they found Hitler dead; it looked like he killed his own self."

Names: Prime Minster Berger, Adolf Hitler, Prime Minster Hitler

Prime Minster of German Term served: 1936 – 1945

Gender: Male

Height: five foot eight

Build: Heavy

Nationality: German

D.O.B 17/07/1892

Cause of death: suicide bullet to head

4th of July 1945

Queen Elizabeth returned back to England back to Buckingham Palace, to find Blunt Supreme there, Queen Elizabeth looked surprised.

"How was your trip to Belgium?" asked the Queen.

"Dangerous like always, I have something I like to show you," replied Blunt.

7th of January 1942 Japan, Hiroshima Prison Camp

X-Ham sliced down the rest of Okuma allies, leaving only the second in command left to Churchill to deal with.

"Stop."

Churchill shot the blade out of the General's hand, it landed on the floor away from him.

"Kill me, kill me now."

Churchill flashed over to the General with his blade inside him, and then pulling it out quickly, the general dropped to the floor.

"He's coming."

"What did he say Churchill?" asked X-Ham."

As X-Ham and Churchill walked out Churchill dropped to the ground, and turned into his true form, X-Ham looked back at Church went to move towards him, but a blade came down towards him. X-Ham moved backwards to realise he was surrounded, X-Ham looked around without a worry in his bones, he smiled confidently.

"Your General is dead, I will let you walk away free."

"That is not our General."

"X-Ham, go, run now."

"I won't leave you, who are you?" asked X-Ham.

"I am Fate Between."

"Between?"

"Yes, I'm alive."

Chapter Thirty One

Sanctuary

2nd of August 1945 location England, London

"Blunt, I love what you have done with the Palace, in such a short space of time," said Queen Elizabeth.

"This will truly help the people get back their trust in you again," replied Blunt

"Director Supreme."

"My Queen I must go now," said Blunt.

As Blunt walked away he press a wireless head set which was placed in his ear, and said "Yes Commander."

"We have reports; X-Ham and Churchill are in Hiroshima."

"I'm on my way, did you just say Hiroshima?"

"Yes why?"

"President Johnson, has ordered the use of the atomic bomb, it will reach any moment now."

"Let's pray to god, that X-Ham and Churchill make it out alive."

3rd of August 1945 Tokyo, Hiroshima Prison camp

As Fate placed back his sword in his case, and looked out towards the sky, he zoomed in on one plane with a bomb attach to the bottom of it, with a dozen beside it, it would take the planes a couple more minutes until they are closer to the Island.

"It looks like, our time here is done," said Fate.

"Brother, stop this, this isn't you," said Church."

"You know how long, I've been trapped in this fake world, well do you, no you don't, for hundreds of years."

"Yet it hasn't made you weak."

"That's because father gave me extra lessons, because I was his favourite, yet next in line."

"Listen brother, together we can stop Eight and her Cyber-Plus."

"Brother, brother, It'll be over in a few minutes, for now goodbye."

Fate vanished away the Japanese soldier looked around shocked out his brain, then seeing aircrafts coming towards the island, he quickly sounded the alarm. Church screamed so loud with power freeing himself from the locks, but on the floor were gold sand, so he pushed himself forward not landing on the gold sand, but on top of a table instead.

"What's wrong Church?" asked X-Ham.

"It's the floor, it has gold in the sand, if I touch it I'll lose my abilities for a while.

"Watch out."

A Japanese soldier came in blasting his rifle of at Church, but Church flipped up in-between the bullets, catching two and throwing it back at the soldier killing him.

"Oh shit, we need to get the hell out here."

"What is it?"

"Do you remember the plans, about the atomic bomb?"

"Yes."

"While America is about to use it on Hiroshima."

"What the fuck."

Church threw the other bullet breaking off X-Ham's locks, and X-Ham kicks the cell door open, more soldiers come out, but X-Ham quickly grabs a samurai and slices them. As Church jumps on X-Ham's back, and he carries him out of the room, Church sides off, and X-Ham looks around.

"X-Ham, we haven't got time to find your weapons."

"How do you know?"

As they were running Church was explaining to him.

"When I'm near certain brothers, I become like a Science Being, but once they are gone my full strength comes back to me."

"Look over there."

"It's fate."

Fate looked back and laughed, while sending a force which knocked X-Ham of his feet to the ground, Church came towards Fate but he vanished away, Church dive to the ground where his brother stood. As he did he witness the aircrafts releasing the atomic bomb, Church flipped upwards back onto his feet, racing over to X-Ham. X-Ham was in shock as the bomb hit the other side of the island, nothing happened at first, and then this light flashed, and then this incredible force came rushing towards everyone. Church flew into X-Ham using his teleport abilities to take them to a safer part of the island, which was on the edge of Hiroshima; they witness Hiroshima being totally whipped out.

"What the fuck were the America's thinking?" asked X-Ham.

"Pearl Harbour," Answered Church.

"Ok, how do we stop your brother, the same way like before?"

"Yes, but this time sliver."

"Africa here we come."

As Blunt walked into the Sanctuary his name was called right away.

"Director Supreme."

"Yes Agent."

"Hiroshima has been destroyed."

"Fucking hell."

"If X-Ham or Church were there, they are truly gone."

"Where are you going Director?"

"To see a old friend."

3rd of August 21:30pm Mesink, Mr First's Mansion

As Blunt Supreme came walking into Roman's study room, Everton quickly exited the room, Blunt wanted some answers and he wanted them now.

"Tell me everything."

"It doesn't work like that."

"Make it work Roman, I need to know."

"X-Ham and Church Between, are they dead?"

"No, no way, if so the bomb didn't kill them."

"You might be right then, Fate Between."

"Fate Between, another one of Church's brothers?"

"Yes."

"Is he bad?"

"No, He's just upset."

"Why?"

"He's been trapped in this world for a long time."

"How do you know this?"

"He's my friend."

"What does he want?"

"To return to a world which is no more?"

"What does that even mean?"

"It means a lot of things."

"Stop with all this nonsense, and tell me the complete truth."

"You really want to know."

"Yes or I wouldn't be here."

"Church will die, that's his legacy, and Fate will die that's his density."

"How?"

"If Church is still alive, give him this sliver bladed samurai, it will empower him, but also kill Fate."

"Isn't fate your friend?"

"Yes, but a good friend truly lost, two more things, find John Warrior he should have returned now, and insure not to come back until the year is nineteen sixty six."

"Almost twenty years from now?"

"Go Blunt, your running out of time."

As Blunt exit the room Everton enters the room, Everton looked at Roman, and he was confused.

"Why are you doing this Roman?"

"History needs to change, so that the history I saw can come true."

"I will talk to your doctor about your meds; you are sounding very unwell "Sir."

"Do what you want Everton, but no cure will save me, from this illness."

Chapter Thirty Two

The Future Foretold Part 2

Sometime in 1990

In one of the boroughs of London something strange but yet brilliant had just happened, as the traffic lights pop this electronic force appeared. The force then impacted into itself creating a bright blue and green portal, someone came out of it, struggling to walk suddenly dropping to the ground. This Caucasian male had black hair stood around six foot tall, also was in excellent shape. The best kind of abs you could ever imagine in your whole life time, the male wasn't wearing anything at all, as you looked closer you could see his blood racing all around his body, but his blood was a bright green and blue colour. The man stood up tall looked around, he could see people looking at him they looked very worried. A police car pulled up near to him he looked very confused, and then the two officers got out of their vehicle with their guns aimed at the un-known person.

"Wait, wait don't shoot me please," said the un-known person.

One of the officers asked with a rough low tone, "Who are you?"

"I am Phillip Armstrong, a scientist who works for Roman James the First."

"Nice try mate, but that won't cut it with us."

"Please don't shoot me please."

"Don't worry Mr Armstrong; we ain't going to shoot you just yet."

"His name's Armstrong "Sir."

The other Officer had a look on his face like, don't fuck with me look, and then carried on to say "We're taking you in for questioning."

One of the police officers grabbed a piece of clothing from the boot of their car, and covered Phillip also handcuffed him and placed him in the back seats off the car.

"Agent Thomas……."

"Yes I know Commander Robins; I'm on my way to the police station now."

"Thomas."

"Yes, Agent Jay?"

"Do you think it's him?"

"Hmmm, listen. Even if it is him, I won't let him slip away again. I know you're a rookie, and all this is new to you. You will be just fine by my side."

"I heard he nearly killed you and your bro……."

"Hear me out, why are you listening to rumours, and weren't you the one requesting to be partnered with me?"

"So it was a lie?"

"No."

Phillip was in a darken room with two officers, one which arrested him earlier and a new one He's never seen before. As Phillip looked around the room he saw a mirror but he knew better than that. He knew it wasn't just a mirror, and that their where people behind it. As he looked closer he could see through the walls, by doing so he used the electricity running through it which opened his eyes further allowing him to see the energy of three people standing up behind the mirror by their vibrations. Like example like breathing or by them talking to each other or the electric partial within their bodies he knew one of the three people were just human but something else he had encountered along his journey.

"Listen here, you told us your name is Phillip Armstrong, and it does check but that name you gave us was a whole lot of bull shit, wasn't it?"

"No, why would I lie to you?"

"Listen here sunshine, we do the asking around here, so tell us who you really are, and why you appeared out from nowhere scaring the people of Tooting?"

The light in the room started to flipper one of the police officers noticed, so he back away a little.

"Garry, ease up on the man, gosh, your such an animal at times."

"Well Mr, are you going to tell me?"

"I am Phillip Armstrong; I work for Roman James the First."

"Yes that name checked, in fact Phillip Armstrong was one of the world first famous scientist who did work for Roman, but had mysteriously died nearly over fifteen years ago. So that's why I need to know who you really are, and how the flip you appeared out from this portal people are saying."

"When I disappear it was because I was working on a task for Mr First; however it went badly wrong as you know, and I've been elsewhere different timelines through different dimension, different futures past and present."

"Who the fuck this is guy, if you're an acting you really need to work on your graft, listen up?"

"Wait, what was the task you were working on?"

"It's top secret."

"Enlighten me then."

Sometime in the 1970's

"Everton what is the status on the Diamond Machete?"

"Roman the scientist, they are nearly finished, with all three items."

"So their managed to melt the Magical Diamonds with the gold from Inspiron, creating the golden ring?"

"Yes."

"Bring me Mr Armstrong, the time has come."

Everton collected Mr Armstrong for Roman as he took Armstrong to Roman's study room, the scientist did not have a clue why Roman had asked for him.

"Hello, I am……."

"I know who you are; you are Roman James the First."

"Yes I am."

"May I ask another question?"

"You just did, and of course you can. Everton can you please leave my study."

"Yes Roman."

"Go ahead and ask."

"I didn't ask you this before, but why have you made us create these dangerous weapons?"

"You see them as weapons, you are correct with the right knowledge, it all came from a dream I had."

"Oh I've heard about that, you have dreams off the future right?"

"Yes, and in this dream I saw a very dark but yet powerful being using his wrath to end all live here on Earth. Also in this dream I saw a Hero a Warrior saving everyone from this dark and powerful being."

"Don't you think your dreams, are just dreams."

"Yes you would say that, but my dreams have come true, as you can see me knowing off these diamonds, and the power within that rock, even the gold which you know is not off this world."

"That power in that rock is evil, pure evil, it looked into my soul."

"Then I must ask of you to promise me something."

"Hmmm" thoughts came from Armstrong minds (Am I meant to just go along with this, am I so naive to believe what is ill man is saying to me)

"You will never ever refill what we have done here, as you can see I am very ill and I will die soon, and by my death Agents will take over the Sanctuary. They will only know a little, until the time is ready for them to know all."

"What's to say I don't keep this promise, and sell it off to someone dangerous?"

"You work here has made you become famous, but yet also a dangerous person, you have done some much to brought this world forward. My contacts I have are protecting you and your family, So you would do kind to understand the situation at hand, and keep this promise or I won't be able to provide that protection for your family."

Phillip grabbed a piece of metal picking it at Mr First.

"No, you will do kind to remember what I have done for your representation, and the technology that nourish this world, technology from an un-harmful entity.

"For the safety and security of this world."

"No, no Mr First, I won't promise you anything. You will have to just trust that I won't say anything to anyone."

"This world, this universe and others depend on that, best believe."

"If that art true why would you make us create the mask, with the dark and evil elements from the rock?"

"It's just a part of a puzzle which will connect, which will complete the puzzle."

Phillip Armstrong drop the metal object to the ground and started to walk out but before he left he turned around and face Mr First at last time, "I have no more questions, I do understand what you have told me. Goodnight "Sir."

"I really do hope you did."

Later into the night Phillip Armstrong was in the lab, the rest of the scientist was clocking off.

"Phillip, the shift is done, do you need any assistants?"

"No I don't, I can handle this last task on my own, I will lock down the lab."

Phillip placed on some safety gloves he grabbed the Diamond Machete, as he didn't notice there was a cut in the gloves. As he grabbed the Diamond Machete handle his finger tip touched it, he could feel it, over powered him. This bright force came out of the Machete forcing him backwards through a special type of glass which sliced all over his body, allowing these electric partials, gain access into his bloodstream, also the Diamond Machete shot out this bright blue and green light into his chest slowly burning a hole in the Centre of his chest, at the same time he was healing. The alarms went off, and the doors to the lab closed, the other scientists raced back to the lab but all they could do was watch as Phillip screamed and then burst into pieces, and impacted into itself. The doors opened back up to the lab they went in but Phillip was gone. Nothing left but a photo of his wife, and son the photo was half destroyed.

"Yesterday a great Scientist mysteriously died, but he did not die in-vane, what he performed with all of you will one day save the future of man-kind. So do not be drain with his lost, make sure his life was not wasted for nothing."

"Everton, how did the speech go?"

"It would have been better coming from you, but you are a very ill man."

1990's England, London Police station

"Well who are you?"

There was a knock on the door one of the police officers opened it, and then step outside. He came back in and whispered something in the other officers" ear, and then both of them walked out of the room. As Phillip looked at the mirror also the three people standing in there walked out of that room as well, as Phillip looked at the door it slowly opened up.

"Well hello Mr. Armstrong, it's very fantastic to see that you're looking healthy."

"Aha, Agent Thomas, How's your little brother keeping?"

"Oh, he recovered very quickly lucky enough."

Phillip clocked the other Agent he took one look at this agent, and could tell by the sweat marks on his forehead, also hands shaking even though to a normal human's eye you wouldn't be able to see it also blood pumping to his heart that this agent was a rookie.

"How very excellent of you to bring me a rookie."

"Shut up."

"Calm down Agent Jay."

"Ha ha ha ha ha, this is too good."

"We're taking you back."

"Remember last time, the second time I returned?"

Sometime in 1986

"I've got him corner Jar."

"Watch this Strictly!"

Strictly was behind a door with a handgun ready to take down this wanted man, so he was ready to until Jar Warrior came smashing through the window. The wanted man quickly armed himself, but Jar rolled over to him, disarmed him kicked his leg making him drop. The wanted man pulled out an army knife went to slice Jar's leg, but Strictly shot the knife out of his hand.

"Come on now Text, what is this like your tenth time breaking out of prison, and robbing a bank?"

"He's coming, and all your love ones will softer."

"Aww, there you go with that crazy talk."

"Especially, you're son, Blood Warrior."

"What did you just say, and how the fuck do you know my son's name?"

Jar grabbed Text picked him up slam him back to the ground, and started to punch him until Text's face was soaked in blood. Strictly had to trickle Jar of him and then the agents came into the factory and took Text away.

"What in hell names just happened, why did you do that?"

"He mentioned my son's name, his full name. He knows something, and he isn't talking crazy this time."

"He's just......"

"Noooo, Agent Blair, he is not just an old nitty, he knows something big."

"Jar you need to go cool down alright."

"Fine I will."

So Text was in the Sanctuary in one of its interrogating rooms with Agent Thomas, trying to get answers out of him.

"What did you mean? talk."

"Me to know you to find out very soon."

"Listen, stop with your crack head games, I will knock fifth shades of bloodclart out of you."

"Go right ahead, because you won't get anything out of me. I will die for my master before I give him up to you."

"Who's your master?"

"No, no, no."

"I fucking hate nitties."

A strange but yet powerful noise which Thomas hear coming from outside of the Sanctuary, Thomas stood up went over to the window looked back at Text. Text just smiled at Thomas and Thomas rushed out of the room, moving towards the sound with a few other agents plus his brother. Outside of the Sanctuary kneed a naked man as Thomas looked through the window, he knew who it was.

"This man could possibly be dangerous, so be careful Agents."

Strictly followed Agent Thomas and Blair outside of the Sanctuary, as they surrounded this naked being with their guns aimed towards him. He raises his head up looking very confused, in what just happened.

"I know who you are, you are Phillip Armstrong right?"

"Yes, but I don't know how I got here."

"You're the scientist who went missing, can you remember everything?"

"Yes it was the Diamond Machete, and the glass, the electric partials."

"What happened?"

Phillip started to have flash backs then suddenly all around him was this electronic force, as the agents looked back at the Sanctuary seeing it's energy getting drain out of it. Phillip used it and force down the agents to the floor. Strictly got back up aimed his gun fired it of, and as the bullets came speeding towards Phillip the bullets burned to pieces before they could get near to him. Phillip forced Strictly back into some of the agents, As he did that Agent Blair rolled forward aimed his gun.

"NOOOOOOOOOOO, brrrrrroooooottthhheeeerrrr!"

Phillip used the energy from the lamppost and hit Agent Blair with it, as he did Agent Blair went flying over to the other side of the field. All the agents plus Thomas started to fire upon Phillip, as they did this force was release again and Phillip was gone.

Sometime in the 1990's Location Police station

"I remember that day you bastard, my brother was in a comer for two years. I nearly pull the plug on him."

"I'm truly sorry to hear that, he wasn't a part of my mission."

"Well, whatever mission you are on, I will have to stop you right here."

"Your just Science, you have nothing special within you're biological status."

Phillip quickly used the energy from the light bulb and threw it towards Agent Jay, but Agent Thomas jumped in the way of it.

"What a fool!"

Agent Jay quickly drew for his handgun but Phillip transformed himself into these electric pieces, and went up into the building's electricity he then came out in the main hall of the police station.

"He was right, my powers are getting stronger."

"Garry, did you just see that."

"See what?"

Officer Garry turned around and saw Phillip standing across him, Garry went to move but the other police officers stopped him.

"I don't think you want to pursuit this one."

"Let go of me what's wrong with you."

Officer Garry was moving over to Phillip as he got closer, Phillip used the electric energy in the food machine and hit the officer with it. Forcing him back through a door as he did that, Agent Thomas and Jay came racing out of the room after him. A few more Police officers got strike down by Phillip, and Agent Thomas quickly placed his ring into his handgun. Phillip turned around to him and stopped Thomas, Phillip started to smile and laugh.

"What do you think you will do with that powerless weapon?"

"Hmmm, you got a good point there. Oh well, what the heck maybe this."

Agent Thomas aimed at Phillip and Phillip did nothing, as Phillip closely looked at the gun. He could feel a familiar but yet dangerous energy coming from the gun, Thomas fired the handgun and these very bright bullets came rushing at Phillip. All the bullets went into his chest, making him drop to one of his knees. Agent Thomas again went to fire of his gun, but this time Phillip made the lights above Thomas pop blinding Thomas allowing him to escape. Agent Thomas looked around and Phillip was gone again, Officer Garry's partner came over to Agent Thomas.

"What was that?"

"This is grown people business, I'm sorry but you guys are just the small timers."

"What do you mean by that?"

"I mean get the fuck out of my way."

"Alright easy."

"Agent Thomas, do you have a clue on where He's going?"

"One guesses the Sanctuary."

"Why there?"

"He's the only other person which can find the locations of all three weapons."

1990 Mesink the Sanctuary the battle continues

Agent Thomas didn't know that Agent Blair had moved the Mask from the Sanctuary to somewhere else, Phillip did not know of this until Thomas alerted the Sanctuary, Phillip used his power by doing so he could hear through the phone line as the electric waves went upwards into the sky, so Phillip listened to Thomas's sound through the electronic waves in the air, he heard him informing the Sanctuary.

"Master can you hear me?"

"Yes my solider I can."

"I have a location for one of the three weapons of Darkness, should I pursuit or carrying on with my true mission."

"Collect the Mask of Darkness first, and then carrying on with your true mission to kill the kid."

Phillip was across the field from the Sanctuary with his normal eye he could see nothing it looked empty, but as he used his electro eyes he could see the blueprint of the building also agents placed all around inside of the building.

"Aha these Science are truly foolish."

Phillip touched the energy box outside of the sanctuary teleporting himself inside, as he was about to turn a corner a group of agents was paroling the area. As he transformed himself into the electricity travelling through it trying to locate the Mask of Darkness, he could not find it at all. In fact it was like it weren't even in the building, as he carried on searching he found where Agent Thomas was, and a whole load of Agents plus Thomas's brother Agent Blair.

"Strictly How's that Razor Blade weapon?"

"Well to be honest I haven't used it yet."

"Aha, well prepare yourself, today you may need to."

As all the lights in the area where they was went off, all you could hear and see was flashing lights from the guns of the agents. Then you heard screams noises from the agents, Thomas and Blair plus Strictly placed on their energy vision goggles special design for spotting Phillip also seeing in the darkness, they could see Phillip killing off the agents. The lights went back on blinding them as Agent Thomas and Blair switch their googles to other mode allowing them to pick up on Phillip energy, Strictly got forced to the wall. Thomas and Blair started shooting at Phillip he tore a pole from the wall, and made an electric force rush up and down it.

Phillip blocked the bullets with the pole burning them to ashes, Phillip quickly moved over to Thomas disarming him and tripping him to the ground. Phillip held the pole up against Thomas chest, and Blair had his two handguns aimed at Phillip.

"You should know by now, that bullets can't harm me."

"Release my brother now."

"Where is the Mask?"

"Somewhere safe, now remove that from my brother."

"How about I do this?"

Phillip swing the pole towards Blair hitting his hand electrocuting
him, making him drop his guns also Thomas got up went to kick
Phillip but he twisted Thomas back down to the floor. Blair took out
his Diamond ring placed his hands around a handle on his back, and
pulled out his Samurai sword as he did he placed the Ring inside the
Bottom of the Samurai handle. Phillip turned around to him and
smiled at him.

"Magic Vs Electric, I guess you don't know." Blair looked at
Phillip, "Know what?"

"That Magic has no power over Electric."

Thomas turned to attack Phillip, but Phillip could feel his energy,
Phillip used the electricity in the room to force Thomas through a
wall knocking him out. Strictly got up and grabbed his Razor Blade
Agent Blair came running at Phillip with his Samurai swinging
towards him, Phillip blocked the Samurai with the electric pole. The
Samurai left a slice mark on the Pole, "What kind of magic is that?"
asked Phillip.

Strictly kicked his back making him move forwards, Phillip turned
around throwing the Pole near to Strictly body, but Strictly bend
under it, and hit it away with his Blade. Phillip was in the middle
of Agent Blair and Strictly, they both had their weapons aimed at
him.

"Well, well, well, isn't this a beaut? Two guys fighting over me,
aww aren't I lucky. "

'shut the hell up Mr. Armstrong."

"No Agent Blair, why don't you go back into your comer?"

Phillip quickly looked at Strictly he analyzed him by the way he was
standing, he could tell that Strictly's leg was hurting him, and
also he saw a sharp pain in his lower back which was giving him
problems.

'strictly do all off us a favour, and go sit down and rest, you're
in no fit mind of state to battle with me."

"I don't understand."

"Yes, you're wondering how I know right?"

Strictly came at Phillip but Phillip shot of this electric force
towards Strictly, but Strictly blocked it with his Razorblade
sending the force somewhere else. Strictly came in with his attack
upon Phillip, but he blocked each and every single attack of his,

and then Blair came in with his attack and Phillip had to dodge and moving out of the way. Phillip then transformed into electric pieces forcing both Blair and Strictly back, Phillip went back to normal.

"It's over now Agent Blair."

Phillip raise up his pole with the electric force growing more powerful, and went to strike Blair but as he did Thomas pushed a button making water come out of the ceiling covering Phillip and weakling him. Thomas quickly moved in and injected him with this different type of liquid, which merged into Phillip's bloodstream attacking it weakling his abilities causing him to faint.

"We've finally got him, well done everyone."

"Everyone it's only us three."

Thomas looked around himself looking at all the agents which died by Phillip Armstrong hands, he was disappoint that he could stop Armstrong without losing a few of his men.

"That was too much of a hard job."

"The job only just got hard."

Agent Thomas threw Phillip into a special design cell with water running through the walls, ceiling and floor. Also every few hour's this special air would spray out onto him, when breathing it in would stopped him from using his other abilities e.g. feeling people's energy, hearing voices through walls, also airwaves conversations and transforming himself into his electric elements.

"What have you found out so far?" asked the Director of all Sanctuaries world-wide.

Commander Jones looked upwards onto a massive screen, showing the Director standing with five other people dressed in combat outfits behind him.

"Director Patrick, we do not know his true intentions yet."

"Well get back in there, and do whatever is needed, Earth is at risk as long as He's here."

"Yes Director."

Jones walked out of the room as he did Thomas and Blair came towards him, "What did the Director say?"

"That we must use, any force necessary to get the answers out of Phillip."

"Any force necessary, he was a human before?" replied Blair.

"Do you have a problem with that Thomas?" asked Commander Jones.

"Commander and chief, I am hundred percent comfortable in executing you're orders."

"Great job, for you Blair, you will need more training. Maybe it's you're thinking which nearly got you killed last time."

"Brother."

"Fine, yes Commander."

"Brother, Captain Thomas, shouldn't we use the transparent blade?"

"You know it's not fitted to our DNA."

"Well, shouldn't we go get him?"

"The book."

"You are right."

"I know I am, I'm always right."

"You don't need to be an ass about it."

"You don't need to like fucking men."

"That's not cool, really not cool."

Chapter Thirty Three

MR. *Warrior*

Mid 1946 location Mesink, Town Sevenhampton

This young tanned man with long brown curly hair reaching his shoulder length in his mid-twenties was training in his back garden, somewhere on Mesink an Island down from England, and across from France, the Young man had his shirt off. The sun was beaming down on his skin which was sweaty, he had scars all over his back and arm, like He's been fighting against others that where much stronger, but obviously not better than me. The young man had two short sticks in his hand, and he was hitting them against a solid wooden thick pole, as Blunt step forward the young man threw back one of his sticks at Blunt, Blunt twisted around catching it. The young man moved forward clicking his fingers together, and what it seems like his girlfriend or wife, threw him a sword to him he catches it and points it towards Blunt.

"Mr Warrior?" asked Blunt."

"Yes I am a member of the Warrior family, who in rats uncles are you?"

"John Warrior, I'm Blunt Supreme the director of an secret agent company known as the Sanctuary."

"So you're basically a spy."

"Well, this spy with his little eyes wants to see what you got."

"You want to fight me."

In the background the woman laughs grabs a glass pours some kind of juice from a glass jug and walks over to her seat sitting down. John dashes towards Blunt without Blunt thinking it shocking him a little how fast John was, Blunt placed up his stick blocking John's attack, but siding him back along the grass.

"John, go easy on the old boy."

"Let me have a little fun, I haven't fraught no one for about five days now."

"What are you?" asked Blunt."

"I'm a Science Being just like you."

"Where did you learn that term from?"

"A friend called Apollo Mars."

"Jason Mars?"

"If that's what he's calling himself these days, then yeah."

"I am not here to battle you to the death, only wanted to see your skills, I am here to recruit you."

"Hold on, by you recruiting me do I get to fight?"

"Yes."

"How much fighting, one to million?"

"About nine hundred and ninety nine thousand."

"Where do I sign?"

Blunt took out a paper and said, "Here."

"Wait."

"Hold on Blunt, let me say goodbye to my girlfriend first."

"You've got one minute."

"Don't do that to me, I'm not a minute man."

The next moment John walked into his bedroom, his girlfriend jumps onto him naked, legs wrapped around him, whispering in his ear "take all of me." A little while later Mr Warrior walks out to his back door to see Blunt standing there, 'this juice is nice, what is it?"

"It's called sangria, made with red wine and fruits, my girlfriend she's Spanish she loves making it perfect for this heat."

"It's really nice."

"Don't drink too much, you will get drunk."

"Okay, let's get out of here, this way."

As Blunt showed Mr Warrior to an Hover-Craft, Mr Warrior stopped immediately "It looks like a Magic-Craft."

"The blueprints were kinder from its design, came from a whole different world, we had two people redesign the first Hover-Jet."

"I thought I wouldn't see something like this again."

So they boarded the Hover-Craft John quick moves over to the controls, "Yet I know how to fly this."

The scene changes to Blunt walking into the very first Sanctuary along with John Warrior, John looked around amused to see how advance his Science race has gotten, since he left.

"So this is under the Bank of England, that's pretty cool."

"How do you even know Apollo Mars?"

"Last year, I was taken away, every thousand years these species known as riddance, pick worthy Warriors to fight in his Arena."

"His Arena who's Arena."

"That's a big spoiler, and anything else I could say."

"Hold on, we're not in a movie, we're not doing Netflix and chill nor Amazon prime don't commit a crime, so tell me?"

"All I can tell you is, Apollo and his friend, well my great grandson saved me."

"Interesting, so how long have you been back?"

"Five days."

"Five days, what the heck?"

"I didn't even ask, who are we going after?"

"Yes, now we get to the juicy part," Blunt passes John a folder and John opens it and starts reading what's on the papers.

"She goes by the name Eight, she's highly dangerous not only that she has an personal Machine she named it Cyber-Plus, not only that but she's working with Fate Between."

"You said Eight and Fate?"

"Do their names mean anything to you?"

"Yeah, Eight is Zero daughter, Zero is better known as Zindus, his family conquered the Galaxy known as Sub-Zero, and Fate Between well all the Between brothers should be dead, the last one Jappy Between was in the Arena and Fate killed him."

"Slow down, slow down, too much info, and just tell me how we stop Eight?" asked Blunt.

"We shouldn't stop her, but instead imprison her," said John.

"Why?" asked Church.

"Mr Prime Minster," said John as Church walked in.

"She's important, Roman told me something, but we can stop Fate, I have a Sliver bladed Sword," said Blunt.

"That's great, but we need any one of his brothers to use it against him," replied John Warrior.

"What like me?"

"Impossible?" asked Blunt.

"Yes, I'm alive." replied Church Between.

"X-Hamstring you're here too?" asked Blunt.

"So what's the plan?" asked Mr. Warrior.

"We……

"John, what is it?"

"They are coming, I feel them."

Everything in the Sanctuary froze, however Church and John didn't, they looked at each other, and then this portal opened up behind them forcing them upto the ceiling crashing into it, and then crashing down to the floor. Out step two Beings and everything went back to normal, straight away the Agents armed their selves and aimed their weapons towards the two Un-known Beings.

"Agents, hold you're fire."

"Truly fascinating, kinder shit I've been missing," said John.

"Who are you guys?" asked Blunt.

One of them walked forward, this Being was in an all navy blue protected combat suit wearing a mask, with a blade attached on the back in a holder, and two small blasters in the Beings hands. Before the Being spoke the next few words three agents fired of their handguns, but the bullets burned to pieces in front of him, and then the other Being which was in a protected flexible Samurai suit red, yellow and black. Holding a blood orange bladed Samurai sword, spoke out.

"We are the children of the R.E.L.O.A.Ds."

"It's true, she speaks the truth," Said John

The one dressed like a Samurai bel down to John, Blunt looked at John and was totally confused.

"What are the R.E.L.O.A.Ds?" asked Blunt.

"A team of Heroes which inherited their abilities from their parents, they gathered together to defeat one of the most powerful nemesis anyone has faced before, throughout all dimensions."

"What's your names?" asked Church Between.

"I am E-Blud, Son of Blud-Fire and E-Chick, also a member of the T.O.R.E.L.O.A.Ds, from the year 2187."

"I am Samurai-KB aka Kyoko Blair, daughter of Director Dwayne Blair and Akemik Yamauchi Blair.

"What does that mean T.O.R.E.L.O.A.Ds?" asked Blunt.

'Together Over Ruling Evil Lords Of Any Dimensions," Replied Samurai-KB

"What's the plan?" asked John Warrior.

"We must travel through time, twenty years ahead," replied E-Blud.

"What about time, wouldn't that be affected by it?" asked X-Hamstring.

"Not if Time itself allows one to use time," answered Mr. Warrior.

"He's right about Time, but not in this case, one of my abilities allows him to travel through any Dimensions, however there are a few rules."

"So you're not even here to help us stop Eight and Fate?" asked Blunt.

"Not the main purpose, but we will to ensure Time is not damage," answered Samurai-KB.

"Then why are you here?" asked X-Ham.

"For you to help us stop Cyber-Plus, and slow down something else, until he returns," answered E-Blud.

"Until who returns?" asked Blunt.

"We cannot say anymore, until we have helped you first," answered E-Blud.

"Hhmmm, why travel ahead in time, and not stop them now?" asked Blunt.

"History instructs us to," replied Samurai-KB

"History, a person, who is history?" asked Blunt.

"This time, history is a living planet," replied Samurai-KB.

"One more thing, travelling ahead will erase you from this moment, it will feel to others that knew you, you no longer was. However you will gain all memories, like you did live the twenty years but you won't age," said E-Blud.

"However the feeling and the knowledge will be very real to you," said Samurai-KB.

"Wait, let me say goodbye to my girlfriend one last time," said John Warrior.

"No, need you won't be going nowhere, only stepping forward for a short moment a moment that does even count," replied E-Blud.

Everything froze in the Sanctuary again, but this time, John Warrior and X-Hamstring wasn't, a portal opened up. As they all walked into the portal, and it closed behind them, the rest of the agents in the Sanctuary went back to normal moving again. Moments later as they were travelling inside the portal, you could see all the events that would have went down, if they choose to not go with E-Blud and Samurai-KB. It would have been a long and tiring goose chase, just like that the portal opened up in a very heated location in which the sun was beaming down towards them, they all came walking out but not with E-Blud and Samurai-KB, as they were already standing in front of them.

22nd of October 1966 Egypt, Africa

"I can tell this isn't England, no more?" asked Blunt.

"You are right, we are in Africa, Egypt," said Samurai-KB.

"What year is this?" asked X-Hamstring.

"What's that on your wrist?" asked Church.

"My mother had one as well, it's a TDC, but it's been damage slightly in a previously/future fight," answered E-Blud."

"What does it do?" asked Blunt."

"It would have help the future heroes, keep a track on me, ensuring I am following the right path."

"What's the future like?" asked John Warrior.

"Its real focus," answered Samurai-KB

"Let's keep moving."

Chapter Thirty four

A Future Foretold Part 3

15th of August 1986 A graveyard, Mesink

A future unknown a future that none of the heroes in that time, could ever imagine. This future was not of any darkness but of a true end, an end from some new kind of greyness, things were not kind in this period.

"I remember when my father, took me to his father's gravestone, and I did not understand at the time why."

"Jardon, Jordan, Jar, let's go, I can feel there is too much pain here for you, it's not good for the boys," said Elizabeth.

"Babe, the boys must understand what was giving for them, why they breathe why they are living right now," replied Jar.

"You stay then, let me take the boys."

So Elizabeth Jar's wife took the boys and headed into the car, sitting there waiting for Jar, to do or say whatever he needed to say so he can let rest his father which meant a whole deal to him.

"Father, you were always right, and I never listened, I am so sorry."

"Yes you better be."

"Impossible, you're dead."

"Oh sorry, let me make this clear to you."

John Jar's father moved forward towards him transforming himself into no other than Ultra-Mist, this greyness surrounded Ultra-Mist.

"You are real, they spoke of your name," said Jar.

"Yes I am very real, but you are not as afraid as you should?"

"You look so much like him, are you him?"

Jar could see what he was looking at but to us it was just greyness surrounding the being, Jar pulled out a mini dagger throwing it towards Ultra-Mist, as it flew towards Ultra, the dagger stopped and Ultra-Mist moved through while it froze in place, tapping it away and it dropped to the ground.

"Why did you kill him?"

"It was his time Jar, but not yet yours, I need you around."

"What do you want?"

"To watch over him."

"Blood?"

"Yes."

"Why, why him?"

"He's important for me to gain back something dare to my Being."

"You talk as if; you are not from this time."

"I am lost in pasture, no time belongs to me, peace that was once upon me has complete left."

"How is this even possible?"

"Your son must stay alive, until he has done what is needed."

"When does he die, just tell me?"

"Only I keep that information, I erased it from the Library of all histories."

"Why here why now?"

"To protect my interest of course, I promise you I will not harm any of your bloodline, that's not my intentions at all."

As Jar's sense slowly came back to him he noticed he was surrounded by agents, but Ultra was gone, the agents spoke out to him. At first it was a blur until he heard his wife's voice, this knocked him back to Earth.

"What happened Agent JA201?" asked an Agent.

"I'm not sure, he was here, something happened but I cannot remember," answered Jar.

"You pressed your watch, was Armstrong here?" asked another Agent.

"Maybe, it's all like a dream fading away," said Jar.

"What did he want, why are you unharmed Agent?" asked the first Agent.

"To protect his interest, but I don't know what interest that I am supposed to protect," answered Jar while glazing over at his sons in the car.

"Mrs Warrior, we will need to take your husband in for more questioning, at the moment In-Pulse could be anywhere, and everywhere."

"I understand just get him back to us, I don't want him to miss Blood's birthday," replied Elizabeth.

As Jar headed into one of the Agent's car, and it drove off, Elizabeth headed back to Sevenhampton Jar's hometown, but however something else was happening in England, Bedford.

"Do you like our new home?" asked Strictly to his wife.

"Why do we have a safe room, what are you involved in Steve?" asked Emma.

"It's not what I'm involved in; it's what I'm protecting you from."

"Baby, please, talk to me."

"Remember in seventh nine, where I rescue you from them."

"Yes I do, the army forces the scientist the poison my village, the beings not from this world."

"I always kept this to myself, but when I say the next few words, history will record it."

"What is it Steve?"

"I and Jar fraught against them with our other squad members, he can't remember anything of that battle, as one of them whipped his memory clean."

"I remember you saving me, but not fighting them."

"Well, I find out who they were."

"Who were they?"

"They are from a Galaxy called Sub-Zero, one of the beings is called Low-Rider."

"What about the other one?"

"The person, who told me, couldn't refill the other ones name."

"A person, what are you talking about?"

"Yes, that person was indeed, our son."

"Blake?"

"Yes his older self, he came back to give me a message, from the most high."

"What was the message?"

"Train Blake with everything I know, He's also holds the key, to defeating him for good."

"Honey, I am always grateful what you've done for me, changing my name and marrying me so that I can gain a new start. The first moment I met you my feelings towards you were strong, I love you."

"I am happy that I could have done that for you, but my job is dangerous, I deal with unexpected terrorist individuals or groups worse than terrorists, I love you too."

"Please, just don't bring them home with you."

"Of course, I wouldn't, I'll never do that to you."

"Did you remember to visit your other son, France is not far."

As Emma said that to Steve in ran Blake full of joy, "Dad, dad."

"What is it, Blake?"

"I saw a shadow moving, at the front of the house, through the window."

"Emma, take Blake and yourself to the safe room, and lock it."

Strictly grabbed his machine gun and handgun also threw on his protected amour. Strictly opened the front door peaking around it, seeing if anyone was there, but no one was. He came out of his house as his wife and son was in the safe room, they could see on the screen mentor, a shadow like being approaching him from the side.

"Hello, old friend."

Strictly turned around blasting off his machine gun, but the bullets did nothing, the Being with force only lift Strictly up dashing him onto the top of his car, and then making him float in mid-air, and then crashing him back against the house wall.

"Are we done now?"

"What do you want?"

"The Warrior family are in danger; I need you to go, assist them."

"You informed me that he killed my father, why should I help his son or believe anything you say?"

"You're Son and Jars are connected, you will do this, or I will kill your wife in front of you."

"You cannot do me let this please."

"I know I have put you in a situation, that is unlikely, but this will benefit the right outcome in the future."

The Being floated over to Strictly touching his neck, healing him and giving him back his strength, "Go, go now."

As Jar Warrior came back to his house, things started to play on his mind, something his brother said, it came to light. Jar opened the door he indeed missed his son's birthday, but that wasn't what was on his mind he rushed upstairs, as his wife was sleeping he woke her up.

"He's not mines is he?"

"What do you mean?"

"Alex, that's why I felt he had no love towards me."

"That's not true, you came back that one night, remember?"

"I never left the base; I was there for the whole thirteen months."

"It couldn't have been a dream, He's real, He's living."

"I haven't got time for this, I'm taking Blood."

"No you can't, stop, let's talk."

Strictly was in traffic on the bridge which led onto Mesink, as he looked in the mirror he saw him sitting in the back, but as he turned around the being wasn't there. Jar was outside holding his son Blood in his shoulders; stirring dead at himself across the pathway, Jar moved backwards quickly throwing Blood onto a soft bush but as he hit the ground Blood was cold out.

"Boys, you deal with my brother, I need to get my son."

Strictly knew he was too late as he pulled up to the house as it was burnt down already, and no one was around until he heard a weird sound, little did Strictly know but one of G-Man's men, watched from a far. A while later Blood was inside Strictly house, as Strictly went to open the door, and a foot kicked Strictly back down to the floor, Blood's eyes slowly closed, and then once it opened back. He was in the Sanctuary's on Mesink in front of his brother Alex, and his father Jordon, as strictly exited the Sanctuary the being appeared grey surrounding him blurring out his face.

"You bastard, my wife is dead because of you."

"No, because of G-Man, I understand this is a sad period for yourself and Blazing, however you have changed something important in the future."

"Tell me the future?"

"Blazing, will have a daughter called Flo."

"Why is she important?"

"Blood's son Kenco, and Flo will have a child called Leo."

"Leo?"

"Yes, Leo will help him escape from Darkness."

"Who is he?"

"Dawn of a New Warrior."

"Father, who is this person?"

"Oh, young Blake, what you see before you isn't a man, "

"What are you?"

"I am the original first ever soul, all of you are a part of me."

"That's really cool."

"Go, don't bother us again."

"For you Strictly, I should know."

"Whatever it is, I do not wish to gain that knowledge."

"It was about your future, but you are right."

"I will kill G-Man."

The being vanished in thin air without a trace like he was never there, Strictly got into his car, and drove off.

"Father."

"Yes Blazing?"

"I felt something odd about that man."

"Blazing, let it to rest, you not need to worry about him no longer."

Sometime in 1972 he shows up again in London, England

Ultra-Mist was standing in front of E-Blud, Samurai-KB, and X-Hamstring.

"Why did you kill him?" asked X-Hamstring.

"He killed his brother, it was his time," answered Ultra.

"What about us, is it our time now?" asked Samurai-KB.

"T.O.R.E.L.O.A.Ds, you know it's too late to stop me right?" spoke Ultra-Mist

"Not if B Warrior is alive," answered E-Blud.

"So let it begin."

X-Ham moved forward Ultra-Mist with only a blink, moved X-Ham to the ground pinning him to it, with only his mind.

"His power has increased unbelievable faster than we imagined," said Samurai-KB.

"We just work as a team this time." replied E-Blud.

So both of them together headed towards Ultra-Mist, while Ultra-Mist still had X-Hamstring pinned to the ground, Samurai-KB plus E-Blud came swapping towards him. Ultra-Mist opened a portal in front of himself sending X-Hamstring into it, as X-Hamstring went into it from his point of view he saw Ultra-Mist moving them away.

"X-Ham."

"Blunt Supreme?"

"Huh, no it's me Johnson, his grandson, I'm heading into the station." X-Ham looked passed Johnson to see Cross Between standing there, "Yes, I'll handle Cross." Moments later X-Hamstring found himself standing in front of Cross Between.

Future Timeline Blood Warrior and the Era of Darkness

"I will end you X-Ham."

X-Ham came towards Cross with his Machete, Cross blocked it and kicked X-Ham backwards making him slid along the ground, X-Ham stopped himself pushing himself forward again. Swinging his Machete at Cross Between which faded through it, and behind X-Ham slicing his back, and kicking his arm which his Machete went flying out, X-Ham turned at Cross which sliced his arm and leg, making him dropped to the floor. Cross move over to X-Ham with his Axe, X-Ham looked up at Cross, "I told you." Johnson saw Cross slice of X-Ham's head, and it rolled to the ground, however everything rewind back to just before Cross Between was going to cut of X-Ham head.

"Ultra-Mist," said Cross.

Chapter Thirty-Three

Beth's Army of dead

22nd of October 1966 Africa, Kenya

A future changed many times, to benefit different Beings, a future unknown likely to be the same as ones we have experienced already, are the new heroes of this time ready to step up to the mark, and defend Earth from the wicked leadership currently ruling?

Time Will Tell

"So where do we need to go?" asked Blunt.

"Kenya," answered E-Blud.

"Why there?" asked John.

"The Army of Dead," said X-Hamstring.

"Impossible how could you know?" asked E-Blud.

"Roman, told me, he had a vision but the King of Africa didn't want to listen."

"Hhhmmm, not to burst any of your bubbles, but who the hell are they?" asked John Warrior.

"It's the Army of Africa, we should be fine," answered X-Hamstring.

"You just had to go and say that didn't you," said John Warrior.

As the Army came up on to the heroes from basically every angle possible, three high position leaders of the army step forward the soldiers ready their weapons into fighting mode.

"If any of you guys have some sort of trick up your shelves, please do use it now," said Blunt.

"We come in peace," said Samurai-KB.

"Bloody hell, they aren't aliens," said Blunt.

"Hand over you're weapons, you have broken Jabkinulake restriction, if you do not, we will before to acted."

"Well guys?"

While that was happening Beth walked forward standing high in the Temple of Kano looking down at her Army of dead, on the other side of the field the King of Africa army had recovered from the mysteries rock which hit the battle field, causing his enemy's army to turn into dead soldiers in which Beth gained ruler ship over.

"King."

"Yes soldiers."

"You must return back to Egypt, you need medical help, your bleeding."

"No, I must finish this now; I just can't believe Elizabeth has turned her back on us."

"She is Hitler's daughter after all."

"King."

"Yes Captain Emmanuel."

"Word has travelled back; we may have some kind of heroes back in the Kingdom, which can help us defeat this Army of Dead."

"No one can help, we must attack now."

"What about your son?"

"If anything happens to me, he will become the new King of Africa; he has instructions on what to do."

"Yes, our noble one."

As the two children of the R.E.L.O.A.Ds, and the heroes were in the Kingdom eating resting up, the Queen and Prince came to them.

"Again I am sorry about earlier, with the generals," said the Queen of Africa.

"It doesn't matter, it's good to have our weapons back, and that we reached an understanding with each other, our majesty" replied Blunt.

"I like this one a lot, bring him twenty girls," requested the Queen.

"Damn boy, you lucky as hell haha," said X-Ham.

"We've sent back word to England, a friend is coming," said the Prince of Africa.

"Friend, we don't have any friends," said Blunt.

"Blunt, Blunt, hey, Blunt are you okay?"

Blunt dropped out of his seat landing onto the floor, his vision become very blurry and his eyes shut. Everything went dark for a second, as he opened back his eyes, he was laying down on the floor, and hurting.

"What's going on, this feels too real," said Blunt to himself.

Ahead of Blunt was Churchill standing holding the Sliver bladed Samurai, and his brother Fate, Blunt looked down at himself seeing a massive cut going down his chest and he was bleeding out a lot.

"It ends here brother."

"Fate, it doesn't have too."

"You die or we both do, your choice brother?"

"Our father wouldn't want this from us."

Blunt looked backwards through the door leading out towards mountains, he could see a Hover-Craft flying in, he then looked back at Church and Fate, Eight walks in with her Cyber-Plus.

"Go Eight, I have it under control."

She looks at her Cyber-Plus and it moves so fast to the side of her, you might have not noticed it, and then they faded away. The Hover-Craft comes in close to the mountain, and the doors slide open John and X-Hamstring fly out of it, landing into the room Blunt looks back at them and they grab him all Blunt sees is Church and Fate running into each other. As they came flying back onto the Hover-Craft Blunt moves his arm out, X-Hamstring moves Blunt's arm back in.

"We need to help him," said Blunt.

"It's too late, He's coming," replied Samurai-KB.

As Church stabs Fate with the sliver bladed Samurai, and cracks starts to appear all over Fate, Fate drops both his golden daggers to the ground, Church turns around to the Hover-Jet readying himself to jump up into it.

"What's going on, why he isn't jumping up here?" asked John.

"Get us out of here now, He's here," said Samurai-KB.

"Samurai-KB, E-Blud, you're here," said Blunt.

"Whose coming?" asked X-Ham.

Church was force to turn around as he did, this greyness being blurred out stabbing him with the golden daggers, Church's eyes shine out a grey colour and his mouth, Church bursts to pieces and the figure steps forward pointing at Samurai-KB.

"That's Ultra-Mist."

The Hover-Craft speeds of into the air and Ultra-Mist vanishes away, the hold mountain then gets blown to pieces.

23rd of October 1966 Egypt inside the Kingdom

"Blunt, Blunt."

"Yeah, what was that?"

"He's experiencing the after affects, whatever truly hurting memories he has regained will come back to him but at full intensity," said E-Blud.

"History recalls normal Science beings have died from experiencing it," said Samurai-KB.

"Will I experience that?" asked John.

"Depends," answered E-Blud.

"Are those Hover Crafts, I can see coming?" asked John Warrior.

"Yes, Everton should be on one," answered Samurai-KB

"How's Blunt?" asked X-Hamstring.

"He's fully recovered."

"X-Ham, it felt so real, I do never want to experience that again," said Blunt.

As the Hover-Crafts landed Everton walked out of it, and towards John Warrior shaking his hand, as we're getting escorted into the kingdom Everton saw lions, elephant, giraffe and other animal living amount the humans here peaceful unchained free to roam the whole Kingdom.

"Roman, informed me you be needing these," said Everton.

"Indeed, we will be," said Blunt.

Blunt and Everton stopped at a pearl design desk, "Welcome to Egypt, will you be staying the night?" asked the Ambassador of Africa.

Everton looked around him diamonds in the floor in the wall, gold all around him; it was a piece of art inside the Kingdom.

"Yes, I will leave in the morning, thanks" replied Everton.

"Okay, right this way, one of the Kingdom's assistant will help you to your room, also would you like me to send through some entertainment for yourself?"

"Entertainment, well yes please do," replied Everton.

Over in Kenya the King had fraught his way to Queen Beth of Kenya as she claimed it for many years, but it was near impossible to battle against her Army of Dead as they could not be killed soon simple, so outside the Temple of Kano his army was holding back hers.

"It's good to see you again old man."

"Old man, I may be, but a bitch you sure are."

"You think I would make it that easy for you to get to me?"

Behind Queen Beth a few ton of her normal soldiers came towards the King, but Captain Emmanuel could see from outside, as he went to move. One of Beth's soldiers of dead stabbed him in the side, Captain Emmanuel turned around slicing that soldier's head off, and kicking the body over the edge falling to the ground. The King moved in killing a few of her normal soldiers, but he was truly outnumbered even for his skill and strength, as he sliced and dices them down. He was out of breath landing to his knee, trying to catch his breath. However, Captain Emmanuel bashed open the doors throwing one of his knives towards Beth in which he sliced this gold device from her wrist. Captain Emmanuel looked back at the Army of Dead, it looked like she lost control over the Army as they started attacking each other, as Emmanuel turned around one of her normal soldiers rammed his sword up through his chest, Captain Emmanuel dropped to his knees.

"You bitch, I hope you die in hell."

The King looked back at his Captain as the soldier was about to slice of his head, the King used some of his last strength to throw a dagger into the soldier's back causing him not to slice of Emmanuel's head. As the soldier's went in for the attack, they heard a weird sound; they looked back at their Queen. Beth noticed she had a dagger in her chest; it was from Emmanuel he then dropped to the ground. The noise the soldiers heard was the army of dead rushing into the Temple, as the King looked upwards he could see them outside the Temple floating in mid-air was a Hover-Craft. E-Blud jumped down on top of the Temple, as the Jet flew around to the front, blasting the Army of Dead back, E-Blud landed onto the floor next to the King, a few Soldiers of Dead came towards the King.

"Don't you worry you royal, I've gotcha."

E-Blud blasted the soldiers of dead away from the King, and then moved in on him, pulling out his blade slicing three down to the ground in which they turned too ashes, his blade itself had electricity running through it and surrounding it. E-Blud grabbed the King around him, and powered jumped up onto the top of the Temple.

"You need to place the two-golden devices, into the hole on the wall, to stop the Army of Dead," said the King of Africa and then died in E-Blud arms.

E-Blud looked back down and with his eye sight he could identifies the two golden devices, he dropped into the Temple landing in-between four Soldiers of dead, quickly killing them and moving over to the devices. As he went to grab them one of the soldiers of dead slice him, but his electric force field surrounding his outer body melted the blade, and he grabbed the devices. He then slid towards the wall in which there was a massive open space, and he put the devices together and placing it into the wall, as he looked back he was surrounded by hundreds of the soldier which were now frozen. This massive door open everything went complete cold, and this large icy storm came out of the massive open space and sucked all the army of dead into it.

"E-Blud are you okay?" asked X-Hamstring

"Yeah the King is on top of the Temple, I'm coming up now."

The massive door closed but and everything went back to normal with, E-Blud powered jumped up on top of the Temple outside. The Hover-Jet landed on top of the Temple, X-Hamstring, Blunt and Samurai-KB came out of the Hover-Jet, E-Blud looked at them.

"It wasn't a success I guess?" asked Samurai-KB.

"The King of Africa is dead," replied E-Blud.

As they returned to the Kingdom it would have been morning time, carrying the King on a board Samurai-KB using her abilities to able it to float, placing him down gently onto a table, the Queen cried out and the Prince run down the stairs into the room.

"Papa."

"We are truly sorry," said Samurai-KB.

"We were just too late," said E-Blud.

"Did you stop the Army of Dead?" asked a General.

"Yes," answered Blunt.

"What for my brother?" asked the Queen.

"Brother?" asked E-Blud.

"Captain Emmanuel?"

"We have no record of seeing him," replied X-Hamstring.

"You are Libran, right?" asked the Queen of Africa.

"Yes I am, what's the interest?" asked X-Ham.

"I will make you Commander and Chief of Libya."

"I haven't been back there for over fifty years."

"How old are you?" asked the Queen.

"I should be almost eighty, but I'm twenty eight," answered X-Ham.

"You're the science experiment, the Americans and Russians worked on?"

"Yes I am," answered X-Ham.

"We heard so much about your hometown, as we were defending the Kingdom, and our other twenty four roams, the King's army came to your town too late, the Nazis really did…………"

"No, please stop, I do not want to hear it."

"For your offer, I will have to decline it."

Everton walked into the room and the Prince looked at him in so much pain, the Prince rushed over to him.

"You bastard, you bastard, you knew this would happen. Why didn't your master convince my father the King to reach out to his allies," shouted the Prince.

"Prince, you are now King of Africa, Roman did as much as he could you're father knew he was an ill man, that's why your father didn't believe," replied Everton.

"I will travel to Mesink with you, and personally take that rock to Roman, I don't want nothing from it it's full of evil, only evil will come of it."

"E-Blud, where to now," asked Blunt.

"We will return to the Sanctuary," said Samurai-KB

"My sons, I have sons?" out spoke Blunt.

"Yes you do," replied Samurai-KB.

"Blair and Thomas Supreme, they're twins both Seven," said Blunt.

"Jardon, I too have a son?"

"John, John, John, what's wrong?" asked X-Hamstring.

"He's experience the time affects," said Samurai-KB.

As John's eyes went blurry and the voices around him went funny, John opened his eyes up again, he couldn't move at all but he was in the Bank of England.

"Oh, why did I do it," said John to himself out loud.

"Do what? You really need to stop drinking that coffee brand, got you tripping all kinds," said X-Hamstring.

Chapter Thirty-Five

I killed Luke Nescote Norman

During 1964 John Warrior's Time Memory

As John walked into the Sanctuary he noticed a broad with a familiar face on it, he looked back at X-Hamstring and he looked drained, X-Hamstring came up close to him.

"John, are you okay, drinking this."

John hit it out of X-Hamstring hand and races into the toilet, he quickly washes his face, and he came back to normal, he wasn't feeling weird anymore.

"Wait, this is a memory, why does it feel so real," John said to himself.

John came back into the room X-Hamstring looked at him, "Man you're looking much better now," John nudged at him.

"Looks like we found the guy," said Blunt.

"Yeah, Luke Norman, father of Stephen Nescote," replied John.

"Okay then, you is right but we haven't mention nothing yet, anyway moving on," replies Blunt.

"Church, is that you?"

What Blunt heard next was all slow, "Yes, what's good, you're not look yourself Mr Warrior?"

"Just trying to figure out some stuff man," answered John.

"So did you all write that down, in your little pretty pink notepads, we arrest him tonight," said Blunt.

John looks down at his desk looking at his pink notepad, with writing on it saying, but the notepad wasn't pink it was black with white paper inside.

8th of June 1964 Portsmouth Harbour 9:00pm Mr Norman meeting with contractor.

"Just to make sure you all know Church will deal with Fate Between, we need Mr. Norman for questioning," said Blunt.

X-Hamstring walks over to John still sitting there, with everyone gone; X-Ham touches John's shoulder.

"John, mate?"

"Yes X-Ham."

"You've been sitting there for five minutes; everyone has left gone back to their family."

"I didn't notice."

Next minutes John was sitting in X-Hamstring car driving over the bridge which led from Portsmouth, England to Mesink, John looks at X-Ham.

"All this spy shit is fun," said X-Ham.

"I'm just wondering why an ex Russia/Chinese Scientist is working with Fate."

"Money I guess, he has a family to provide for, and jobs aren't that easy to find in his field of employment, if you know what I mean haha."

"It's ten thirty a.m, this meeting supposed to go down at nine pm."

"You've written it in your pretty little pink notepad, like Blunt informed us to do."

"Yeah I'm just going over things, like why?"

"Don't worry John, you rest up, see your family. The Hover-Craft will be at the Mansion waiting for you, at 20:00 hours."

"Maybe I should see Roman."

"Is that where you want me to take you, because you know I haven't got any family,"

"Not a woman at least?"

"You can't trust any of them."

"Don't you need to release though, feel good when you're up inside?"

"That's why you go to those special venues right?"

"Bloody hell mate, I think you should get yourself a lady, before you end up catching something. I know you're a super-human, but god I'm sure you can still get something it's the 60's man."

"Look at you sounding all British, looks like Blunt's warned off on you after all mate."

"I've spent most my time in England, it's not a surprise, if I'm going to pick up the slang, and really be careful them ladies are rank proper nasty."

"You're right; I'll find a lady one day."

"Okay, maybe two or three, as you age slowly like a motherfucker."

As the car pulls up outside the Mansion Everton was waiting there for them, John looks at Everton weirdly talking under his breath,

"Righhteous."

"What did you say?" asked X-Ham.

"Nothing special."

 However, Everton heard what John said, but acted normal.

"Welcome back to the Mansion, Roman is expecting you," said Everton.

"How comes?" asked John.

"He had a vision that you needed to speak to him."

"So his illness is getting stronger?" asked X-Ham.

"You could say something like that," said John.

X-Hamstring looked back at John, John carried on ahead as they got to the room, and Everton looked back at X-Hamstring.

"I'm afraid to say this conversation, will be only with Roman and John."

"Where should I go?" asked X-Ham.

"I will make something for you to eat, please come this way with me," answered Everton.

"Do you have any of that Jerk Chicken Rice and Peas, I first tasted it in Jamaica last summer," asked X-Hamstring.

John looks back at them walking away having the most weirdness conversation he ever heard, and then he opened the door, "I preferred the curry goat," said John to himself.

"Welcome Mr Warrior."

"This is the third time meeting you right?"

"Yes it is."

"Your standing, you're not in your wheel chair?"

"No I am not."

"That's interesting isn't it?"

"I see your body is younger than your mind, soul and heart, you are only using this body as a vestal."

"You are truly amazing."

"No I am not, he gives me these abilities."

"Ultra-Mist?"

"You say his name freely."

"Am I meant to be afraid?"

"You tell me."

Suddenly everything went upside down John found himself on one knee, kneeing to a grey figure standing there blurred out, and Roman in a wheel chair looking out of the window.

"I let you see what you want to say; even Righteous is blind to me."

"What do you want?"

"What do I want, no, what do you want?"

"Why did I do it?"

"Haha, if you don't know now, how are you meant to know after."

"You kill me don't you?"

"Nope, that's someone else's path."

"Why are you here?"

"Looking after my interest."

"Impossible."

"It's so funny the kids are using you lot, but you can't see it can you."

"We will defeat you."

Knock, knock came from the door, everything went back to normal however Roman was in his wheel chair facing outside, Everton comes into the room.

"Everton I need to speak to you."

"No."

"Roman?"

"Forget it."

John faints to the ground and then the next minute he was in X-Hamstring car, outside his house.

"I tell you one thing, Everton can make some banging fried chicken."

"Can he?"

"Yeah, I placed some aside for you, here you go."

"Thank you X-Ham."

"Take care, I will see you later tonight."

As John stepped into his house his son came tackling him down to the ground, John looked up at his wife as she smiled with joy.

"Oh, how I've missed you both."

From behind his wife was his other son too.

"Don't you worry, I've missed you too Goy."

Goy smiled and laughed as well.

"It's good to have you back John."

"It's been two years, it's good to be back."

As John rested his eyes, his eyes opened back up in the Hover-Craft, with X-Hamstring, E-Blud and he looked around himself.

"Where's Blunt, Samurai-KB and E-Blud?" asked John.

"Samurai-KB and E-Blud who are you talking about?" asked Blunt.

"Wait, is that Luke Norman? asked John.

"Yeah we've captured him, we're going back to the base," said X-Ham.

"No, Blunt and Church need our help," shouted John.

"What do you mean?" asked X-Ham.

"We need to go to peak's edge now," replied John.

"That's almost thirty minutes away, in the Hover-Craft," said X-Ham.

"Yes."

As John said that he was forced back, his eye shut and once opened again, he was in the base outside the room where Luke Norman was, John looked down to his hand holding a dagger.

"Kill him, or they will all die."

"Why?"

"His children needs to grow up without knowing their father."

"Why me?"

"Just do it."

John now felt like he had no will over his body, as he walked into the room, Luke quickly tried to kick the chair at him, but John moved it around.

Blunt, X-Ham and Church watch from the screen mentor.

"What is he about to do?" asked X-Ham.

"We need him alive, He's the only one which knows where Eight and Cyber-Plus hide out is," said Blunt.

Luke kicked the dagger out of John's hand in which the dagger landed onto the table, but John punched Luke to the ground injuring him, X-Ham turn the corner to see the room, but John picked up the dagger, kneeling down placing it against Norman's throat and slicing it, X-Ham came in and shouted out.

Name: Luke Nescote Norman

Retired Scientist: Age 44

Last residents: Cornwall, London

Height: Five foot Elven

Build: Average

Feature: Bold head facial Hair

D.O.B: 19/03/1910

D.O.D: 25/06/1964

Cause of death: Throat sliced

M.B: John Warrior

"Impossible," said Blunt.

"John, but no, why?" asked X-Ham.

"John, put down the dagger," said Church.

John got up turned around to X-Ham, his eyes were greyed out, and Church noticed that the weapon was the Dagger of Dreams, X-Ham went to move forward, but this force came out of John's body like a shadow figure. This force knocked X-Ham out of the room through a wall, putting him in a coma and John dropped to the floor passing out. As John opened his eye he was in a cell in the Sanctuary.

"Hello, anyone, hey."

"Calm down John."

"Blunt, Church, what's going on?"

29th of June 1964 London, England

"You've killed someone important which would have help us find out where Eight and her Cyber-Plus hideout is, also you've put X-Hamstring in a coma."

"He's on life-support, it's at forty seven percent, if it drops any lower we may have to pull the plug."

"Guys it wasn't me, I'm sure of it, please believe me."

"Do we have to consider you an enemy now?" asked Blunt.

"Something doesn't add up," said Church

"What is it?" asked John.

Samurai-KB and E-Blud appeared across from Blunt and Cross, Blunt draws for his handgun and Church sword appears in his hand.

"Who are you guys?"

"KB and E, help."

"We know it's Ultra-Mist, he's here."

"You need to wake up come back to us."

John's eyes close again.

28th of August 1967 Egypt, Africa

"Luke Norman was a scientist who help build Eight's cyber-Plus, and I murdered him," said Mr Warrior to himself.

"John, John, you've finally recovered," said X-Ham

"Yeah, how long has it been?" asked John.

"One year," answered Blunt.

"Time memory thing, is a real kick in the ass."

"Tell me about it," replied Blunt.

"Where are we?" asked John.

"The Sanctuary," answered X-Ham.

"That's a prison, isn't it, over there?" asked John.

"Yeah, the one we're going to put Eight in, E-Blud is helping to build it," said X-Ham.

The telephone rang Blunt walk over to it picking it up, "Director Supreme, this is Agent Jones of the London branch."

"Yes, Agent Jones."

"A message from Mr Blair, He's in danger."

"Leeroy, no his son, He's in Jamaica with him," Said Agent Jones.

"X-Hamstring, what is it?" asked John.

"Director, we have a location on Mr. Blair."

"Where is he?"

"His beaconing is saying Japan, Tokyo."

"Who is this really?" asked Blunt Supreme

The other person on the other line hang up, as all of the heroes and two children's of the R.E.L.O.A.Ds, boarded an Hover-Craft heading towards Tokyo. A while later they were in Japan in fact they were flying pass Hiroshima as there was now peace between the USA and the Japanese, Japan was no longer a threat but an alley.

29th of August 1967 Tokyo, Japan

"Pilot go around Hiroshima, the air is still poison," said Blunt.

"No go through it," said E-Blud.

"Are you mad or something," replied Blunt.

"Maybe or not, I have place a force bubble around the Hover-Jet, we are fine breathing," replies E-Blud.

"Fine, carry on forward pilot," ordered Blunt.

"What's wrong with X-Hamstring?" asked John.

"He can't be, He's experiencing a time memory," answered Samurai-KB.

"Right fucking now?" asked John.

"Yes," answered E-Blud."

"Where is he?" asked Blunt.

"Right here, He's in 1964 Jamaica, Montego bay."

Montego Bay Jamaica

18th of May 1964 X-Hamstring's Time Memory

Jamaica, wickle wickle Beach an explosion hit the defence base people started to panic, out to sea there was a dozen Spanish warships.

"Waston, listen up now, get word back. The Prince must leave to England, from there they can protect him, more than we can."

"The British have sent us some help."

"What kind of help that is."

"Look."

"A few hover-Crafts, who's on it?"

"Isn't the weather so gorgeous here, haha," said Blunt.

"X-Ham, are you okay?" asked John.

"Not sure," replied X-Ham.

"Where's Elizabeth now?" asked Blunt.

"Director, Church, has tracked her to Egypt."

"Why would she be there," said John.

"The King the temple," replied X-Hamstring under his breath.

"X-Ham, what was that?" asked John.

"Nothing."

"Director Supreme, Prince Diovan wants us to help near the beach."

"I heard He's only sixteen years of age," said Blunt.

"Beth truly has done a number on us," said John.

Elsewhere in an airport a man was moving fast passing people carrying a child.

"Dad, pappa."

"Not now Dream."

"Where are we going?"

"Mesink, we must leave Jamaica, through Mesink we can go England start our new life."

"Dadda, me love here, me nah want to go."

"Ardrine, listen up it's not safe at the moment, too much chaos, as you are a half-blooded princess you are safe, you don't consider you royalty but you are."

As the hover-Craft floated over the Beach the Spanish and Jamaican soldiers looked up at it.

"Comrade, fire it down."

"Incoming."

"Director, shields at ninety four percent."

"Hold on who are they?" asked Blunt.

"I can't get a clear vision," answered John.

"The King and Cubans."

"X-Ham you didn't even look, how do you know that?" asked John.

"WATCH OUT," shouted X-Ham.

X-Ham moved forward drawing for his Machetes but the bullet burned because of the shield surrounding the Hover-Jet, and then X-Ham dive out of the Jet crashing into one of the warships.

"What's up with X-Hamstring?" asked John.

"Thought he was acting normal to be honest," replied Blunt.

"John help him," shouted Blunt.

"You've lost it as well, I'm not a super-human like him," replied John.

"Use this then."

X-Hamstring was on the ship with both his Machetes in his hands slicing and dicing him way through, as he turned around he was surrounded by Spanish soldiers all aiming their rifles at him.

"John!"

John moved forward to the edge of the Hover-Jet ready to jump out but another Hover-Craft flew next to theirs, "Let me take it over from here." Church moved his hands using his abilities to control the water, slashing the soldiers surrounding X-Ham off the ship. X-Ham looked up but then at the King crashing into the other ship, X-Ham started running jumping from warship to warships.

"The King," said Blunt.

As he said that the ship he was on blew to pieces X-Ham was forced back, X-Ham went flying into the water, but Church used the water to lighting his impact guiding him back into the Hover-Jet.

"Director Supreme, the Spanish have taken over Wickle Wickle Beach, they are heading to the Kingdom."

"Whats X-Ham status?" asked Blunt.

"I'm fine."

While on the airplane in the air leaving Jamaica the half-blood princess said, "Dad, are we safe yet?"

"Babygirl we are will be fine, I'm sorry I never told you the truth before."

"It's okay papa, I understand, we will be okay right?"

"When we land in Mesink, now sleep we soon reach."

Back in Jamaica, Montego Bay in the Castle the knights approach a young boy, "Prince."

"Yes."

"Its your father."

"He's dead isn't he?"

"Yes."

"I guess it's time."

"Watch out Prince."

The knight jumped in the way of the Prince taking the explosion the Prince was force backwards, as he hit the ground everything slowed down his hearing was cloudy his vision was blurry. He could barely hear or see anything the footsteps moving towards him, and people screaming dying, but with all his last strength the Prince got back up.

In Spanish all of the soldiers were saying.

"Stand down Prince, stand down."

The Prince kick one backwards into another one then moving forward grabbing the last soldier's rifle moving it upwards out of the way from his body, and then drawing out his Machetes slicing that soldier down to the ground. As the Prince went to exit through the hole in the wall a dozen Spanish soldiers stood in his way, the only thing the Prince had was his Machetes in his hand soaked in blood and the blood hitting the ground.

"I am General Castro, your defences have been whipped out, this country now belongs to President Rimus, give up little Prince."

"You all can go suck your mother's dutty pumpum out."

"Kill him."

As the soldiers placed up their weapons and the Prince held his hand tight around his two machetes, and started pacing towards the soldiers suddenly all the soldiers in front of him dropped to the ground.

"What the bludclart wagwarn?"

The Hover-Jet lands down onto the floor not so far from them, and outcomes X-Ham, Church, Blunt, John.

"So the British Empire does care about Jamaica?"

"Yes, in fact a few dozen ships should be hitting the Caribbean Channel any point now," said Blunt.

"What's the plan?"

"Your father is dead."

"I end all of them."

"Prince, we are here to find someone."

"Mi stay ere, mi deal with these pagans 2 rashole."

"Did you hear us, Prince?" asked Blunt.

"No, I have the rest of the Caribbean Island coming, they soon reach."

"Do you know of this person," as Blunt showed the Prince the photo just like that Leeroy came rushing in with his son rightful King of England."

"The King of England."

"King of England, you kid that boy, he's just Tyrone, my fisher man's son," said the new King of Jamaica.

"Long story King, we got to fly, good luck on your battle."

As they all boarded the Hover-Jets and flew up into the ship a dozen Spanish warships came entered Jamaica's channel but as they did the other Caribbean Island surrounded them with their battleships. As that happened the airplane which the other survives landed down on Mesink, they all got rush into the airport by agents and army forces.

"Fahter?"

"Yes Dream?"

"Where are we going?"

"To see an old friend of mines."

"Why?"

"He'll help us with new IDs so we can live in England."

19th of May 1964 London, England

The Hover-Crafts landed down on top of a building, X-Ham, Blunt, Church, John, Leeroy and Prince of England all headed into the building making their way down in a secret lift, to the Sanctuary.

"Everything has been already sorted," said Blunt."

"If anyone askes any question to you, about who you are, what do you say?" asked Leeroy.

"My new name is Malcom foster, born in Africa, Ghana, and I am thirty two. I study property and Management," said the King of England but now known as Malcom Foster.

"That's believable, I think this will work."

"All that sounds great but when will I have my life back?"

"As you are her son, you can never have a normal life, until she is dead or locked away for good, we are sorry Mr Foster." replied Blunt.

"What about you father?" asked Mr Foster.

"I am no longer your father, until the day she is not a threat, just call me Leeroy or Mr Blair."

As that happened Samurai-KB and E-Blud appeared to the side of Leeroy and Blunt, they all armed their weapons at them but X-Hamstring step forward, "Hold your fire it's just them."

"Who are they?" asked Blunt."

"No story short, you're in a Time hole, it has many names. Only you know of us but not anyone else, you need to wake up X-Ham," said E-Blud.

"Wake up."

Chapter Thirty-Seven

Tokyo Japan

29th of August 1967

"How's X-Ham doing?" asked Blunt.

"He's fine, He's recovering," answered E-Blud.

"He needs to recover now, we about to land in 3-4 minutes."

"Snap," said John.

"E-blud," said Samurai-KB.

E-Blud moved over to X-Ham placing his hand over his chest, and making this electric force appear, Blunt looked back.

"What's he doing?"

"This will give X-Ham temporally strength, as his natural healing ability will merge with this."

E-Blud sent the force into X-Ham chest waking him up with full energy.

"X-Ham?"

"Yes guys I'm back and I remember something,"

"What is it?" asked Blunt."

"Malcom Foster is Leeroy's son as well," answered X-Ham.

"Wait that means I should be the Queen of Newer England in my future, as I have English royalty in my blood line?" asked Samurai-KB.

"Your mother was a princess wasn't she?" asked Blunt."

"Yes of Japan."

"Director Supreme, we are landing the Jet."

"Hold on, something has alerted me."

"E-Blud, what it is?" asked X-Ham.

"It's Eight and her Cyber-Plus, there are in Washington DC."

"Okay, E-Blud, John, Samurai-KB, use this Hover-Jet and go to Washington, I and X-Ham will deal with this situation."

"It would have been a lot easier if we could have teleport us there, but the TDC has affected my abilities."

"Pilot, do indeed request for the Sanctuary to send another Hover-Jet."

"Yes Director Supreme."

So as the Hover-Craft flew off into the sky heading to America, Blunt and X-Hamstring headed into the building to find it empty, they both draw out their weapons.

"Be on high alert X-Ham."

"Why this place is totally empty."

The light turned off and seconds' later back on with both of them truly surrounded and outnumbered one to hundred.

"Place down your weapons."

"What is the meaning of this?" asked Blunt.

"Mr Supreme, it is finally nice to meet you."

"Who the hell are you?"

"You don't remember me do you?"

"Bounty, your Generals Okuma's son, isn't it," said X-Ham.

"Excellent job, you were always on point."

"We have an agreement; peace is with both our countries?"

"You are wrong; Mr Supreme, Japan has a strong agreement with America, and Queen Beth not England, rest in peace her soul."

"So what do you want?" asked Blunt.

"I only have a few months left, so it isn't much more than revenge, bring me Mr Blair."

Mr. Blair came out of the shadows struggling to breathe looking warned out, while for a sixth something year old, you couldn't blame him for what state he was in.

"Guys, get yourself out of here, don't worry about me, I've lived my life" said Leeroy.

However one of the troopers hit the back of Leeroy's head making him drop to the floor.

"I personally will kill him, if you don't deliver his son to me."

"His son, what are you talking about?"

"The real King to be, so stop fucking around with me."

"He's dead."

"Do not lie to me again, we know you took him back to England, and changed his name furthermore," Bounty walked forward placing his handgun against the back of Leeroy's head, Leeroy looked up at them.

"I have a son?"

"Yes, you had a son, with Beth," answered X-Ham.

"She took him to Jamaica, so we couldn't find him, when we went there to assist them from an all-out war against the Spanish. We didn't make it in time, they killed him," said Blunt.

"Mr Supreme, why lie, why fucking lie," shouted Bounty.

As he shot Mr Blair in the back of his head, making him drop to the floor, blood was pouring out from his wound created by the force of the bullet.

"Take them away," ordered Emperor Bounty.

30th of August 1967 Washington Dc, the White House

"What are those?" asked John.

Missiles after missiles hitting the Hover-Craft making it crash down in the front yard of the White House; before it hit the ground E-Blud shielded the Hover-Jet ensuring John and Samurai-KB got out safely as it blew to pieces with him inside.

"He can't be can he?"

"He's fine, it's E-Blud he's so dramatic," replied Samurai-KB

However they got surrounded by the secret services and more. And then E-Blud came up under the wreck.

"What the heck is going on?" asked John.

"Eight and her Cyber-Plus," answered Samurai-KB.

As they got escorted into the White House, into a room where the President, Eight and Cyber-Plus was standing also with a handful of secret service men behind them the door closes. Over in Tokyo Blunt and X-Ham were placed in two different rooms next to each other, with a transparent glass between them. As X-Ham turned around towards his door it opened up, and the room was flooded with troopers fighting him, all Blunt could do was watch. As X-Ham took them on taking them out one by one, until they started hitting and warning him down.

"Hold on X-Ham, hold on."

X-Ham looked at Blunt as he did one of the men hit X-Ham in the face with a metal stick, knocking him out to the ground, Blunt yelled out. The troopers picked X-Ham up carrying him out of the room, Blunt moved forward to his door, shouting.

"Where are you taking him?"

Back in Washington DC, inside the White House, the heroes were disarmed from their weapons, and in front of the enemy.

"Who's going to speak first then?"

"President, I guess you did," answered Samurai-KB.

"Why haven't you killed us yet?" asked E-Blud.

"We have a common enemy, in fact two," answered Eight.

"Two common enemies, Samurai-KB, what is she talking about?" asked John.

"It can't be possible, but even if it was, we were sent back to aid them in stopping you both," said Samurai-KB.

"Samurai-KB, are you going against us?" asked John.

"Yes, are you joining them?" asked E-Blud.

"E-Blud, you know what we've seem, you know what will happen, do we have a choice?" answered and asked Samurai-KB.

"She's kinder right John, let's hear them out first," said E-Blud.

A device on E-Blud arm was going off; he looked at Samurai-KB and then John.

"What is it?" asked John.

"X-Hamstring, is in danger, real danger," replied E-Blud.

"You two leave, I will carry on the conversation with them," said Samurai-KB

John looked at E-Blud and Samurai-KB nudged at E-Blud, and E-Blud turned to John grabbing his shoulder as the Secret Services threw them their weapons. E-Blud tried to teleport, "How embarrassing, like really," said Eight. Cyber-Plus open a portal for them E-Blud looked back, "Yemini," said E-Blud and John grabbed E-Blud and they both disappeared into the portal and out in Japan, E-Blud moved away from E-Blud.

"What in hells name are we doing, we can't leave her," said E-Blud.

"E-Blud, you know well enough she can look after herself, we must rescue the others."

"Damn it, come on let's go."

Blunt Supreme got dragged to the floor in front of X-Hamstring which was locked down into a chair, as Blunt got up his feet and arms were locked so he couldn't move.

"What the fuck is wrong with you."

"Now, now, Mr Supreme, all you have to do is get me, Leeroy's son."

"How, why?"

"If you don't, X-Hamstring will die your move Mr Supreme."

As Blunt couldn't move at all he watched as this massive torch came down in front of X-Ham, he tried his hardest to move but nothing was happening, as this massive torch turned Blunt shouted out.

"So you're going to burn him to ashes?"

"No more talking, any last words?"

Blunt looked pass X-Ham to see a Hover-Craft flying in, so Blunt quickly said, "Yes, yes."

"Yes, yes, what?"

"I will give you his address."

"Excellent."

As Blunt told him Bounty had spies already in Britain, moving in on Malcom Foster's address, word got back to Emperor Bounty. All Blunt saw on Bounty's face was a smile, and as Bounty moved to the side out of Blunt's vision, Blunt heard him say kill them both. Blunt turned his head back to X-Ham, and X-Ham looked at him with a face impression saying goodbye, but Blunt winked at X-Ham which confused him. As he did that this blast impacted destroying the massive torch, and killing some of Bounty's men also forcing Bounty down. E-Blud came into the room quickly freeing Blunt and X-Ham, Blunt notices Bounty escaping through hidden passage way.

"E-Blud, get X-Ham back to the Hover-Jet, I'm going after Bounty."

"Okay."

As Blunt followed Bounty into this dark area lights completely off, Blunt felt movements around him, as someone came to hit Blunt, But Blunt moved around it disarming him and kicking him back.

"Blunt, it's too late, my forces has his son."

"Nothing is never too late."

Blunt heard footsteps it sounded like Bounty was running as this door opened Blunt saw light, and followed after, as he exit the room Blunt was force back with a gunshot.

"Emperor."

"Hold on, let me see."

"Emperor we must leave now."

Emperor looked at Blunt on the floor out, and then boarded onto a hover-Craft, as that happened another Hover-Craft came flying down near the other hover-Craft in the speakers Emperor Bounty said.

"Stop me or save him."

Just like that the Hover-Craft Bounty was in flew off, and E-Blud quickly ran through the door to see Blunt lying there.

"Move the Jet away, now," shouted E-Blud

As he saw flames coming his way as the island blew to pieces, E-Blud found himself and Blunt on the Hover-Craft, Blunt's eyes opened up, but E-Blud vanished away reappearing in front of the Force and Light, inside the pasture.

"My end is now?" asked E-Blud.

"Neither, the future has yet changed."

"Dimensions are rebuilding destroyed timelines, creating new strains within those timelines."

"He did it then?" asked E-Blud.

"Not quite yet, but the path is on the narrow."

"So what for me then? Asked E-Blud.

Just like that E-Blud was back inside of the Hover-Craft with Blunt,

"Where did you go?" asked Blunt.

"Where did who go?" asked X-Ham

"E-Blud."

"You saw me disappear?"

"Yes."

"Somewhere no being should ever go," answered E-Blud.

"Where are they heading?" asked John.

"I have no clue," replied X-Ham.

"Surrey, Croydon," said Blunt.

"Croydon?" asked E-Blud.

"What's the matter?" asked Blunt.

"The time I come from, there's no London at all, yes England, but no London, and in fact it's called Gravesend."

"What happened to London?" asked Blunt.

"In my timeline's history, all boroughs of London and more were destroyed, and after a while turned into one massive Graveyard, renaming the whole of London Gravesend, and England Newer England."

"That doesn't sound too pleasing, Croydon may be full of nitties but it's home." said Blunt.

26th of October 1965 Moscow, Russia

"I've finally found you."

As Church Between was standing in a hall across from Eight and her Cyber-Plus he had his sword in his hand ready.

"Let's not pretend here."

"Pretend what?"

"That you're going to kill us."

A portal suddenly opens up next to Eight nothing happened at first, and then out walked a being standing twelve feet tall, wearing a very large armour and holding a very large sword.

"Superior Cosmic."

"He has found me, I will no longer be the guardian of all timelines."

Church raced forward as Cosmic dropped to his knee with two swords in his back, as Church looked passed him and into the portal he saw the being standing there, as the being started moving forward Cosmic closed the portal.

"I have come to the wrong time; you must leave with me Church."

Cosmic opened up another portal walking forward into it, Church turned to Eight and her Cyber-Plus and then walked into the portal disappearing as it closed behind them.

1ˢᵗ September 1967 Washington DC, the White House

Inside the White House, Samurai-KB was given back her weapons, and escorted to a Hover-Craft.

"We will be joining you in England, at the palace like we agreed," said Eight.

"It just to get the others on side, but I believe I can," replied Samurai-KB

As she got onto the Hover-Craft and it flew away, Eight walked back into the room where the President was.

"You can refill your true self now, father."

"Impossible, how did you know?"

"My Cyber-Plus, informed me."

"I can see it in your eyes, something is wrong, so let me ask you this have you missed me?" asked Zero.

"Yes father, but I know you are not the Being, I know yet, you're much younger, even though you look the same like all the time."

"You are very wise indeed my daughter."

"Please just call me Eight."

"So are you going to ask me?"

"I wasn't but how did you do it, how did you brain wash her."

"That doesn't matter right now, what does is my perfect plan, having them altogether."

"What about In-Pulse?"

"Hasn't you're Cyber-Plus, begun its final upgrades?"

"Yes."

"It advanced so quickly building its own species, just like Yemini AI System, but I know once the Cyber-Forces are created it will help slow In-Pulse down, making enough time for us to do what we need to do."

"Something changed didn't it, I became something else, but it's not something but someone."

"Ultra-Mist?"

Everything went grey in the room also started to rot away, as this figure merged out of the wall standing in front of Eight and Zero, having them being weak from his appearance.

"Ultra-Mist, please."

"I am always watching, as I belong between, everything."

"We are not going against you."

"Enough, even if you did, you couldn't."

"Why are you doing this to us?"

"So you know your place, don't you think the heroes are bored of you, future, past, present. You're always an object in their way, which they always defeat."

"I can go back to the Galaxy?"

"I gave you that Galaxy, for that very reason, and yet you keep coming back here."

"We will leave?"

"No yet I am waiting for him to come to me."

"Lord Warrior?"

As this grey figure blurred out moving through Eight making her whole body shake, and with force turning her body around to watch the next moves.

"Please Ultra-Mist, please."

Surrey, England

As the Hover-Craft landed down in a park called Beddington location outskirts of Croydon, Emperor Bounty opened the doors to find the King to be being escorted over to him.

"We don't have much time Emperor."

"Where are they?"

"Five clips out."

"Then we take the boy to the location."

"Yes Emperor."

As the Hover-Craft flew up into the sky the their Hover-Craft wasn't that far from it, as the Hover-Craft speeds off but finding themselves in a chase, dodging and moving between landmarks and other things.

"E-Blud."

"I'm trying, hold on."

"Finally, I was beginning to believe you betrayed me."

"I told you I foretold the future."

"What's the matter E-Blud?" asked Samurai-KB.

"I feel, yes I feel him."

"In-Pulse,"

"Phillip Armstrong," said John.

"Hold on, don't do it," said Blunt. .

E-Blud teleported into the Hover-Craft, standing away from In-Pulse, Emperor Bounty and a few of his armed men. Little did E-Blud know but In-Pulse placed an electric field around the Hover-Craft, blocking E-Blud abilities to teleport out of it, also making the Hover-Craft completely disappear.

"Where has it gone?" asked Blunt.

"It's his greater great grandfather, In-Pulse he's placed a shield around the Hover-Craft, making it invisible to our eyes," said X-Ham

"How do you know that?" asked John.

"E-Blud did it once himself," answered X-Ham.

"What can we do?" asked John.

Chapter Thirty-Eight

A sudden Death

E-blud also Malcom Foster, have been kidnapped for more than three years, but before we start let's go back to the moment it happened.

1967 somewhere in England airspace location on Hover-Craft

"Blunt, it's not even on the radar," replied X-Ham."

"Your device is beaconing," said John.

Blunt answered it.

"It's Samurai-KB, I'm at the palace, and everyone needs to come back right now,"

"We're in a tricky situation at the moment."

"What's happening, in fact just meet me here at the palace."

"Okay."

As the Hover-Craft turned around, the scene changes to the other Hover-Craft inside as E-Blud fades forward towards In-Pulse, In-Pulse had the same ideal as well. In-Pulse moved E-Blud out of his fade grabbing him, and pinning him up against the inside of the Hover-Jet.

"Oh dear boy, who do you think you inherited these powers from?"

"You, however you weren't around long enough to advance yours."

E-Blud pushes a force into In-Pulse moving him back off him, but In-Pulse had other plans, and flipped E-Blud to the floor forcing them through the bottom of the Hover-Craft. As In-Pulse was still holding E-Blud they both were falling downwards form the sky, In-Pulse pulls E-Blud close to his body, and teleports them back onto the Hover-Jet, E-blud was on both of his knees, as In-Pulse walks over to him placing his hand on to his shoulder.

"You're family, why are you doing this?"

Without any words In-Pulse strict E-Blud from his powers, and then disappeared leaving E-Blud on the floor crawl up into a ball.

27ᵀᴴ of July 1973 Unknown place Tropical Island

"Stand up E-Blud."

E-Blud looking drained and slow forces himself upwards onto his feet; he's also age heavy with grey strikes in his hair.

"This time you will face five of our unskilled guards."

As the five guards surrounded E-Blud in this temple arena, and without any words, they came rushing towards him, E-Blud flips upwards kicking one away but not landing correctly, in doing so the other one rugby tackles E-Blud to the floor. E-Blud was trying to move out of the ways of this guard, kept on stamping on him, E-Blud kicked out the guard's leg then grabbing him into a head lock snapping his head. E-Blud pushes himself upwards as he does, the next guard punches him to his chest, forcing him down to ground, other two grabs him pinning his legs down, while the other one was on top of him pounding him with punches.

"Alright, enough, stop, I said stop."

As the guards moved away from E-Blud, his face was soaked in blood.

"Take him back to his cell."

As they dragged E-Blud along the floor to his cell, they went pass where Malcom Foster was, but Malcom was looking stronger than before.

"Bring me, Malcom."

As Malcom got escorted into the room, the guard force him to kneel down towards Emperor Bounty.

"Hello Malcom."

Malcom quickly disarms both guards from their weapons, killing them and then aiming it at the Emperor; however dozens of guards flooded the room behind Malcom aiming their guns at him.

"I've trained myself for three years, for this very moment."

"Guards, lower you're weapons."

"Foolish move."

"Hand over the guns to them, and maybe you live to see tomorrow."

Malcom looked at Bounty and then at the guards.

"I am truly outnumbered I guess."

Malcom threw back one handgun, but with a grenade attached to it, as it landed behind the first guard, the rest noticed it too late, and it blew all of them away. Malcom then turned around to the Emperor which was now out of his seat standing up, all E-Blud heard was three gun shots.

"E-Blud."

"Over here."

'That was all you?"

"Yes, as you were weakling your grandfather, I had to train, and prepare us for our escape."

The alarms went off but Malcom and E-Blud was outside not too far from the Hover-Jet.

"E-Blud, what are you doing?"

"I can't move no further."

"What is this blue force surrounding us?"

"Energy."

"Who are you talking to?"

As Energy spoke to E-Blud it vibrated around the force field, the sound of Energy's voice came from different points within the force field, plus only E-Blud could hear Energy's voice.

"E-Blud, do something we are surrounded."

"Nothing to worry about."

As the bullet came towards them they burned into ashes, even the rocket launches all the flames spread around the outer force field.

"Are you doing this?"

"No."

"You were never given your abilities, the power of energy was always within you, and no one can ever take your powers from you."

"In-Pulse did."

"Your Grandfather has been punished for his actions."

"What punishment was he dealt with?"

1. Energy sources are forbidden to take another who wills energy.
2. Ones with energy can kill others who will energy.

"These laws are different for time as you know time should not be abused by someone who wills energy."

"Wait, wait."

The force field went away Malcom quickly went behind E-Blud.

"Please tell me you have your abilities back?"

"My powers have been reinstalled, greater than before."

As the troopers and guards begun to fire at them again, E-Blud place an electric force up, and then sent it travelling towards them all, frying their whole bodies.

"What's the plan now?" asked Malcom.

"To get you back to England, and for me to get back to them," answered E-Blud.

"Well, the Hover-Craft is just over there."

"You still do not know me."

At the Sanctuary the system was going off, agents running away, in fact one of the agents came to Director Supreme's office.

"Director, Director Supreme."

"Blunt, isn't here, what is it Agent Jones?"

"It's Eight we think, she's lit up on the systems."

"Where?"

"Well, here in England, Centrale London, a building known as Netcreed."

As the agent said that this blue force appeared knocking everyone down to the floor, and out came E-Blud and Malcom Foster.

"You both are alive."

Everyone gets back up to greet them.

"Ok, Agent Jones, get everyone together. I will inform Blunt."

While that was happening Blunt was in Roman James the First Mansion, on the outside also inside it was being rebuilt, as papers were being signed, Everton was concerned with this idea of Roman's.

"Roman, are you sure?"

"Everton, how long have we known Blunt for?"

"Many, many years."

"Sent him back in."

"Ok, "Sir."

Everton opened the door Blunt enters, and Everton exites looking weirdly at Blunt.

"What's up with him?"

"He doesn't trust you, maybe like the fact that the Agents will be taking over this mansion after my death."

"It is a bit odd, why did you call for me?"

"You founded the Sanctuary, but that location isn't safe anymore, here you can do a lot better, and take on my apprentices."

"We will definitely turn them into great scientist, Mr First."

"No, you won't."

"Wait, what do you mean?"

"I've already done that job."

As Blunt was about to walk out, he looked down at the papers, noticing his name wasn't there, but too names which weren't of great meaning too him.

"Roman, what kind of sick game is this?"

"I know what you are worried."

"I hope for your good you do."

"You won't be taking over this Mansion, and turning it into the new location for the Sanctuary."

"Our agreement?"

"The agreement is there, can you not see the names."

"It's not my sons, but others, unknown to me,"

"For their safety they cannot inherit the Sanctuary Thomas and Blair Supreme."

"That I understand but they will still become agents working here, what sick game is that come one, this is their birth right."

"No it was your birth Mr Supreme not theirs."

"You just can't do this; you can't just get two random two people and make them owners of this, I built the Sanctuary."

"You don't understand do you, Mr Supreme you die today, she kills you. Cause of your death your kids would have been unsafe, but you hid them away you set in motion, for them to become who they do. They will enrol into the agency, as junior agents."

"You are truly sick, I can't have nothing to do with this, has your illness sent you this far off the edge."

Everton came into the room Roman looked pass Blunt at Everton.

"What's the matter Everton?" asked Roman.

"Blunt."

"Yes, Everton."

'They have a location on Eight, just Eight she's alone."

Without any thought Blunt came flying into the Hover-Craft, Everton and Roman watched from the window.

"What did you say to him?"

"Noting that I wasn't meant to be said."

As Roman and Everton watched from inside his Mansion as the Hover-Jet speed of into the sky.

"This will be the last time we see him."

In the Sanctuary in London X-Ham and E-Blud was about to do something, "E-Blud, do your thing," said X-Ham."

"I won't be able to get inside the building, but outside I can do."

'That's good enough," said Samurai-KB.

As they all teleported outside of the building, above them they saw a Hover-Craft floating, and as someone came flying out of it smashing through a window.

"Blunt."

"He can't go in alone."

"Cyber-Plus."

Cyber-Plus vanished away in front of them, and as they came into the building troopers flooded the main entrances, all the heroes had to battle their way up as troopers after troopers were blocking their way.

"Eight, stop, just give up."

"Isn't this a pleasure?"

"I'm not here to play games."

"You're too late, and not wise, coming here alone."

"What about you being here alone?"

"Am I."

Blunt shot Eight in her shoulder making her flip over a desk, and then came flying over the desk but as he did he got hit away. Blunt came sliding to the ground hitting the window, cracks spread to appear on it, Eight stood back up.

"Blunt, I like to introduce you to my few Cyber-Forces."

Blunt looked all around as Eight fire of her gun, he flips pass her bullets, which hit the window breaking it. As the window smashed by the impact of the bullets, the air nearly sucked Blunt outside, but Blunt rolled forward as he did one Cyber-Force punch him to the ground. Another one grabbed him flipping him upwards in the air, and then punching him over to the broken window, as the few Cyber-Forces arms transformed to blasters aiming down towards him Blunt placed up his hand.

"Goodbye Mr Supreme."

As their fire of their blasters Blunt flipped upwards, but the impact of the blasters on the ground force him outside of the window, everything slowed down as Eight moved forward in front of her Cyber-Forces aiming her pistol at Blunt shooting him three times in his chest. E-Blud E-punched a few troopers down as he turned around he saw Blunt falling, Samurai-KB turned at E-Blud and nudged at him. Before Blunt hit the ground E-Blud flashed in front of him, catching him and diving to the ground.

"Blunt, Blunt."

"He was right, he is always right."

"No, Blunt, Blunt, noooooooooooooooooooooooooooooo."

Name: Blunt James Supreme

Founder of Sanctuary: Erased

Height: Erased

Build:Erased

Features: Erased

D.O.B: Erased

D.O.D: Erased

Cause of Death: Erased

This unlikely rage was travelling through E-Blud, in fact all his body lit up, E-Blud then teleported away appearing behind Eight and her Cyber-Forces.

"Oh, hello……..

Before she could finish her sentence E-Blud was off attacking,
destroying each Cyber-Force one by one, until he was in front of
Eight with this rage. Eight was shaking where she stood E-Blud moved
forward, but she couldn't move.

"E-Blud, stop."

"This wouldn't be what he would want."

As E-Blud went to strike Eight Samurai-KB blasted him back, but it
wasn't enough as he moved forward, she tried to blast him again but
he block it. John and X-Ham came forward but E-Blud force them
backwards through a wall, E-Blud raised his hand but Samurai-KB came
in front of him.

"Stop, stop, E-Blud."

A while later Eight came into the Sanctuary escorted by the heroes,
into her prison.

"Until we know what to do with you, you will stay here," said
Samurai-KB.

As Samurai-KB came out of the prison, and the prison then was moved
downwards into the darkness hole fifty feet downwards.

"Do you think the prison will hold her?"

"X-Ham, it will do."

"Look at E-Blud, will he be okay?"

"He'll be fine he just needs time."

"What do we do now?"

"We stop Cyber-Plus, and its Cyber-Forces."

"What do you think Cyber-Plus, next move is?"

"I have no clue."

"I guess, all we have to do is be prepared, for any attack."

"I agree."

One week later the heroes were at Blunt Supreme's funeral, across
stood his two sons, and their mother and a bunch of Agents. As
everyone walked away E-Blud approached his sons, the Agents step
forward he looked at the mother, and the Agents stepped away.

"Why didn't you protect our father?" asked Thomas.

"I am truly sorry; your father was a great man, he will always be a great man."

"That's not good enough, when I am older; I will stop men like the ones who killed my fathers."

The young teenage boys walked away with their mother, being escorted by the agents.

"E-Blud, it isn't any of our faults," said X-Hamstring.

"We knew he wasn't a part of the T.O.R.E.L.O.A.Ds, we just didn't know this outcome, history didn't recall it," said Samurai-KB

"I could have saved him, I'm sure of it," replied E-Blud.

"Don't destroy yourself over this, history is set," replies Samurai-KB

Chapter Thirty-Nine

Future was Foretold Final part

14th of March 1975 Sevenhamton, Mesink

Two years passed by, as John was in his bed slowly waking up, he heard a noise from downstairs. He looked back at his wife, and then went to his sons room to check on them. The noise came back again John quickly equipped himself, and headed downstairs.

"Hello, great Grandfather, this is the first time meeting you."

"Who the fuck is you, and why are you in my house?"

"Now, now, with the bad words, they call me Ultra-Mist."

"Haha, get the fuck out of here."

"Have you got any of that sangria, I need to catch my thirst?"

Ultra-Mist faded forward towards John without him even knowing, chopping his throat, and moving back to where he stood, John dropped to one of his knees choking.

"I know, I know, it's a shock to your system."

As John fired of his bullets Ultra-Mist merged through them, slowly walking over to him, John quickly pressed his device.

"Director X-Hamstring."

"I know it's John, where's E-Blud?"

"Director."

"Yes, Commander Jones."

"We have great trouble here."

"What is it?"

"Look."

"Cyber-Plus, and all its Cyber-Forces, outside."

"Yes."

"E-Blud you go with a few agents, I, Samurai-KB and the rest will defend the base."

Without a word E-Blud teleported away with a handful of agents, on the other hand John was chucked through his living room wall. His partner and their sons, came downstairs, John looked up over at them he saw a flash of blue energy on the corner of his eyes.

"Go back upstairs, it's safer there."

"Oh, look at little Jar and G-Man; I'm not harm for them. After all we need to keep Jar safe, don't we?"

John's partner and their sons run back upstairs, and then E-Blud came through the door as he did, Ultra-Mist sent a force but E-Blud dodges around it and it hits all the agents killing them.

"Damn it, you beings are always so slick."

E-Blud came at Ultra-Mist, and John fired of his rifle, bullets were bouncing of Ultra-Mist amour. Ultra-Mist held out his hand holding John in place, while he slammed E-Blud through the floor.

"Your journey ends here, Mr Warrior, I have no need for you to be alive."

"So you control time?"

"I am everywhere at once, but nowhere at the sametime."

"Pasture."

Ultra-Mist floated over to John ramming his blade inside of John, E-Blud flipped upwards seeing what just happened.

"Not again."

Name: John Dangelo Warrior

Company: Erased

Height: Erased

Build: Erased

Features: Erased

D.O.B: Erased

D.O.B Erased

Cause of Death: Unknown

E-Blud came at Ultra-Mist but everything went slow, E-Blud then found himself on a mountain, with Ultra-Mist behind him.

"Do you know why I am doing all of this?"

"Yes, because you have pass being evil."

"I am broken, he broke me, my own son."

"You sound mad."

"I am, but also more."

"Kill me then, get it over, and done with."

"No, it's not your time yet."

Ultra-Mist flashed forward punching E-Blud off the mountain, as E-Blud was in the air, Ultra-Mist came flying of after him, but E-Blud teleported. E-Blud landed inside the Sanctuary, the agents moved away aiming their pistols at him.

"It's just E-Blud."

"Come on; get yourself together, we going out there."

Eight stood up as she could feel Cyber-Plus.

"Cyber-Plus, give up, shut yourself down," said X-Ham.

"Never, you are not my creator."

"It speaks."

Without an order one of the Cyber-Forces fired of, blasting away a few agents, then seconds later it was an all-out war, outside of the Bank of England.

Ultra-Mist was now standing in front of E-Blud, Samurai-KB, and Hamstring.

"Why did you kill him?" asked X-Hamstring.

"He killed his brother, it was his time," answered Ultra.

"What about us, is it our time now?" asked Samurai-KB.

"T.O.R.E.L.O.A.Ds, you know it's too late to stop me right?" spoke Ultra-Mist

"You erased the part of history, which told us who killed your wife," said E-Blud.

"Do not mention anything about her," said Ultra-Mist

Ultra-Mist came out of his shadow form refilling to these heroes who he was, "Impossible, Warrior?"

"B... Warrior is alive," answered E-Blud.

"So let it begin."

X-Ham moved forward Ultra-Mist with only a blink, moved X-Ham to the ground pinning him to it with only his mind.

"His power has increased unbelievable faster than we imagined,"

"We just work as a team this time,"

So both of them together headed towards Ultra-Mist, while Ultra-Mist still had X-Hamstring pinned to the ground, as Samurai-KB plus E-Blud came swapping down at him. Ultra-Mist opened a portal sending X-Hamstring into it, as X-Hamstring went into it from his point of view he saw Ultra-Mist forced them away. Samurai-KB tried to hold out her hands, but Ultra-Mist grabbed it forcing her upwards.

"We failed greatly," said Samurai-KB.

"It's time for all three of us to go back."

Ultra-Mist open the Dimension Pull throwing Samurai-KB into, and then grabbing E-Blud sending him into it as well as himself, Ultra-Mist was the first to come out of the Dimension Pull on the other side landing on his feet in front of an android known as Mind.Swapper.3 looking very human like, Yemini and his children.

Future Timeline

"Ultra-Mist," said Yemini.

"Do not spoke another word," replied Ultra-Mist.

"Father?"

"My children, it's been so long."

"Don't look into his eyes, my kids," said Mind-Swapper.3.

"Too late, darling."

1975 Bank of England

X-Hamstring stood straight up all his friends were gone, Blunt Supreme, John Warrior and Church Between, he was completely lone in the world so X-Hamstring got himself together and disappeared.

1977 Roman James the First Death

Two years later Right Ultra-Mist appeared in Roman James the First study room, but this time you could see who Ultra-Mist was he was no other than Blood Warrior.

"You have done well Mr First."

"Will you tell me?"

"It's done; I've erased any knowledge of what happened."

"You've bless me with all knowledge, I know only a little, and a few others know as well."

"That's why you die."

"Bone Warrior, he killed your wife didn't he, you finally found peace and he came along and took it from you."

Roman started floating in mid-air you could see him slightly being erase from history, Roman James the First was going to become another myth.

"He didn't kill her, he murdered her but I saw it in his eyes, he never knew what I became. Instead of death I was curse with life of eternity, who would really wish for that a never ending circle."

As Ultra-Mist vanished Roman body burst to pieces blood all over the place, Everton ran into the room as he did his Diamond Machete appeared, and he was transformed into his armoury.

"Roman, Ultra-Mist."

1977 the office

The man passes all the files onto the floor sweating heavily, "That can't be how it ended, where is X-Hamstring."

"I am here, Hudson."

"What did you do to my guards?"

"They've been built with?"

"You know you can't kill me right, I have it flowing through my blood."

X-Hamstring moves aside and In-Pulse appears.

"Phillip Armstrong."

In-Pulse creates a electric force sending it into Hudson ridding Hudson of his stomach, and leaving one massive hole which you could see through.

"X-Hamstring, destroy the files, it's the only way the past can be kept safe."

"Hold on, where are you going?"

"To a battle that I may not win."

"You've help me, so let me help you."

"You are by staying behind, and watching over him."

"Thanks In-Pulse."

Chapter Forty

T.O.R.E.L.O.A.Ds

**A future which has not yet come, in which I may not see, but a
present Time for you maybe, and a past time for them**

E-Blud and Samurai-KB returned to see that Mind-Swapper.3 was
fighting her children, with the help of Yemini,

"Get back to the base, Samurai-KB," said Yemini.

"What's going on?" asked E-Blud.

"Quickly, go," shouted Yemini.

As E-Blud opened a portal both of them watched as, Ultra-Mind blast
Yemini away, and they inserted wires into Mind-Swapper.3's mind.

Golden said, "Ultra-Blud the Defence is down."

Ultra-Blud replied, "its ok, I can see the Cool Protectors, what to
prove to us that they can handle their shit."

Golden replies, "shouldn't we help, Zero's Seven Acts, are pretty
strong."

Ultra-Blud replied, "Golden stand down, the two people we have
catched, seem to be more important to protect."

Ava said, "You're sounding right like a Protector."

Ultra- Blud replies, "Ava, please."

Blood Warrior said, "so you're their leader?"

Ultra-Blud replies, "You interest me Blood Warrior, but I never
trusted you."

Ultra-Blud punched Blood Warrior to his stomach and then races his
knee into Blood's face making him flip backwards.

Ultra-Blud said, "Zero."

Blood was in some much pain but he couldn't understand why, was it
the battle he had with Blazing, did Blazing do something to him, or
was his powers reduced by being in this Timeline.

Blazer said, "So it's Zero then?"

Ultra-Blud replies, "Only Zero has the guts, to come inside here."

E-Boy said, "Just for that object."

Leo replies, "That's not Zero, that's Blood Warrior, what are you doing?"

Ultra-Blud replied, "We still haven't figured you out yet, while we do, please enjoy the show."

As the tank was racing towards the Firm Sanctuary, Press touch the floor, making the floor come up moving the tank off the ground, as it was in the air Quick-Feet sliced through the tank. Out flew Zero's Seven Acts Rex grabbed Hope to the throat, slamming her into the ground, Tempa smashed Heavy in through a wall, Nine started to attack Sliver-Strike.

Ultra-Kid kicked Press backwards siding along the ground while E-Tank transformed herself back to normal, and started to fight Quick-Feet, while Captain-BMT sent a force sending Peace backwards. Rex came up behind Press went to stab him, but Press merged through it, grabbing the back of Rex's neck and kicking Rex's back forcing him downwards, Press jumped towards turning his knife into a sword going to slice into Rex's throat, but Ultra-Kid, trackled Press downwards.

E-Tank turned into a cannon blasting off towards Quick-Feet, but Quick-Feet rushed in-between the blasters, force travelling over to E-Tank, in which E-Tank transformed back to normal, grabbing Quick-Feet, legs spinning him around and flying him down to the ground down to Tempa, Tempa looked behind him as he did Heavy, made his fist go large smashing Tempah backwards and into Hope as he was about to ram his blade into Captain-BMT's side.

Ultra-Blud said, "Damn, the Cool Protectors can fight, can't they?"

Golden replies, "Yes Blud they can."

Ultra-Blud replied, "I wasn't talking to you, Golden, I was talking to him."

Blood Warrior replies, "Why do you believe me to be Zero, Zero's dead."

Ultra-Blud replied, "I think you're a fool, Zero never dies, he just hides."

Blood Warrior replies, "I killed him, I killed him, I changed history."

Leo said, "Blood we're in a different timeline, Zero can be pretty much, alive in this one."

E-Chick said, "I know who you are, you're Beware, Goy's son, the Goy I killed."

As E-Chick's armed started to spark up the gateway in the Firm Sanctuary turned on, as it did E-Chick stopped, and then outside a black portal opened up.

Ultra-Blud said, "What the hell is going on, arm yourselves ready."

Out of the black portal came the Children of the B.E.C.A.U.S.E.

Rex said, "About time, come on let's end these Protectors."

Press said, "Everyone in a line."

Leo said, "Look outside, who are those?"

EE replies, "Impossible, I sent them away, I trapped them."

Ultra-Blud said, "It looks like you didn't do a good job."

EE replies, 'stop getting on my back all the time man."

Ultra-Blud replied, "You're just a machine, you shouldn't talk back."

EE replies, "Am I just a machine."

Out of the gateway came Yemini dropping to the floor, EE transformed himself into a Morden looking Zero, racing towards Ultra-Blud, while Ultra-Blud grabbed his sword handle Zero trackled Ultra-Blud with all his force through the protected glass window dropping from great height.

Blazer said, "Watch out."

A blast came out from the gateway blasting E-Chick backwards from Leo, and destroying her.

E-Boy shouted, "My sister, no."

Out of the portal came Ultra-Mist throwing his Blade into E-Boy's side, burning him to ashes, Blood Warrior rolled backwards and away, from Ultra-Mist blast, Ava moved around to Leo cutting him free, and Dawn jumped backwards through a grip.

Leo was free he grabbed for a weapon Ultra-Mist blasted it away.

Ultra-Mist said, 'step back."

While moving behind Yemini getting her upwards sending back his other Blade into his hand, and placing it into the back of her neck.

"If any of you move, she dies, does everyone understand," said Ultra-Mist.

"Kill her she's not important," said Rex.

Quick-Feet said, "Get back to the Firm, Press and Sliver-Strike protect the object."

The rest raced off towards Zero's Seven Acts and the Children of the B.E.C.A.U.S.E, all Press and Sliver-Strike could see, was chaos as bodies after bodies were dropping.

Leo said, "What do you want?"

Ultra-Mist replies, "That object, so that the Epilator will work."

Leo replied, "I cannot help you like that."

Ultra-Mist blasted Leo backwards making him dropped into Golden, making them dropped off the edge, through some glass. Ultra-Mist moved Yemini round to face him, as he drives his blade into her, but Ava blocked it away kicking Ultra-Mist backwards.

"Mother, the T.O.R.E.L.O.A.Ds defences are down, we should attack."

"I agree."

As Press and Sliver-Strike got to the front of the Firm Sanctuary these force opened up, and sent them backwards to the ground, Press rolled sideways grabbing Sliver-Strike moving him away from the blast.

Press said, "Mind-Swapper.3, Ultra-Mind and Ultra-Swap."

Mind-Swapper.3 said, "Kill them."

Ultra-Mind dashed off towards Press hitting him back, and then twisted Sliver-Strike over to Ultra-Swap, which took out his leg flipping him to the ground, and getting on top on his slices and dices came down towards Sliver-Strike, but he was moving in-between and from them.

Mind-Swapper.3 got to the door and it opened up making her way through the Firm Sanctuary over to the control Centre, where she saw a familiar character.

"E-Blud and Samurai-KB."

"Mind.Swapper.3, stop, what has gotten into you?" asked Samurai-KB.

"I've just been reawaken, that's all."

"The real enemy is Ultra-Mist," said E-Blud.

Ultra-Mist blasted the floor next to Ava making her move backwards and through some glass, Mind-Swapper.3 sent a force over to Samurai-KB also Ava, as Ava turned around the force merged into her, and then this light surrounded her. In slow motion Samurai-KB held out her hand, but Ava blasted to pieces, and Samurai-KB dropped to her knees.

"It looks like you're little adventure didn't work," said Ultra-Mist.

"Samurai-KB, get up, get up," shouted E-Blud.

In his mind he was saying he can't fail her like he did Blunt, so he faded towards Samurai-KB taking Ultra-Mist's blade inside him, which froze him in place. Samurai-KB turned around to see E-Blud with a blade out of his chest, looking down at her.

"See, I am not useless after all, goodbye good friend."

E-Blud energy impacted inside him completely destroying him, Samurai-KB wasted no time moved close to Ultra-Mist slicing him back.

"Ouch, that really hurt."

"You bastard, you've taken everything away from me."

Samurai-KB tried to move forward again, but Ultra-Mist held her blade and burned it into ashes, grabbing her close to him.

"Another Mind-Swapper?" asked Ultra-Mist.

Samurai-KB blasted Ultra-Mist flipping off him, sliding to the ground, as Ultra-Mist then blasted the core which powered the Control centre, and he jumped through a portal. Yemini dropped down to the ground as she did, Dawn climbed back up and grabbed Yemini getting her from the Control Centre as it blew to pieces.

"Samurai-KB, watch out," shouted Dawn.

As Ultra-Mist came out from another portal, behind Samurai-KB, Press stabbed the side of Ultra-Mind, but Ultra-Mist also stabbed Samurai-KB, Press kicked him backwards in the air, and then travelled jumped into Ultra-Mind Slamming him down to the ground. While Sliver-Strike was about to slice open Ultra-Swap's throat, Sliver-Strike got forced backwards into a building, and the building came down on top on him, Ultra-Swap looked behind him and it was his mother Mind-Swapper.3.

Press moved forward as he did Mind-Swapper.3 sent a force, but Press merged through it, or that was he thought as the force sent him backwards to the ground Press sword flew out of his hand along the ground.

Samurai-KB body then faded away like History whipped it, and Ultra-Mist stood up tall watching down at Dawn and Yemini.

Mind-Swapper.3 said, "We must leave your father, to finish them of."

Ultra-Mind replied, "Let us destroy them together."

Mind-Swapper.3 replies, "You two are not ready yet, you both would have been, killed by those two."

Mind-Swapper.3 opened a gateway disappearing into it, Press got back up time jumping over to his sword, and Sliver-Strike forced himself up from the dirt, rubbish and crumbles which trapped him down.

Press said, "The Firm Sanctuary has been destroyed."

Sliver-Strike replies, "What now?"

Press replied, "Earth has been cooperies, we must leave to go to the Galaxy."

Sliver-Strike replies, "The others?"

As Sliver-Strike said that a Craft came landing down to them, as the door went transparent standing there was, Dawn, Golden, E-Boy, Blood Warrior, Yemini and Leo.

"Where's, E-Blud, Ultra-Blud, E-Chick, EE and Samurai-KB?"

"Long story, what about the other protectors?"

They got into a Craft flying over the battle field, all there was' was bodies after bodies, and the Magic-Craft scanned the battle field, but no live sign, until it started beaming.

Blazer said, "Over there."

The Craft landed and Press and Sliver-Strike walked over to where it was scanning, they saw Hope laying on top on someone, they moved Hope and it was no other than Rex. Press grabbed Rex forcing him upwards holding his blade against his throat, cutting into it.

Blood Warrior said, "Hold on don't do nothing, let's take him with us, we can question him."

Press looked backwards and replied, "Who's that guy?"

Dawn said, "He's on our side, He's a good guy."

Sliver-Strike replied, "Ever since they got here, all this badness has happened, I don't trust them."

Leo replies, "Where we come from we've lost our friends as well, we must work together, so there won't be no more."

Dawn said, "I agree."

Press replied, "Ultra-Blud was the leader, I don't agree, but I'll follow, at my own risk."

As they scanned around the rest of the field finding a few dead bodies off the enemies, E-Boy said, "Ultra-Blud went through the side of the Firm Sanctuary, he might still be alive."

Dawn said, "We'll go scan that area, and then come back, but we must leave Earth."

So Dawn, Blood Warrior, E-Boy and Leo got back into the Craft flying around near the edge off where Ultra-Blud drop to, but no live force at all.

Dawn said, "It looks like He's gone for now."

Blazer replied, "You're Brother will be fine, come on let's get the others.

So the T.O.R.E.L.O.A.Ds, C.O.O.L.P.R.O.T.E.C.T.O.Rs, Blood Warrior, Leo and Yemini travelled into outer-space heading towards the sun, where a massive metal ring was, which powered up and this green force shot out of it, they travelled in through this a Dimension Pull which was built especially for this trip, so that there was an easier way to get to the Galaxy.

Press said, "Home Sweet Home."

Sliver-Strike replied, "It's good to be home."

Blood Warrior replies, "Where too now?"

Drawn said, "The Courts of Sanctuary."

Blazer replied, "The Peace roamers will get the truth out of him."

Leo replies, "If not I guess the old fashion way."

Rex said, "What's the old fashion way?"

Blood Warrior replied, "I don't think you're going to like that answer."

E-Boy replies, "I like these two."

 "I like them as well," replied Dawn.

So as the Children of the R.E.L.O.A.Ds and N.E.W.P.R.O.T.E.C.T.O.Rs flew to the high courts of the Sanctuary on their mission to stop Ultra-Mist, a New Age of superheroes in the future was merging.

Printed in Great Britain
by Amazon

42775646R00138